A Hearthfire Historical Romance

BOOK 1

Counting Stars
All the Stars in Heaven
My Lucky Stars
Captive Heart

A Timeless Romance Anthology: European Collection

Timeless Regency Collection: A Midwinter Ball

Hearthfire Romance Series:
Saving Grace
Loving Helen
Marrying Christopher
Twelve Days in December

Forever After Series:
First Light

Power of the Matchmaker series:
Between Heaven and Earth

MICHELE PAIGE HOLMES

A Hearthfire Historical Romance

BOOK I

Copyright © 2017 Michele Paige Holmes

E-book edition
All rights reserved

No part of this book may be reproduced in any form whatsoever without prior written permission of the publisher, except in the case of brief passages embodied in critical reviews and articles. This novel is a work of fiction. The characters, names, incidents, places, and dialog are products of the author's imagination and are not to be construed as real.

Interior Design by Heather Justesen
Edited by Cassidy Wadsworth Sorenson and Lisa Shepherd
Cover design by Rachael Anderson
Cover Image Credit: Brekke Felt, Studio 15 Portraits
Cover Model: Kara Moore

Published by Mirror Press, LLC
ISBN-10: 1-947152-12-2
ISBN-13: 978-1-947152-12-0

Prologue

The Scottish Highlands, September 1746

Collin

"Is this the lad?" A wizened man seated at the head of the long table squinted, bunching the skin surrounding his eyes into folds. His coarse, grey beard dragged across his knees as he pushed back his chair and angled toward me.

I suppressed a shudder. Liam Campbell looked older than the stone walls of his keep, but he appeared every bit as fierce as rumored. The infamous scar he'd earned during the early days of the Watch crisscrossed his left cheekbone and traveled up to where his eyebrow should have been. His jaw set in what appeared to be either anger or hatred—likely both—and I wondered uneasily whether he'd taken me of his own accord or if he acted under the direction of the English.

Either way, this couldn't be good.

And either way—

I'd meet my fate head on as Da met his. I straightened as best I could, which wasn't much, held on either side as I was and with my hands still bound behind me.

"He must be the MacDonald rabble," one of the men restraining me said. "Watched him spend the better part of yesterday digging Ian MacDonald's grave."

My chest burned at the mention of my father. The crude

hole I'd dug for him hardly qualified as a grave. I glared at the old laird, my own hatred surfacing. When it came to the dead, Scotsmen usually had some sense of respect. But not Campbells, as far back as any history I'd ever heard. Probably the only reason they'd allowed me to care for Da at all was weariness from their own journey.

But I'd scarce placed his body and added a few handfuls of dirt when they'd come at me from behind. I'd not even been given a chance to find a suitable stone for a marker. And now my father lay cold and stiff, his body unmarked and unprotected on one of the Highlands' endless moors.

"Release him," Laird Campbell ordered.

I stumbled forward with sudden freedom, only just catching myself from falling. Beside me the men laughed, and the jeers and titters of others echoed throughout the vast hall.

I looked up to see intent grey eyes studying me closely. Laird Campbell was not amused.

"Untie him and get him some food."

A woman hovering near his chair hurried away as I felt a dirk slash through the rough rope binding my hands. Just the mention of food was enough for the hollow ache in my gut to flare to life, reminding me that I'd not eaten in three days.

Since Da and I had shared the mush he made from the stolen barley. I pushed the thought from my mind and set about rubbing my wrists, attempting to restore circulation.

Laird Campbell turned his attention to the clansmen who'd brought me in. "The lad's fair starved. Instead of watching him labor you ought to have helped, then given him some bread." His voice was sharp with reprimand. "It's a miracle he hasn't followed his father to the grave yet."

Yet? Because you plan to see to it personally? Did he want me fit enough to endure whatever torture he had in mind, or did he want me alive to hand over to the English, who were well known for their own cruelty and punishments? I wasn't sure what he thought either option would accomplish. At this date there was nothing left to tell, no secrets the English had not uncovered. Bonnie Prince Charlie had safely fled Scotland, leaving his loyal supporters behind to suffer the consequences of his failed bid for England's throne. I met Laird Campbell's steady gaze and kept my focus there, though I heard the uneasy shuffle of his men.

The one on my right spoke up. "We passed half a dozen English patrols on the way. Could have turned him over to any one of them and received a nice purse."

"It is well you did not." Laird Campbell's ominous tone sent a shiver up my spine.

The man on my other side cleared his throat. "You didn't say—"

"Must I *say* everything? Some things ought to be obvious!" The laird's words reverberated off the walls. He grabbed a staff leaning against the table and slammed it onto the stone floor. "You were to bring me Ian McDonald's son, alive and *well*." He pushed a tankard down the table toward me. "Drink."

Wariness that this was some sort of trick was no match for my overwhelming thirst. I stepped forward, took up the cup and gulped down its contents—lukewarm water.

"Fetch him another," the laird ordered, and the cup was whisked from my hand by a second woman lingering nearby.

"How long since you've last eaten?" the laird asked me.

Yesterday's PROMISE

"Three days." It hurt to answer. The half cup of water hadn't been nearly enough to soothe my parched throat.

"Three days." The laird pointed the staff at the men on either side of me. "That is when each of you shall eat again. While you are awaiting your next meal, you'll have ample time to think on following orders. Take them below."

I didn't turn to watch the proceedings behind me but registered that they occurred without protest or fight. Liam Campbell was both respected and obeyed, it seemed. I kept my eyes on him, appraising, wondering if he was still as tough as the wounds he'd earned, or if age had made him vulnerable.

I could only think that if his wrath kindled at so little a grievance from his own people, things did not bode well for me, a MacDonald and therefore an ancient enemy. But the tone the laird used next was different from the one directed at his men.

"What's your name, son?"

My eyes snapped to his as Da's bullet-riddled body sprang to mind. I stepped closer. "Collin MacDonald—*Laird* MacDonald now, since you've murdered my father." I spat and watched with satisfaction as my saliva hit near its mark and slid down the laird's cheek.

A collective gasp echoed around the room. I jerked backward as my arms were seized again.

He shook his head, and his men fell back. "So we ended up with Collin, did we?" His gaze was upon me once more. "You should be grateful. Your brother mayn't fare so well. And I shouldn't be certain of your status as laird just yet—second born, as you are."

"Ian's dead." I thought of my twin brother as I had seen him last, a fortnight ago, his body still and twisted at the bottom of a ravine near Munro lands.

"Is he, now?" Laird Campbell said slowly, and in such a manner as to make me question what I'd thought to be true.

Da said to leave him, that there was naught to be done. I pictured my father's grief-stricken face as he'd scrambled back up the hill. The watch had been just behind us, and we'd barely made our escape that night—the only time I'd ever heard my father cry.

"All is not always as it seems," Laird Campbell said, bringing me back to the present.

What was he talking about? Did he have Ian here, too? I glanced around, half-expecting to see him brought in wearing chains, or to see a man with an axe approaching, or to feel a pistol held to my head.

But Laird Campbell had made no move to wipe his face, and appeared, if anything, less hostile than when I'd been brought before him. If his aim was to make me uneasy, it was working.

He drummed his bony fingers on the table as he stared at me. "Bravery—an admirable quality." He nodded slowly. "But pride is foolishness." He shook his head. "The downfall of many great men, many a MacDonald." He lifted a rag from the table and held it out to me. "I've no desire to start off on the wrong foot. I'll take your apology and my face cleaned, or you'll be taking a trip outside with my men for a thrashing."

Because he was too old to do it himself? My hands clenched into fists at my sides. Da barely in his grave, and the man responsible for his death expected an apology? Next he'd be wanting my fealty.

Yesterday's PROMISE

I lifted my chin and met his gaze steadfast. "Whatever purpose you've brought me here for, you cannot succeed. You'll not have me. Do what you'd like to my body, but you'll not have an apology or anything else."

A wicked smile curved the old laird's lips. "Did I want a body to do something with, it would not be yours, lad." The hall erupted in laughter.

I felt my face burning scarlet but told myself not to mind. What was humiliation compared to what I'd been through these past months? I'd survived the English dogs this long. I wasn't about to let one of my countrymen—traitor though he was—take any satisfaction from me.

Pursing my lips, I steeled myself against what was to come. *How bad can it be?* It wasn't as if I'd never been beaten before. Da had taken a switch to my backside more than a time or two. I'd just pretend it was him. *I'll take it for you, Da.*

"Stubbornness," Laird Campbell said. "Another questionable trait. Though I suppose I should expect no less from a MacDonald."

I fought the urge to spit on him again. "The MacDonalds are strong, too. We're the oldest, most powerful clan in the Highlands."

"Once, long ago," Laird Campbell said. "But now . . ." His voice trailed off, almost as if he didn't wish to recount the obvious. For our loyalty to the prince, we had been nearly annihilated.

Laird Campbell's gaze seemed to soften. His mouth turned down, and his eyes drooped as if sorrowful. For a fleeting second I wondered whether he regretted the punishment he'd handed down or if he was mulling over the current, sad state of the Highland clans and Scotland in general. Either way, he'd no one to blame but himself. Had his clan sided with the Jacobites we might have had success instead of slaughter.

Another minute passed, and I sensed he was still waiting for me, giving me one more chance. I would not take it. I'd not grovel at the feet of my enemy. *Not yet, anyway.* Unease that had nothing to do with hunger stirred my innards. In the past year I'd seen men brought low under torture. I'd never experienced that suffering myself, but I'd seen pain reduce grown men to bairns. I wanted to believe more of myself than that. But at fourteen, I'd not yet been tried.

At last Laird Campbell nodded to his guards, and I almost felt relief when they took my arms and made to take me from the room. It was always better to get a punishment over with. Sometimes the dread was half the agony. Though, noting the strength of the two men who held me, I somehow doubted that would be the case.

"Wait!" A shrill, yet tiny voice halted our procession.

I glanced over my shoulder as a lass, little more than a bairn herself, appeared behind the laird's chair. She reached up onto the table and grabbed the cloth Laird Campbell had held out to me just moments before.

"Don't hurt him." She spoke as if she was used to ordering others about. "I'll clean Grandfather's face." She looked directly at me. "*You'll* only have to say you are sorry." She turned to Liam Campbell and, standing on tiptoes, reached to wipe his cheek. He bent closer, allowing her better access, and a broad smile—genuine, this time—formed on his mouth, transforming the fierceness into a face nearly bearable.

Yesterday's PROMISE

"That was very kind of you, Katie lass." He picked her up and settled her on his lap. They both turned to look at me.

"Well," Laird Campbell asked. "You aren't going to let my granddaughter's generosity go to waste, are you?" A sharp look at his men, and they released me, one of them muttering beneath his breath as he did.

"I–" I wasn't sure what to say. I faced Laird Campbell and the girl. I'd not expected to have a waif of a child—and a lass at that—come to my rescue. It was humiliating, and any form of apology still went against grain. "I cannot apologize to the man who killed my father."

"I didn't fire those muskets, lad."

"You might as well have," I said. "You turned him in. You handed him over when you knew they'd kill him."

"I did only what your father asked of me."

"Liar!" I burst out. "That isn't true."

"It is." Laird Campbell's voice sounded heavy—tired. But also truthful, and as his arms wrapped protectively around the child in his lap, he didn't look like a man capable of such brutal treachery.

Don't be fooled.

I reminded myself that his gruesome scar told another story—one of his early betrayal, an encounter with Grahams before they, and the other clans, realized that the Campbells were working for the English and had formed the black watch.

A nice way of phrasing the word spies, Da had said. A justification for using brutality against the other clans and in return receiving favors from the English.

"My father wouldn't ask for his own death. He wasn't a coward." I thought of the cave and the supplies we'd been gathering there. We would have made it a few more months, at least. And while a life in hiding wasn't the one Da was used to leading, I felt sure he hadn't been ready to give up. He'd still had some fight left in him.

"No man as brave as your father chooses to die—without a reason," Laird Campbell said. "But sometimes we wish those we love to live more than we care about our own lives—or deaths. Your father chose to turn himself in so you might live. He came to me and asked me to betray him, so you'd be given into my care, and so you'd be spared the fate of nearly every other MacDonald male."

"That's not true." My breath left me as if I'd just been punched. I suddenly wished I was outside feeling the sting of a lash against my back instead. That was pain I could live with. The thought that Da might have faced a firing squad in order to save me was not.

The Campbell laird had to be wrong. *He's lying.* "I wasn't in any danger. I'm only fourteen. The English were only interested in the men—in those who fought."

"You don't *look* fourteen, lad." Laird Campbell's gaze strayed to my feet—large by any standard—then traveled up my lean body to the top of my head, nearly equal in height with most of the men in the room. "Your father sensed you were in danger, and he was right. As son of a laird, your name was listed on that execution order, alongside his."

No, I wanted to cry out. It wasn't true. It couldn't be. I wasn't in any danger so long as Da and I were together. And we were good at evading the English soldiers and watch alike. My father knew the hills and crags of the Highlands as well as anyone. We could have lasted a long time. *He could have still been alive.*

Yesterday's PROMISE

"MacDonalds were there to welcome the prince when he arrived, and MacDonalds smuggled him away at the last," Laird Campbell continued, as if he thought I didn't believe his claim about the price on my head.

"I know what we did." I'd been there for most of it.

"Well, the English do not take it lightly, son."

I bristled again at the use of the endearment. I couldn't figure Liam Campbell out, or what he wanted from me.

Not for the first time in the past two days I wished I'd disobeyed my father. *If I hadn't listened, if I'd come out of those bushes with him . . .* I squeezed my eyes shut tight, closing out the light of the room and the strangers surrounding me. But all the darkness brought was the image of Da being led away and the echoes of shots.

"Aren't you going to say you're sorry?"

I opened my eyes to find the wee lass staring up at me.

"It isn't nice to spit on people," she said matter-of-factly. "Even when you're sad or angry—or frightened—you should still be nice."

My ire rose further at her reprimand, and I placed my fists on the table, leaned forward, and glared at her. "What does a little bit like you know about sorrow?"

Laird Campbell's expression changed swiftly, to a twisted mass of scar tissue, even uglier and more frightening than the face that had first greeted me.

I've gone too far.

"She knows plenty," he said, his voice deceptively quiet. "Her mother lies in that casket behind me." He turned toward the dais at the back of the hall.

I followed his gaze and glimpsed the long, wood box laid

out across the trestle table. Flowers adorned the top of the casket, and candles burned nearby, on either end of the table.

It was a shock to see it there, to realize I'd not noticed before. With some consternation I realized I'd not taken stock of my surroundings. A quick glimpse around the room revealed no additional caskets, and my eyes returned to the lone box on the table. It was laid out with such respect—*on the table they eat at, no less*—that I felt neither remorse for my earlier words nor sympathy for the laird or his granddaughter.

At least her mother will have a decent burial. I hadn't even a blanket to lay Father in and had lowered him into the ground with nothing covering him but his own, filthy, blood-smattered clothing.

I glanced from the casket to the child and saw that her impertinent look had dissolved into one of uncertainty and fear. With a tremulous sigh, she turned from me, burying her face in her grandfather's shoulder.

At least she still has someone, I thought, further justifying my unkindness. But the thought didn't carry the bitterness of my previous ones. I hadn't the strength to hate the child. I didn't *want* to hate her—or, at the moment, even Laird Campbell with the compassionate look he bestowed upon the lass and then me.

He is my enemy. I tried to rouse the anger I'd felt just moments before, but somehow the girl's reaction had taken it from me. It wasn't right that she had lost her mother. It wasn't right that my parents were both dead and that what few clansmen I had left were strewn about, hiding and starving on their own land.

Yesterday's PROMISE

"How long?" I asked, looking past Laird Campbell toward the casket. "When did she—"

"Three days ago," Laird Campbell said. "She was my only child. I would have gladly given my life for hers, so you see—" He paused, shifting his granddaughter's weight before meeting my eyes again. "So you see how I could not deny your father's request. When he asked me to see that you lived, that you were safe, I had to agree."

I read the truth in Laird Campbell's eyes even as my own smarted. I looked down at the weathered wood of the table and wished, more than anything, that I didn't know the truth, and that I wasn't beholden to this man for my life. *That Da had not given his for mine.* But there was no changing that now.

I swallowed the painful lump that had formed in the back of my throat and blinked rapidly to keep foolish tears at bay as I uttered the belated apology. "I'm sorry."

Part One

Marry in June when the roses grow,

And over land and sea you'll go.

Wiping my mouth with the back of my hand, I looked up from the trencher and glanced around the hall, relieved that no one appeared to have been watching as I consumed more food than I'd had in at least a fortnight. I still didn't feel quite full, but I'd eaten everything they'd brought me, and it appeared there were no plans to bring more. If this was my last supper, I intended to make it as good a feast as possible. And if it was not . . . well, I'd need all my strength to escape. I'd no intention of being on Campbell land for long. But the thought that my father might have intended just that niggled uneasily at the back of my mind . . .

Chapter One

Alverton, England, June 1761

Katie

"Katherine Christina Mercer, come down here this minute—"

"—and help," I finished in a nasally tone matching Mother's when upset. I made no move to answer her summons that sounded as if it was intended for a nine-year-old instead of a mature, independent young lady of nineteen.

Independent and artistic. I could not afford to be

interrupted. Whatever chore needed to be done it would simply have to wait until tomorrow. I'd worked all the morning, as I did most every day, leaving me little time to paint. Leaning back on my stool, I clamped the end of a well-chewed brush between my teeth as I studied the canvas before me.

I squinted, then sighed in frustration as I took in what I'd hoped was—but obviously was not—a completed work. The scene appeared finished, but something about it was not quite as it should have been. And Lady Gotties, to whom I hoped to sell the painting, would surely notice as well.

"Christina!"

"Bother," I muttered, more concerned with what ailed the painting than what troubled my mother. I held one hand up, spreading my index finger and thumb wide in an attempt at crude measurement. Moving my hand in front of the canvas, I checked the distance between sky and mountain, trees and meadow.

The scale is good. That's not it. Pensively I stared harder.

"Do not make me come up there." Mother's voice carried up the stairs again.

Little worry of that. I dismissed the threat as idle. Mother had never once been up to my attic. It seemed highly unlikely she'd start tonight. I glanced out the window. It *was* almost night. The time for finishing this painting—for finding and fixing what was wrong—grew short.

But when I looked back to the canvas my error seemed blatant. The hue of the sky was wrong. No little mistake. And I'd so wanted to finish this piece tonight.

Yesterday's PROMISE

Perhaps, in better light . . . As a last hope, I stood and dragged the easel toward the solitary window—definitely not the best source of light or the best view for capturing the majesty of the sky on a summer day. I'd relocated up here out of desperation. Anything out in the yard or in the house below that was at all moveable had already been taken. Thus far I'd managed to preserve my easel and supplies as well as everything dear to me by stashing my belongings up here. That Mother knew of this and had not put a stop to it was likely because she saw no value in the canvas and paints.

Or anything else I own. That was true enough, at least. Aside from being two seasons old, or one of my few plain mourning frocks, the gowns I had left were mostly in a sorry state of disrepair. The dresses that had once comprised much of our wardrobe were not designed with work in mind. But I had done little else the past year. And with no other clothing to wear while doing that work, the gowns had quickly become worn.

Not to mention, too short. I uncrossed my exposed ankles and knew I'd have to let a hem out and find some trim to add to a gown tonight if I planned to visit Lady Gotties tomorrow.

But there would be no point in visiting Lady Gotties if I did not have this painting completed.

Pulling the brush from my mouth, I continued to study the landscape critically. *The sky is too light—too vast and blue.* The sky in Alverton hadn't looked that way for a long time. Perhaps it never had. It was most often grey, and on particularly pleasant days—rare ones—appeared more of a purple hue. The painting would have to be fixed.

Glancing out the window again, at the waning light, I wondered if I had enough time to mix paints and rework the sky before the sun set completely. There wasn't a lantern left to spare for me to bring one up here, and even had there been, it would only have created more shadows to contend with.

I need to be out in the yard again.

Brisk footsteps sounded on the stairs, jarring me from my contemplations.

Mother?

I jumped up to pull the latch on the heavy trap door, and not a second too soon, as her grey-brown head appeared in the opening. Stepping back, I allowed her to enter the sloped room. Once inside, she looked around the narrow space, crammed with canvases, jars of paints, stacks of books, and the large trunk full of my clothing.

"You've made quite the nest up here, I see," she said.

"It's nothing anyone would have wanted," I said defensively. "It's not hurting anyone."

"No one, except you." Ducking her head, she crossed the room on squeaky floorboards to sit on the edge of the trunk. "Christina, you cannot hole up in here forever."

"I know." I looked across the room at the easel longingly. Outside the sun had nearly set. "I'm almost out of canvas, and three of my colors have run dry. But I have a plan," I added hastily. "During her last visit Emma's grandmother, Lady Gotties, expressed interest in my work. She's coming again this weekend, and I intend to present her with a painting she might wish to purchase."

"You are not going to *be* here at the week's end," Mother said.

Yesterday's PROMISE

"What?" I searched her face, dread in my heart. I had known it might come to this, had known that it *would* come to this eventually—that we would all be forced to go live with some estranged aunt or other obscure relative kind enough to take us in. *But not so soon.* Father had barely been gone six months.

"The last of the furniture was taken an hour ago," Mother said. "Our beds are reduced to blankets on the floor for the night, and we'll be taking our supper at the work table in the kitchen. I sold the last of the livestock, too."

I nodded, not caring a fig about the furniture or the cow that had gone. My horse had been sold three months ago, and I'd just as soon sleep on a pile of blankets on the floor as in the four-poster bed that used to be mine.

"Where will we go?" I asked. "How soon will the new tenants be here?" *Will I be allowed to bring my paintings? Will there be time to visit Father's grave again?* Selfish thoughts, to be sure, when I should have been in the rooms below this afternoon, helping Mother. But it was difficult not to feel selfish when I thought of Annabelle, one year younger than I, touring Europe on her wedding trip right now. She'd done nothing to help Mother settle the estate after Father's death, but had instead created a flurry of work for all of us as we readied her trousseau and all else for her wedding, just a few weeks previous.

"Will we be staying with Anna?" I asked. Staying with my sister wouldn't be so bad. She had married well, and her new husband owned a vast countryside estate as well as a townhouse in London.

"*You* will not be staying with Anna," Mother said. "It

wouldn't be good for you—seeing your sister happily married like that. It's high time you thought of yourself, of your own marriage."

I bit back a harsh laugh. "No one will have me. My prospects were not promising before, and now—without any sort of dowry and with Father's reputation—they are nothing." Which was all well enough for me. What did I want with a husband and babies when I could devote my life to art?

Once, in those years before our circumstances had changed, like any other young lady, I had dreamed of balls and parties, of beautiful gowns and dashing suitors. But Father's fall from grace with the English government had changed all of that and at the worst possible time—just before my London season was to have begun. I had been disappointed, of course. But a conversation with Father out in the yard had changed my perspective.

"Being a wife and a mother is a wonderful thing, Christina. And I believe you will yet have those opportunities. But you are meant for more." He stood behind me, looking over my shoulder as I sat at my easel, adding shadows to a thrilling landscape. Or thrilling to me, anyway.

"Your talent is quite remarkable—as are you. In more ways than you realize," Father continued.

"If you are saying that to console me, it is working." I set down my brush and turned to him. "I suppose we shall not have to travel to London now, and that is something." Riding in carriages did not agree with me in the least.

Father smiled. "No loathsome carriage rides. No stuffy ballrooms or boorish men. I should say you are quite fortunate to have avoided the whole affair." He swept his arm, gesturing to the garden. "Instead you are left in peace to enjoy this beautiful scenery and to paint it as you please." His eyes strayed to my canvas. "Though I must say this looks nothing like our landscape here."

"Oh, it isn't," I exclaimed, only too eager to tell him of my work. "It is a place I imagined—"

"I am sorry you did not get a season," Mother said, bringing me back to the present and the cramped attic.

"It's all right." I tucked away the pang of sadness the memory had brought forth and crossed the room toward her. Truly I didn't mind the loss of a season anymore—hadn't minded since soon after it had happened. Thinking back on that spring now, I realized that my quick recovery illustrated how very little the whole affair had meant to me to begin with.

Instead of enjoying my seventeenth summer in town, spending a fortune on a new wardrobe and attending balls and other prestigious social functions, I'd spent that summer with Father, consoling him, telling him he'd done the right thing in standing up to his superiors when he believed they were wrong. I hadn't understood, exactly, why Father was so strongly against the Act of Proscription against the Scots, but speaking his mind about it had cost him his long-standing post in the military.

Where I had been sympathetic to his cause, Mother had been furious. I'd hardly ever heard my parents quarrel before that, but after his dismissal, it was difficult for a day to pass without them arguing.

"It doesn't matter, Mother. None of it." I sat beside her on the trunk. "I'm not like Anna and probably wouldn't have made a good match anyway." I suppressed a shudder at the thought that I could have been married a year or two by now. *I might have even had a child!*

I could only be thankful for my good fortune in escaping that life, and for Grandfather's limited funds that had rescued us the previous year and provided a season for Anna.

"I wish—" Mother began. "I wish things could have been different. I do love you, you know."

"Of course I know." I laid my head against her shoulder and took her hand.

"We were a fine little family, the five of us." She squeezed my fingers affectionately.

I nodded. "The best." *We still are.* Though it wasn't the same anymore. Father was gone, Anna moved away, and Timothy had been sent to Grandfather's for the summer. I missed him racing around the house. I missed my evening chats with Father. Occasionally I even found myself missing Anna. *Or Anna as she used to be.* Growing up we had been the best of friends, and only in the past few years had our differences surfaced enough to drive a wedge between us. But Mother was right. For many years we'd been a fine little family. We'd been happy together.

I wondered, not for the first time, if it had started out that way, if my parents had always been in love or if they'd found each other out of necessity—Father, a widower in the military who needed someone to care for his daughter, and my stepmother, a young widow with her own child. Whatever their beginning—and they never spoke of it—there had been many good years and a son of their union. But all that was before Father's humiliation. Before his actions that somehow seemed the beginning of the end of everything I knew and loved.

Mother straightened and turned to face me. "You are nineteen years old—nearly twenty."

"Yes," I ventured warily. Mother was using her no-nonsense tone, the one that brooked no argument.

"It's time you were married." She held a hand up, cutting off my protests before I could speak. "It's time you were married, and you shall be." She took in a deep breath. "Tomorrow."

"*What?*" I jumped up and hit my head on the sloped ceiling. Eyes smarting, I stepped away from the trunk and Mother. "Have you gone mad?"

"Your father perhaps did at the end, but I am quite sane. As was he, apparently, when this was decided." She removed an envelope from her apron pocket. "He intended to speak with you before he died, but he never got around to it—leaving the task to me." Bitterness laced her words. "Lord Collin MacDonald will arrive at ten o'clock tomorrow morning. You will be packed and ready to go with him."

"I don't believe this." *An arranged marriage? Father wouldn't.* "What about posting banns? Where are we to be married? What of—"

"It's all explained in this letter." Mother held it up but did not yet hand it to me. "Lord MacDonald has arranged the license and will be bringing the proper clergy with him, and you will be married here before your departure."

"*Departure?*" I demanded. "Where is this stranger I am to wed taking me?" I couldn't be hearing things correctly. This couldn't be happening to me, of all people. *Me married? To a stranger? Absurd!*

I snatched the letter from Mother's outstretched hand and made my way toward the window, to read it in what little light was left.

"Supper will be in the kitchen when you're hungry," she said.

I didn't bother to reply but waited until the sound of her steps on the stairs had faded away. Only then did my trembling fingers unfold the paper. Father's writing, sloppy in his last days, stared up at me, and I felt my eyes fill with tears, not only with dread at what the letter might reveal but because he was not here to tell me himself.

My dearest Christina,

My time is growing short, and I should speak with you in person but, coward that I am, cannot bear the thought of our last days together being filled with contention. And so I ask your forgiveness before I even begin.

When you were very young I took you from your mother's people, but not before giving my word that you would return to them someday. Among them is a fine man named Collin. As a youth he risked his own life to protect yours when he believed you in danger. He has waited these many years for you to grow up and for me to contact him regarding your whereabouts.

I have done so now and requested that he wait until the summer to take you to his home—your first home. I know you will protest this; I am certain you will want to resist your mother's plea for this marriage and Lord MacDonald's good intentions. I beg of you not to. Instead, consider the promise you gave me in my parting days, that you would be mindful of the welfare of your mother and brother. Your marriage will provide a settlement for them as well. As for your situation, I am comforted in knowing that you will marry well. You will be the wife of a lord and will lack for nothing. I only wish I could be there to see you in your wedding finery and to kiss you farewell.

I pray you will give this situation a chance. That you will honor me as I honor a promise made long ago.

Your ever loving father,
William

I read the letter twice more and even turned the paper over, certain I must have missed something. But that was all—no further explanation. I knew only that this Collin MacDonald had known me as a child and waited for me to grow up. *How old is he? And a lord?* A chill that had nothing to do with the dropping temperature ran up my spine. What did I know about being the wife of a lord? I didn't want to know anything about it, about being a wife to anyone.

If only Anna was here. At least she could have told me what I might expect of marriage to a nobleman. *What might be expected of* me. I did not think I could ask anything of Mother, private as she tended to be. Yet going into such an enormous undertaking as marriage so completely blind seemed to doom the arrangement from the start.

Or doom me, at least. Turning from the window, I sank down on the stool before the easel. Had I, only minutes before, been concerned about the color of the sky I'd painted? Had I once spent an afternoon crying when my horse was sold? *Have I not spent months mourning and missing Father, who is sending me to such a fate?* Along with the hopelessness I felt engulfing me, a burst of anger flared to life. *How dare he! How could he?*

"How could you, Papa?" I cried aloud, using the name I had as a little child. *How could you betray me so?*

My shoulders slumped, and I stared at the canvas, wishing I could disappear into the landscape and never be found. It was no more of an option than my disappearing anywhere else. There was nowhere to go, no one who might take me in.

Perhaps, if Lady Gotties had been here already and she liked my work well enough . . . But no. It was a foolish thought, and I knew it. The likelihood of a woman surviving on her own—and one without any practical skills, at that—was not good.

Anna was out of the country and could not help, even if inclined to. And that was doubtful, given her egocentric, self-preserving nature the past year. She hardly ever allowed her then-fiancé and now-husband to so much as converse with me. *How likely is it she'd welcome me in their home?* Mother and Timothy maybe, but never me.

There was no one else who might help. The servants had all been dismissed, or I might have tried finding work elsewhere with them, however unqualified I was.

I rose from the stool and walked over to the trap door, closing it, letting it fall with a deafening slam. The sound did little to appease my agitation. I lit a candle and lifted it high, staring around the cluttered room. *My attic. My art.* I would have to leave it behind.

Yesterday's PROMISE

Tomorrow morning a man was coming to marry me. I would have to go through with it and go with him, or Mother and Timothy would be destitute.

I would have to make promises to a stranger. I would have to give myself to him. *I will have to leave everyone and everything.*

With despair in my heart, I walked to my trunk and began to pack.

"Feel better now?" the laird's hand was heavy on my shoulder, interrupting any thoughts I'd had about escaping.

"Not so hungry, anyway," I muttered. I pushed back my chair and stood, turning and feeling a little more confident as I stood nearly eye-to-eye with the old man. "What do you want of me?"

"Why are you so certain I want something?" He walked past and took up his chair at the head of the table. The wee lass that had been with him earlier was nowhere to be seen.

"No Campbell does something for a MacDonald without expecting something in return."

The laird's brows rose, and a speculative, almost amused look crossed his face. "You're an astute lad."

Sure that I'd just been insulted, I frowned.

A broad smile widened Liam Campbell's mouth. "A clever, intelligent lad," *he clarified.*

Apparently not, if I didn't even know his words. I felt my face flush. "Nothing—astute—about it. MacDonalds and Campbells have been enemies since time began."

"True enough," *he said as the smile slipped from his face.*

Chapter Two

I brushed the dirt away from Father's grave, wishing once again that we might have afforded a more expensive stone, one that stood perpendicular to the ground instead of this one, pressed flat into it. I worried that someday the drifting soil and then the grass might overtake the narrow strip, covering it and wiping away all memory of Father from the earth.

The thought brought a fresh wave of sadness to an already sorrowful morning.

"I forgive you." I placed a bouquet of wildflowers over the stone. "But you'd best help me," I said, as a sort of half prayer, my face raised to the dreary sky and the heavens beyond. "Be with me and help me to endure whatever lies ahead."

Knowing I had little time before Lord MacDonald was to arrive, I got to my feet and turned from the grave. I shook the soil and grass from the skirt of my best dress, a slightly too-short grey silk, as I hurried across the cemetery. I didn't want my mother to worry. It wasn't her fault I was in this predicament. If anything, it was Father's, and after a night of ranting and raving, I could no longer find it in my heart to be angry with him either.

Some minutes later I approached the house and felt alarmed to see nearly two dozen horses tethered by the gate as well as a good-sized, if somewhat shabby, carriage in the drive. The vehicle in question looked as if it might fall apart at any moment, the wheels thin with wear, and the sides dented and scraped as if they'd survived numerous attacks by highwaymen.

What sort of lord went about in a carriage like that? Perhaps it did not belong to Lord MacDonald after all. Perhaps he'd sent a messenger to tell Mother he had changed his mind.

The horses tethered nearby tamped my hopeful thought before it could come to full fruition. I wondered if Lord MacDonald had brought the animals as the settlement to be paid to Mother. If so, she could not be pleased. She'd not know the first thing about where or how to go about selling them, and in the meantime we'd not have the means for their upkeep.

She will not have the means. I will be gone. With whom and where were the questions that remained to be answered.

Filled with trepidation though I was, I felt myself pulled toward the house, my innate curiosity drawing me closer to discover the particulars of my fate.

Gathering my skirts, I walked quickly, eying the carriage with distaste before rushing up the steps to the front door. *So much for my hope that we would not be traveling far.* A large, enclosed carriage indicated otherwise, no matter that it didn't look capable of a journey beyond a mile or two.

With a quick breath for courage, I pushed the door open. I stopped short once inside, just managing to press my lips together to contain an audible gasp.

Heads—far too many of them—turned to look at me anyway. My heartbeat quickened as I glanced around the crowded room. What had always seemed a generous-sized foyer was crammed with men—too many for me to accurately count, moving about restlessly as they were.

Are there fifteen, twenty? I glanced to and fro, alarmed at so many eyes on me—eyes that did not appear overly friendly. Each man had a sword and at least one pistol hanging from his belt. My apprehension heightened at seeing so many weapons so close to my person.

For a second I wondered if they were friends of Father's from the military and he had somehow arranged for them to attend my wedding. But none of the men were in uniform, and on closer inspection, I noted that the clothing they wore was in poorer condition than my own.

"She's the look of her mother," a man to my left said, breaking the oppressive silence. He stepped from the crowd and grabbed my hand, shaking it heartily, the assorted weapons in his belt clanging loudly as he did. I tried not to look at the wicked sword that nearly reached the floor, or the pistol, or the knife at his waist. Instead I did my best to return his greeting, summoning a wan smile, though inside I felt I might be ill or even faint.

"Bonny, that's what," he said, grinning broadly, accentuating the many wrinkles lining his face.

That accent . . . I thought of the carriage and the horses outside. He was not from around here. *From anywhere around here. Not even from England?* I had to be mistaken. Father would never have married me off to one of the barbarians from the north.

The man was also easily twice my age, with a balding head but more than ample auburn hair covering his face, arms, and his legs exposed below knee breeches. He could not be my intended. *Please no.* But when several seconds passed and no one else stepped forward to greet me, I feared it must be.

At least he appears to be possessed of good humor. I attempted to console myself while fighting tears of dismay.

"She does have the look of Katherine. And a more bonny lass I never saw."

At last another man joined us, this one clapping me on the back soundly as if I was both a man and an old acquaintance.

At his overly friendly gesture, four others followed, circling close around me. My arms pressed down at my sides—the men were too near for me to do otherwise.

"Hair like a field of dry heather."

An odd compliment. Though, perhaps it hadn't been meant as one. Given the number of auburn heads surrounding me, perhaps hair of a different color was seen as inferior.

A man reached out, touching one of my painstakingly arranged curls. I tried not to flinch. Father had always said that showing fear was a sign of weakness, and though inside I trembled, I did not want to appear weak in front of these men.

I had decided sometime during the long hours of the night—after realizing that any attempt at sleep was futile—that if I must marry, I would do my best in this endeavor. To that end I had sat before the looking glass by candle light, taking more care than usual with my appearance, hoping, I supposed, for a bridegroom who did the same.

"Eyes like the sky afore a storm," the man who'd spoken about my hair continued.

"Save your poetry for later, Finlay," another beside him said. "What matters is that she's known her sorrows and is sensible to boot. A fine choice in your dress color, Miss Katherine."

"Good luck it is, wearing grey to your wedding," agreed yet another who stood behind our tight circle.

I nodded, though I had never heard such before. Obviously they had not been to London recently to see the latest fashions. The gown my sister had married in had been a beautiful ivory silk, with lace and pearls at the throat and sleeves and a long train that trailed behind. I had envied her that dress. But just now, exclaimed over as I was, I felt grateful for the simple grey. Wherever these men were from—and it most definitely was not Alverton or even Nottingham—they judged my gown as appropriate. A little thing, but it brought a measure of relief. I'd spent the night worrying over what my bridegroom would think of me. To realize I'd at least dressed correctly was something, however small.

I was feeling just slightly better, if not completely overwhelmed about my circumstance, and reminded myself that I only had to marry one of them. Meeting one strange man today had sounded bad enough. *But twenty?* I stifled nervous laughter.

"Marry in June when the roses grow, and oe'r land and sea you'll go," the man called Finlay said, waxing poetic again. I thought of the carriage outside, and my panic returned.

"Just how far are we going today?" I asked. A voyage by sea did not sound so bad—at least once we arrived at the dock. The drive to London's wharfs would be torturous, but standing on deck with the fresh ocean air blowing about as we sailed toward the continent sounded quite lovely.

"Be lucky to make Newark by nightfall if we don't get on with it," a voice behind me said crossly.

"We're having a reuniting with kin, MacDonald," the bald man who'd first spoken to me said. "Hold your peace a minute."

MacDonald? Did he mean Lord MacDonald?

Before I could turn to see who had spoken, my hand was seized once more.

"Name's Alistair Campbell," the bald man said. "And I've—*we* have—" He swept his arm toward the men clustered around us—"waited a long time to see you again."

Again?

"I'm Quinn," the man standing beside him said. "Cousin to your mother and now you." He grinned, revealing a mouth that was missing several teeth.

"Moireach Campbell," another said. "Your mother was a fine woman. She'd be pleased to know you're coming home."

Finlay, Donaid, and Ruaridh came forward next. I gave up trying to keep their names straight after that. Each sounded stranger than the previous, save for the common last name of Campbell, a name I'd heard Father mention a time or two before.

My mother was a Campbell. And she was from . . . I didn't know. Shame and regret and worry flooded my mind. How could I not know where my own mother was from? Father had rarely spoken of her, and I had never bothered to press him. He had provided me another mother, the only one I could remember, and that had always seemed sufficient—until now.

No others came forward to greet me, and I knew a brief moment of relief when I realized that all had failed to introduce themselves as Lord MacDonald.

Looking up at the men clustered about me, I felt strangely touched that they had traveled to find me, to see me wed. Though I'm sure I must have looked utterly confused as I stared at each in turn.

"Are none of you Lord MacDonald?" I asked, wondering who the voice I'd heard earlier belonged to. Maybe the groom had grown tired of waiting or had cried off at the last minute. Maybe I was to be expected to choose one in his stead—a possibility that seemed at least as painful as having a husband chosen for me.

Oh please no, I silently prayed.

"I am Collin—Laird MacDonald."

Laird. A term I'd heard Father use when speaking of the Scottish clans. My heart sank further as I turned toward the deep voice and realized that half of the roomful of men had not moved at all since my entrance. Contrary to the jovial expressions on the faces of those whom I'd just met and who surrounded me, these men looked as if they were attending a funeral or preparing for war. Not one smiled. Several looked positively fierce. I searched the group for the one who'd spoken but felt no reprieve when a man stepped forward.

Like the others in the room, he was armed to the hilt—with sword, knife, and pistol all tucked neatly in his belt.

Had they supposed I would resist? No chance of that now. Were weddings in the north a violent affair?

My eyes traveled up to his and saw rich brown beneath a somewhat shaggy mop of equally dark brown hair. His face appeared young, if not serious, with not even a hint of a smile. But he did not appear to be an ogre, or as old as my father, or horrible to look upon—all worries that had consumed me the previous night.

Our gazes collided midway through our perusal of each other, then held for a long second. *Collin, of course.* My heart quickened as some inner part of me felt a jolt of recognition, stirring my stomach in a not entirely unpleasant way. For the first time since I had entered the house I thought that, perhaps, I could go through with this.

Behind me the front door banged open. "I'm terribly sorry. I cannot find her anywh—Christina!" Mother's hand grabbed mine and whirled me around to face her. "Where were you? How dare you leave me to face this—these—" Her sharp eyes narrowed as she looked at me closely. Disapproval marred her usually pretty face. "What have you done to yourself?" she asked tersely, staring at my skirts.

I glanced down and saw that I had not been entirely successful at ridding my gown of the dirt from the cemetery. "I had to visit Father one last time."

"You speak to the dead?" Lord MacDonald asked behind me, not a hint of humor in his voice.

"Only when I am angry with them." I turned to face him again and had the thought that Father had met my intended before. If only we could have spoken of this. "Or missing them," I added as another clutch of sorrow tugged at my heart. Never again would I speak with Father about anything.

Mother cleared her throat loudly, as if she suspected I had forgotten her presence—not far from the truth. There was something about Collin MacDonald that commanded all of my attention.

"Let's get you upstairs," Mother said. "The least you can do is wear a clean gown to your wedding."

"She is fine as she is."

I looked at Laird MacDonald, uncertain of his tone. *What must he think of me? Traipsing around in the dirt before I am to be married.* I didn't want to care but found that I did.

His eyes had shifted to the front of my skirt. A false, fleeting smile vanished faster than it had appeared. "Your name is Christina?" He sounded perplexed and possibly annoyed.

I nodded, wondering what the problem was, if there hadn't been some mistake after all. Had he come to the wrong house? How many other penniless girls in the province were being forced to wed today?

"Her name is *Katherine* Christina Mercer." Mother gave me a stern, reproachful look.

Yesterday's PROMISE

Belatedly recalling my manners, I sank into a curtsy and held my hand out to Lord MacDonald. He took it, but instead of bringing it to his lips, turned it over quickly and examined my palm, which was quite ordinary save for a thin white scar that began at my wrist and swept up toward my thumb, the result of an accident when I was very young.

"Do you find my name—or my hand—lacking, Milord?" I tugged free of his grasp, alarmed at the startling sensations his simple touch had caused.

"On the contrary. I find you to be just as I had expected."

I wasn't certain what to make of his comment, so I said nothing.

On the other side of the room—the pleasant side, as I was coming to think of it—Alistair Campbell cleared his throat. "Don't be thinking to back down now, Collin."

Laird MacDonald turned a furious look—one I prayed he'd never use on me—on Alistair. "It was not I who was late."

"I'd run away, too, faced with the prospect of marrying a Macdonald," one of the younger Campbells muttered. This time it was Alistair who sent a silent and stern warning to the man.

"Now that acquaintances have been made, shall we begin?" A before unseen clergyman appeared at the head of the crowd, near the stairs. Given his height over the others in the room, I guessed he had to be standing on the bottom step. His accent was as thick and foreign as that of the others, and my horrible suspicion grew.

Laird MacDonald took my hand in his once more, without so much as asking, and towed me forward as the crowd parted—brooding MacDonalds to one side, merrier

Campbells to the other. Once in front of the priest, Collin let go and took a sideways step away from me, as if I'd some sickness he wished to avoid.

I don't want to be close to you either. But I felt almost hurt and strangely lacking with the absence of his touch. I clasped my hands together, the warmth of his hand still lingering—nearly unraveling my composure.

I focused on the priest, noting that he stood on the second stair, not the first, and that this made him only slightly taller than my husband-to-be.

Mother appeared at my side, likely to keep me from running, and I willed my nerves to calm. Behind and beside and all around us the men crowded closer until I knew if I moved at all I would touch at least one. The air seemed to thicken, and I looked at the stairs longingly, wishing I might escape to my attic once more.

The priest began speaking—in a language foreign to me. I glanced at Mother, but she was staring straight ahead, as if nothing was amiss.

As if her daughter was not about to marry a Scottish laird.

The priest droned on, and it was all I could do to keep myself still. Only the thought of two dozen weapons being directed at me kept me from movement. Whenever I had imagined my wedding—a rare occurrence—I had never envisioned anything like this, standing in our foyer, packed tightly with a group of Scottish clansmen I did not know and with whom I would be leaving shortly. It seemed too bizarre to be real, and so it became unreal to me.

I felt disembodied, almost as if I was a stranger looking down on some other unfortunate girl. I knew the moment would soon come when I fully realized that *I* was the one in this predicament, and it was then that things would likely become most difficult. But I held that moment off as long as possible. I did not wish to cry in front of these strangers—or, even worse, give into hysterics. But how else was I to feel with all that was familiar slipping away and a new, and not particularly friendly, husband who spoke a language I did not understand?

To calm myself I thought of the scene as I would one I wished to paint. Several of the men, including Laird MacDonald, would make interesting subjects. My mind turned to my art, and I began imagining bold strokes on a large canvas. *A light background, the men at the forefront. Maybe posing with their swords?*

" . . .take Katherine Christina Mercer to wife."

My eyes snapped to the priest. When had he begun speaking in Latin? I glanced nervously in either direction, but no one appeared to be looking at me. I willed my frantic heartbeat to slow. I'd not missed anything important.

Nothing important! I was about to be wed.

I forced my attention to the ceremony, trying to listen as I should and, for the first time in my life, feeling immensely grateful for tutors who had required me to study Latin.

At last he ceased speaking, and Lord MacDonald turned to me. Following his cue, I moved stiffly within my cramped confines, angling my body toward him. His mouth set with a look of grim determination as he took both of my hands in his, not firmly as before, but with the barest touch.

Nonetheless it affected me. I glanced down at our joined hands, wondering at the tremor I felt at our contact.

It is anxiety. Calm yourself, Christina.

Not quite looking into my eyes, Laird Macdonald began to speak.

"I vow you the first cut of my meat, the first sip of my wine—"

If he intended this to be romantic, he was failing miserably. His voice seemed to lack all emotion—as it should. *We don't even know each other.* I found his promises extreme. I hoped they weren't literal and that I would be allowed to cut my own meat and have my own cup at dinner.

"From this day it shall only be your name I cry out in the night and into your eyes that I smile each morning."

Just the thought of being beside him come nightfall terrified me. But that he might cry out my name . . . I felt a blush steal across my cheeks. I was powerless to cover them or turn away, as Lord MacDonald held me in place with both his hands and eyes, now staring directly at me. *Or through me.* Though his gaze was directed at my face, I felt as if he was looking past me, as if his mind, too, was in another place entirely.

He did not seem to notice my discomfort but continued his vows. "I shall be a shield for your back as you are for mine, nor shall a grievous word be spoken about us, for our marriage is sacred between us, and no stranger shall hear my grievance."

Easy enough for him to promise. He was surrounded by people he knew. Everyone was a stranger to me. I'd have no choice but to keep any grievances to myself.

"Above and beyond this, I will cherish and honor you through this life and into the next."

The room fell silent when Collin finished. I stood there looking at him, moved by his last words, though I tried not to be. What would it be like to be cherished by him? I found that I very much wanted to know, even as I struggled to control my breathing and worried I was expected to know all those vows by heart and say them next. It seemed much to promise someone I'd just met. Yet, strangely, it felt as if he'd meant every word.

"Repeat after me, Miss Mercer," the priest said in Latin.

I managed to nod and struggled through my pledge to Laird MacDonald—Collin—those same vows he had just given to me.

"Above and beyond this, I will cherish and honor you . . ." Might I someday feel such a depth of emotion for this man? And might he feel the same for me? The idea both terrified and enticed me. Perhaps my girlish dreams had not entirely vanished. Or, perhaps he would finish them off once and for all, if the cold stare he gave me now was any indication of the future.

I ended my vows feeling very somber indeed.

Laird MacDonald dropped one of my hands and turned back to the priest. In spite of his light touch, the hand still held in his began to sweat.

"Collin Ian MacDonald and Katherine Christina Mercer, by the authority of the Almighty God and the Church of England, and before these witnesses, I pronounce you husband and wife."

Words so final that a ripple of fear shivered up my spine.

"Bear up, lass. You're almost done," one of the Campbells reassured me. I felt a comforting hand on my back and leaned into it for a second, feeling a slight buckling of my knees.

"She's only just started," a man on the other side of the room said, and when I looked his way I could have almost sworn I saw Laird MacDonald's—Collin's—mouth twitch.

Annoyed with me already? Or merely amused at my nervousness? I hoped for the latter, though I was not overly fond of being a source of amusement.

"Ahem." Finlay Campbell cleared his throat. "You haven't forgotten—"

"No," Laird MacDonald said a bit too sharply for a man who had supposedly just experienced one of the happiest moments of his life. He dropped my hand, and I glanced over at him as he fumbled with a tiny parcel he'd drawn from his pocket. His brow furrowed as he untied the string, and when he looked up at me, I saw a misery in his eyes that I felt sure mirrored that in mine. It occurred to me, then, that I was not the only victim here. My *husband* had not wanted that title today any more than I had wanted the title of wife. Yet he had come all this way, gone to all this trouble, and gone through with it.

Why?

"The ring ceremony is an old Scottish tradition," he said. "Or a Campbell one, at least, and as you're a Campbell—" His expression said the rest.

And as we're surrounded by armed Campbells, and I've no wish to start a war—

But there had been a war, many years ago when I was a child, and Father had fought in it. In Scotland. *Against* Scotland.

I glanced at Mother, whose face seemed to have turned

to stone. *Father was sympathetic to the Scots' plight, because my real mother was Scottish.*

How had I not realized this before now? Why hadn't Father ever told me?

I counted backward quickly, calculating that my father and mother would have been together around the time of the Jacobite uprising, when that imposter Charles came from France to try to claim England's throne. Many English troops had been dispatched to Scotland during that time.

Was theirs a love match? How could that even be possible? *Father is English. I am English.*

Or at least, I'd thought I was. Everything I'd ever known or believed to be true was crumbling around me. Uncertainty and fear crept into the farthest recesses of my mind with a dizzying effect.

Laird MacDonald finished untying the package and withdrew a small, silver ring from the paper. He took my hand once more, his touch no less impactful than a moment before. I closed my eyes briefly, thinking I might have enjoyed it, had the one touching me not been so reticent. He slid the band over the third finger of my left hand. *Over the vein that leads straight to my heart.* My overly sentimental sister had shared with me this tidbit about wedding rings, and I'd thought it a lot of nonsense at the time.

But now . . . The band felt strange on my finger, unfamiliar.

Unwanted.

My heart felt the same, with a queer tugging at it, as if it was no longer mine to control. This ring, or the man who had given it to me, had laid claim to me, body and soul, and I feared or sensed it was my heart that would most suffer the consequences of our union.

He cleared his throat. "I give you my heart at the rising of the moon and the setting of the stars. To love and to honour through all that may come."

More vows, I thought, anguished. *Will this never end?* Even Anna's ceremony at the grand church in London had not seemed to go on this long.

I'd thought Lord MacDonald's voice devoid of emotion before, but now it sounded positively anguished as he rushed through this second set of promises.

"Through all that may come. Through all our lives together. In all our lives, may we be reborn that we may meet and know and love again, and remember." He released my hand, as if holding it had pained him.

It had tortured me.

"Now the lass," the priest coaxed.

"No." My husband's command was swift. "It is enough. She needn't say anything more. We are done here."

The priest glanced toward the Campbell side of the room, then nodded, and the men behind us stood in silence.

It is finished, then. I am married. There was no *we* to the equation in my mind until, beside me, Alistair cleared his throat and spoke.

"Seal it. With a kiss."

"Pagan," the priest muttered. Nevertheless, he cleared his throat and gave each of us a pointed stare.

Slowly Laird MacDonald turned to me. Alistair nudged me so that I faced Collin as well.

Yesterday's PROMISE

He looked as reluctant as I felt for what it appeared was expected to happen next. I did not intend to make it any easier for him. Even if I'd wanted to, I'd no notion how. Having missed my season and any chance at suitors, I hadn't the slightest idea how to go about conversing with, let alone kissing a man.

He closed the space between us. I didn't look up but stared at his chin. A throaty chuckle sounded behind us. "He's not so bad as all that, lass."

Another voice chimed in. "She's a shy'un. You'd best be kind to her, Collin."

Someone jostled me from behind, and I stumbled forward, straight into my husband's chest. He grasped my shoulders, steadying me.

"Sorry. Thank you," I mumbled. Our eyes met, and his were filled with an unfathomable pain. Sharing a kiss seemed the last thing either of us wanted. Yet the onlookers pressed closer, insisting. I closed my eyes, shutting out his look of discomfort and hoping that would make it easier.

Quickly now. Just get it over with.

His lips covered mine gently, in the barest meeting, but filled with such surprisingly sweet promise that I felt shaken. Then he turned away from me, took my hand again, and faced us both toward the crowd as a loud hurrah—from the Campbell side—went up.

"There's the matter of signatures," the priest reminded us, and Laird MacDonald turned us around again and marched us up the first stair, near the papers resting on the newel post. He released my hand to sign his name first.

I felt lightheaded—either from his kiss or all that turning, or possibly trying to decipher the conflicting emotions my new husband was displaying. He'd first seemed impatient with me then angry, and then indifferent. But something painful had followed. Speaking the vows that accompanied giving me my ring had cost him. And his kiss . . .

What could possibly have caused him to look so tormented? Feelings of self-doubt crowded my mind. *The grey dress was not good enough. I shouldn't have been late. I shouldn't have spoken so boldly at first.*

"Ian, you're to sign here," Laird Macdonald said when he'd finished. I moved aside as another of the MacDonalds came forward. Like most of the rest of the lot, his eyes and hair were dark—nearly black, in this case. Shiny and sleek, it fell below broad shoulders. Next to Laird MacDonald, I guessed him to be the best dressed of the men. But there was a look about him that did not speak of anything gentlemanly. The sleeves of his shirt were taut, his breeches as well, narrowing into black boots, one of which boasted the rather ornate handle of a dagger. He didn't look any happier than the rest of them but grabbed the quill and slashed his name across the paper. When he'd finished, he stepped back, casting a loathing glare at me.

A pirate if I ever saw one. I had the absurd thought that I must paint him someday. *Why do you hate me?* I wanted to ask, my feelings of hurt and inadequacy multiplying. Instead I met his gaze with what I hoped was an equally fierce one. Who was this man to ruin my wedding day? Another ridiculous thought. What was there to ruin?

"Ian." Laird MacDonald's voice was sharp. "What's done is done." He stepped between us. "Go sign the document, Katie."

Katie? For a half second I wasn't certain he meant me. No one ever called me that, and it seemed a far stretch from Christina or even Katherine. But a small part of me liked it, liked that so quickly my husband had determined what he would call me, and it sounded personable and friendly. *If I only knew what I should call him.*

I climbed to the second step and took up the quill. With a steady hand, I filled the line with my carefully practiced script. *Katherine Christina Mercer.*

Now Lady MacDonald.

A twinge of panic worked its way to the surface again. I took a deep breath and struggled to tamp it down, while pretending interest in the paper before me. I noted that my husband's signature was fine, but our witness, Ian's, was little more than chicken scratch. Though he'd been upset when signing, I'd have wagered he couldn't have done any better had his emotions been in check. It was funny what one could tell from a simple signature. I'd been studying them a long time, mostly on paintings I'd been fortunate to view in London's cathedrals. In this case, I surmised that Laird MacDonald had some level of education. Ian, on the other hand, did not; his letters were ill-formed and little more than squiggles and lines.

Alistair Campbell came forward next, his grin as welcoming as Ian MacDonald's had been threatening. He signed as the other witness, and then there were no more delays to be had. I sensed my husband was anxious to be off.

I was simply anxious.

The small sea of men parted as I followed him toward the

front doors. I felt a hand on my arm and saw it was Mother's. I leaned forward, wanting to feel her comforting embrace, but she pushed past me to stand in front of my new husband.

"Lord MacDonald, there is the matter of our settlement."

I felt myself pale and blush at the same time. *To so brazenly ask—*

He reached into the pocket of his coat to pull out an envelope. A small square of tartan came with it and fluttered to the ground. I held back a gasp. Though the fabric was tiny, I knew from Father that having even that much of a clan's plaid was open rebellion. But Laird MacDonald seemed unconcerned. He handed the envelope to Mother.

"This is all there will be. Spend it wisely." He bent to pick up the scrap of fabric, which I quickly saw was not one square of tartan, but two, sewn crudely together.

"For you." He pressed the cloth into my hands. "This is the Campbell plaid—your mother's people." He flipped the square over to a brighter, bolder pattern. "The other side is the Macdonald's. My clan. Yours now as well."

I sensed strain as he spoke the last.

"Blasphemy," someone on the Macdonald side said. I feared it was Ian.

Laird Macdonald pretended not to hear. "Keep it well hidden. We've no desire to lose our heads on this trip."

We. The word chilled me. I was one of them now. I had been all along. No wonder Father had protested the treatment of the Scots. His own daughter was one.

My fingers closed around the scrap as a burning began behind my eyes.

Long ago my father had taken me from Scotland, knowing that someday I would return.

"My only child lies dead," Laird Campbell began. "Her only child, my granddaughter, is but four years old. She is a Campbell at heart." The laird thumped his fist loudly over his chest. "But half of her blood is English."

I gasped. I couldn't help myself. Nor could I help the surge of bitterness and repulsion that filled me. "Was her mother—"

"She was not forced." Laird Campbell's voice was eerily quiet again. "She chose this Englishman, a soldier—against my wishes, mind you—but he was her choice."

I couldn't fathom how Liam Campbell was laird when he couldn't even control his own daughter.

"For an Englishman, he was a good man," Laird Campbell said. "He cared for her."

There were no good Englishmen. "Where is he now?" I asked, glancing about uneasily.

Laird Campbell answered with a clouded look, and shaded, almost guilty eyes.

I didn't understand at first; then an awful suspicion filled my mind. "He's one of them, isn't he?" I demanded. "One of the soldiers who killed my father."

Chapter Three

To keep from giving away my overwrought emotions as we moved toward the front door, I looked down at the ring on my finger. The slender band was not plain, as I had supposed, but intricately designed. I lifted my hand, studying it closer.

"This is beautiful," I said, somewhat astonished at the detail on a piece so tiny. Two delicate bands, each engraved with a distinct and different pattern, converged in the middle, crossing over one another and looping together so as to be joined. "Where did you—"

"I made it," Collin said. And in that moment I determined to think of him by that name instead of Lord or Laird MacDonald. Anyone who could create something so beautiful was someone I ought to be able to call by his given name.

"You've found the way to her heart, Collin. Just ply her with jewelry," a Campbell called out.

It's not that. It's not that at all, I wanted to say. I'd been the first one in the family to offer up my jewelry when our funds ran low. I hadn't missed any of it, had never had a piece I cared much about—*until now.*

"Thank you," I said, ignoring the comment and looking at Collin. As before, he did not quite meet my eye. "It must have taken you a very long time."

"I began some years ago," he confided. Or at least, it felt like a confidence to me. "When I received your father's letter, I had only to polish the ring."

"I will treasure it." I clasped my hand to my heart, which had quickened at his words.

I knew the labor a painting required—the hours of sketching, the process of mixing colors, the brush strokes and shading that had to be just right. But this ring was an entirely different type of art, one that had to have required infinitely more time and patience. I thought of the previous evening and my frustration with a sky that had taken only a few weeks to paint. I'd hoped to have fixed it, but had I been working with metal and something so fine and small, there would have been no margin for error, no possibility for change.

A swell of admiration for my new husband—or his talent, at least—took hold inside of me, a spark of warmth on an otherwise cold occasion.

We'd made our way through the crowd of Campbells and MacDonalds, and for the last time, I walked out the front door of the only house I could ever remember living in.

Mother ran along beside us, the envelope that Collin had given her thrust forward in her hand.

"Lord Macdonald, there must be some mistake. This is not what was agreed upon."

"It is what was available." He paused on the step to look over at her. "My people are starving. That I have spared this much is nothing short of a miracle. I suggest you make good use of it." He turned to me, holding his hand out toward the carriage. "Katherine."

Inwardly I cringed at the use of my given name. A few minutes ago I'd been Katie. Why the change? For some reason Katherine had always sounded harsh to me, whereas Christina seemed more melodic. But I supposed now—since I was returning to my mother's homeland, and her name had been Katherine, too—that I ought to get used to being called that.

I also supposed that my situation was not about to improve, as I had been led to believe by both my mother's words and my father's letter the previous night. Had Collin

MacDonald been an English lord, this trickery would have bothered me far more than the twinge of worry I felt right now. But Collin was not English, and I was not just a Macdonald now. I was a Campbell, and my marriage was the link to my past.

"I must have a minute to say goodbye to my mother." I did not ask it of Collin, but expected that courtesy and turned away, taking Mother's arm and leading her a short distance from the carriage.

"Oh, Christina, whatever will we do? Your grandfather is getting on in years. The cousin who is to inherit his estate has already moved closer and begun taking over some of the duties with the tenants. He'll not want Timothy and me there for long."

I opened my mouth to say something but found I could not. I was about to leave—forever, possibly—and my mother was still going on about the money.

"Anna will have to take us in, and she won't be the least happy about it. We'll arrive penniless. There is hardly enough in here to outfit us and get us to London."

"Perhaps you would like to join me—in *Scotland*," I said, irritated and hurt that all she could think of in this moment of our parting was finances.

This seemed to snap her from misery. "Oh, darling, I'm sorry. You must feel more wretched than I. You should not have been forced to this, and now with no money to come of it—If your Father were here, I'd—"

"Don't say it." I held up a hand. "Do not speak ill of the dead."

She tapped her foot on the ground. "He is fortunate to be in that state, at the moment."

"Mother," I gasped.

She waved my protest away. "You cannot tell me you've not had an angry thought about him the night past."

"No," I admitted. "I cannot." I glanced over my shoulder at Collin. He stood with three other men near the carriage. The rest had moved off toward the horses I'd seen earlier.

Mother followed my gaze. "I didn't know about them—about all this. Your father told me very little."

"You might have told *me* sooner," I accused.

She shook her head. "I promised him I wouldn't." She wrung her hands. "I promised him a great many things I think I oughtn't have."

"Like what?" I asked, wary now that there were more unpleasant surprises in store. Though I could not imagine what she might come up with beyond what had occurred already this morning.

"Your season," she said, taking my hands in hers. "Your grandfather—my father—he wished to pay for it as he did Anna's, and your father wouldn't let him. I didn't understand why at the time, and we fought over it terribly. But I realize now—"

"It was because of this." *Because of him.* I glanced at Collin again. Father had not wanted me to have a season, a chance to meet someone and fall in love. *Because of some promise he made long ago.*

"I'm sorry," Mother said again. "So sorry. I think he would have been, too. I don't think he realized how barbaric—" She stopped herself suddenly, as if just realizing what she'd said. "Well, maybe they're not as bad as all that."

"Maybe not," I said drily.

She smiled and squeezed the tips of my fingers. "You must admit, Christina, that a part of you likes this. A part of you has yearned for this very thing."

"I have not!" My whispered denial was harsh. "I did not wish to marry a stranger and leave England."

"Maybe not aloud you didn't," Mother said. "But think of your paintings. You hardly ever paint anything familiar. Your imagination is always taking you to foreign places."

Was it? Her insight gave me pause. I thought of the painting I'd worked so hard on for Lady Gotties, and how it had not come out the way I felt it should. *Because I did not paint the sky as it looks here.* I never painted the sky—or much else—as it looked here. I'd never realized this before and found it a rather startling revelation. *Do I long for adventure?* I didn't know. I hadn't longed for marriage, nor had I been concerned with my heritage. But in the past hour I'd found I *was* curious.

About both, were I completely honest with myself. Collin did not seem horrible—not the old, fat, overbearing lord I'd imagined. I was not afraid of him. He seemed serious but not mean, and was not near as frightening to look upon as some of his clansmen.

Like that Ian.

As for traveling to Scotland . . . It wasn't anything I'd ever imagined I would do. But I could not deny the curious pull I'd felt since the mob of Campbell men had surrounded and befriended me.

"You agree," Mother said, having watched the revelations cross my face the past minute.

"Not entirely," I said, pleased to realize that what I felt most right now was not sorrow or fear, but agitation. I was still upset that I'd been tricked—by Father—and I didn't like not knowing what was going to come next. I vastly preferred being in charge of my own destiny, and at the moment felt anything but.

And I was irritated I could not pull out my easel right now and paint this scene. Behind us, the men had mounted their horses and made all the more impressive a picture, clustered together as they were. Collin cleared his throat loudly, but did no more. I knew it was time to part.

I leaned forward, hugging my mother. "Tell Timothy I shall write to him. And I'll send him something wonderful from Scotland." What that might be I didn't know, but I guessed there must be something of interest there to a seven-year-old boy.

Tears misted my eyes when I thought of not seeing him again for a very long time. *Ever?* I clutched Mother tighter. "I love you," I whispered, regretful that I had not said those words to her often enough.

"And I shall always love you," she said. "Daughter." Her arms fell away, and I stepped from her embrace, hastily wiping an escaped tear. I did not whisper goodbye—it seemed too final—but walked quickly toward Collin and the other men still standing in the yard.

The carriage door was already opened. My trunk had been secured on the back. Collin held his hand out to me, and I took it, grateful for his steady grip as I stepped up into the carriage.

Once inside, I slid to the far end of the seat and turned my head to look out the narrow window. I heard him climb in beside me and felt the carriage rock as the other men clambered on top and behind. The driver called out to the horses, and the reins snapped. We rolled forward with a lurch. I turned toward Collin, saw the closed, latched door on the other side of him, and my agitation burgeoned, intensified by sudden, irrational fear.

I felt a surge of hatred for the unseen Englishman and even his daughter, whom I'd met earlier. Mostly I felt loathing for the vile man before me.

"I sent him to do it," the Campbell laird admitted, and only my shock kept me from leaping from my chair and going for his throat.

"I sent him because I knew he would show your father mercy."

"Mercy?" I gasped. "Is that what you call it?" Da's broken, bloodied body came to mind, and the food I'd eaten earlier threatened to come up.

"There are far worse ways to die," Laird Campbell said. "Do you know what they've done to the traitors taken to London?" He didn't wait for me to answer. "They're flogged, all while a crowd of people look on, leering and taunting. Then, if the prisoners survive that—and some have, God help them—they're beheaded and their heads held up for all to see, mounted on a gate post, while the bodies are dragged through the streets of London." Laird Campbell leaned near to me. "Can we agree now that I showed your father mercy?"

Chapter Four

Spiders. Heights. Sickness. Poverty—Mother's great fear. All acceptable phobias for a person to have. I ran through the list in my mind, hoping to distract myself in any way possible from the one thing I feared.

I imagined myself precariously balanced on the roof of our house or in a very high tree. I imagined what views I might see up there—similar to those I saw from my attic's tiny window, only grander. While it isn't particularly natural for a person to be so very far above the ground, I also found that the idea did not particularly frighten me either—at least not enough to distract me from my present concerns. *I have to get out of here.*

I tried spiders next. Closing my eyes, trying to block out my surroundings, I pretended that I was back in my attic room and a giant, hairy creature emerged from the eaves. Spiders can have deadly bites, and they are disgusting besides. I might scream if I saw such a sight, but I also knew I could squish the spider with my shoe. Thinking of arachnids was not going to distract me. *We need to stop.*

What if I was gravely ill? What if I lay dying of the fever and pox? Sickness could rob even the young and vigorous of their lives, so it was possible. *But I would not care.* I'd watched my father waste away and knew that when the body became so far gone, the mind was like to follow. In his last days he'd been incoherent and unreachable. In some ways it had been almost a relief when at last he'd been free from his ailing body.

I found I could not muster any amount of fear over illness either. *I cannot breathe.*

And what of poverty? Lord MacDonald—Collin—had told Mother that his people were starving. Did that mean I was likely to be starving soon, too? Somehow I doubted that he would fail to take care of me. His vows, though somewhat ridiculous, had also been reassuring. If I was to have the first cut of his meat and drink of his wine, there would have to be meat and wine to be had.

As for poverty in general—I felt I'd survived that well enough the past year. It had caused Mother no little amount of strife, though I always felt her worries about our change in status had more to do with how we were viewed by our neighbors rather than the practicalities of how we were to continue to eat and where we were going to live. At any rate, even her fears were somewhat normal and justified. Whereas—

Mine was not. Not normal or logical or even explainable, yet it existed within me as real as anything I'd ever experienced. And I had experienced this blinding terror on more than one occasion and felt it rear its head now within the close confines of the carriage. *Let me out.*

My forced thoughts—attempts at directing my worry elsewhere—had met with little success and taken up precious little time. We'd not yet passed the edge of what used to be our property, and already I fumbled with the shade covering the largest window on my side, pushing it up so I might see out. Only there was *no* window, or no glass in it, at least. I stared for several seconds before realizing my good fortune then pulled a pin from my hair and used it to secure the shade, away from the opening.

In the crevice of the open frame I could see little shards of glass—remnants from the pane that must once have been there. That it was there no longer seemed an unexpected blessing. Sitting on the edge of my seat, I pressed my face through the opening and gulped calming breaths of fresh air.

"This coach was the best we could find," Collin said,

sounding annoyed again. "The glass was probably shot out by a highwayman."

"A comforting thought," I said, though being attacked was the least of my concerns at the moment. I didn't look at him. I couldn't—couldn't look anywhere on that side of the carriage for fear of seeing the locked door again.

"A man would have to be a fool to try it," Collin muttered.

Thinking of the well-armed Campbells and MacDonalds riding in front and behind us, I had to agree. Still, just in case we were stopped by thieves or otherwise, I folded the square of tartan and tucked it carefully up inside my sleeve. Tomorrow I would see to it that it was hidden even better.

"You should close the shade. We'll be breathing nothing but road dust soon."

I knew he was right but could not bring myself to follow his suggestion. Though the air coming in through the window was a bit dusty, it was still *air*. And the open space was enough that I thought I might be able to endure the ride—for a while at least. I could feel a surge of terror hovering just below the surface of the temporary calm the missing glass had brought.

I could crawl through that space if necessary. *I am not locked in here.*

"I should prefer to leave it open and enjoy the scenery," I said, hoping Collin would not press the issue.

"You may have my seat," he offered. "And look out the glass here."

Silently I cursed his chivalry. "No, thank you. The open window is fine."

"Still stubborn," I thought I heard Collin grumble, but he did not bother me about it again.

Yesterday's PROMISE

We traveled in silence to the main road. The carriage turned north, and had I not been so anxious about being inside, I might have felt excited. I had only ever traveled south, toward London. What lay north beyond Nottingham was both mysterious and alluring.

But I could not appreciate that now. Dust stirred up from the horses ahead of us was indeed coming inside the carriage. I coughed several times before reluctantly pulling my face from the opening. Collin reached over and snapped the shade back in place.

No! I flashed panicked eyes at him, then at the locked door.

"Stop the carriage," I demanded, practically climbing over Collin to reach the door. I fumbled with the latch and was surprised at how loose it was. I was still gripping the handle when the door detached from it and flew open.

Collin grabbed me around the waist, saving me from pitching out onto the road face first.

"Stop the carriage!" he shouted, stomping loudly with his foot.

"Whoa," the driver called to the team as Collin did his best to pull me back inside. But I was having none of it.

"Let me go," I cried, pushing his hands away. We were still moving slowly, but I managed to right myself and jump, landing in a crouch on the road. Collin shouted something at me, but it was unintelligible, and I didn't look back. Instead I stumbled off, through the tall grasses growing alongside and over to a clump of bushes. These I leaned over, gasping and choking and certain my stomach would empty itself.

Alistair reached me first. He'd dismounted and had his

arm on mine, steadying me as he whispered soothing words. I gagged more, but nothing came up. I'd not eaten dinner last night or breakfast this morning and found myself grateful for that, as it would not lead to further embarrassment or shame in front of my new husband and his people.

I was starting to care about that again, and to return to myself now that I was outside the wretched vehicle. I became more aware when Alistair stepped aside and Collin stood there, a guarded expression upon his face.

"Are you ill?"

I shook my head and wiped my mouth with the back of my hand, though nothing had come up. With a resolute sigh I straightened and turned to look at my husband. He was the only one close to me, the other men having placed themselves a ways off—even Alistair had moved back with them. I felt grateful. I was going to have to explain my behavior to Collin, and that would be bad enough.

"I'm not ill—" *Not physically, anyway.* I offered a trembling smile, which Collin did not return.

"It's just that—" I broke off. How was I supposed to explain my irrationalities? He'd realize he married a madwoman, and he'd probably drive off without me.

Even that would be better than riding in a carriage.

Collin said nothing, but one eyebrow rose expectantly.

"I cannot ride in the carriage," I said, as matter-of-factly as I could. Perhaps he would think this a malady of all Englishwomen, and I might be forgiven.

"It is not good enough for you?" His lips puckered with disdain.

"That's not it at all." I shook my head. "It is perfectly fine. But it's a *carriage*. I cannot ride in them."

"Why?" His brows drew together as if he was perplexed. "Explain yourself."

If only I could. "They frighten me." I sounded like the biggest ninny.

"The horses pulling it frighten you? Or the speed at which it travels?"

I shook my head again. "I have no fear of horses. Nor is it the speed. It is the confines of the space and—and the locked door that frighten me. I know it sounds absurd—"

"It *is* absurd," Collin said, turning from me. "I would much prefer to hear the truth. Is it being so near to me? Are you upset at leaving your home? Those circumstances I might understand. But to place the blame on traveling—"

"I *am* speaking the truth," I said, angered that he'd not believed me. "It has been this way since I was very young. I don't understand it, and I certainly do not enjoy it, but every time I have ever tried to ride in any type of closed vehicle, I have been overcome with panic, to the point that I become unable to breathe and my stomach acts ill. It feels—I feel as if I am being taken against my will, and it is frightening. *I don't even understand it,*" I admitted, throwing my hands up in the air.

Collin turned toward me once more. His eyes darkened, and he looked past me, as if he was in some other time and place. When he spoke again, it was without the anger or annoyance of a moment before.

"You've your father to thank for your fear of carriages."

"My fath—"

"How well can you ride a horse?" He took my arm,

steering me toward the men, most still mounted, waiting on the road. "Alistair, you'll be giving Katie your horse today."

If this took Alistair by surprise, or if he was opposed to it, he hid it well, simply walking toward me and handing over the reins.

"She's a mite bit feisty, this 'un. Best tell her up front who's boss, or she's like to bolt on you now and then." As if to prove his point, the mare reared her head and began pulling away from Collin the moment he tried to move her closer.

He frowned as he looked from the spirited horse to me. "Ian," Collin barked. "Get over here."

Ian was slower to respond, plodding along methodically as the others parted to let him through.

"What?" He peered down at us from atop a fine, black stallion. Ian's shirt billowed, and his long hair blew backward with the breeze. But it was the steel in his eyes and the sneer on his lips that most reminded me of a pirate. I suppressed a shudder and looked elsewhere.

"Give me your horse. You and Alistair will ride in the carriage today."

Ian smirked. "Tired of your wife's company already? Or that unsure of yourself?"

"I'm sure enough that I don't trust you on your own," Collin said. "And it would be a bad omen to spill my brother's blood on my wedding day."

"There's always tomorrow," Ian said, swinging down from his perch. His arm brushed mine roughly as he pushed past us to climb into the carriage. "Wedding day or no, you oughtn't press your luck."

Yesterday's PROMISE

My too-short grey silk ended up being a good choice for more than one reason. The full skirt allowed me to sit astride a horse—something Collin insisted I must do if I was to be allowed to ride on my own. The grey was also not a color easily soiled during the rigors of our ride over England's dusty roads. As we dismounted near the day's end, I found that a few swift shakes of my skirts left them looking not much worse than they had that morning. Unfortunately, I feared that was the only part of me not in worse condition. Everything—from my sunburnt forehead down to my aching back and legs—hurt, with my backside feeling particularly sore and stiff. Shaking out my gown had been but an excuse to linger a moment while I attempted to regain control of my trembling legs.

Clothing accounted for, I took to running fingers through my wind-blown hair. *Black Lion Inn*, I read, glancing at the sign swinging overhead. It appeared a respectable enough place, with ivy growing up the sides, covering much of the two-story building. Weathered stone peeked out beneath this, and wooden shutters framed the windows on both floors. A few souls wandered in and out as I stood there, waiting for Collin to finish speaking to the Campbells and MacDonalds assembled around him.

"We'll stay here tonight," Collin said to me when the others had dispersed. He'd not had two words for me since we began our ride, hours earlier. Relieved though I was to be done riding for the day, I sagged as he confirmed my fears that we had reached our destination.

Now what? For the first hour or two of our journey, I'd been far too busy enjoying the new landscape and the thrill of being on a horse again to worry much over the coming evening. As the day had worn on that worry had crept closer, as had my misery and discomfort. The latter being the more immediate of concerns, I had been focused on that—on how to *remain* on Ian's horse as long as required.

Both the pains and pleasures of the day came to an abrupt end when I thought on what pleasures my husband might expect to receive tonight. Along with the knowledge about the wedding band being worn over the vein that led directly to one's heart, Anna had also acquired information about the marriage bed and what occurred in it. At the time, her revelations had been enough to fill me with deepest gratitude that I'd not been granted a season or any hope of marriage.

And now—*I wished she'd never told me.* This evening was perhaps one situation where stumbling blindly into the future might have been best.

Our carriage rolled to a stop behind us, and I stepped aside, wanting to be well away before its occupants exited. I was too late. The door banged open, and Ian jumped down, a scowl on his face that made Collin's frown appear almost cheerful. Ian glanced my way and began marching toward me, his hand outstretched. Instead of fleeing, I stood my ground and held out the reins to his horse. Though I'd have much preferred to have been in Alistair's debt, Collin had not allowed me to even attempt to seat the mare. Feeling particularly grateful that I was to ride instead of somehow enduring the carriage, I'd not felt it prudent to argue the matter. But now . . .

"Thank you for allowing me to ride your—"

Ian snatched the reins from me. "You'd best find some other way to transport your Campbell bride before tomorrow," he snapped at Collin, then pulled the stallion along with him toward the stables near the back of the inn.

Avoiding Collin's gaze, I turned toward the carriage in time to watch Alistair descend the steps, somewhat stiffly. That both he and Ian made it all the way here without any harm coming to at least one of them seemed something of a miracle, given Ian's outburst this morning and what else I'd seen of his disposition.

Thinking of poor Alistair, who'd been nothing but kind and pleasant to me since our first meeting, I sought him out, intending both thanks and an apology for my part in his unfortunate circumstance today.

"I must thank Alistair," I said, by way of explanation to Collin then ran—or rather hobbled along—to catch the group of Campbells heading off down the road. When it became apparent I was not going to catch up, I called out to him.

Alistair stopped and the rest of the Campbells with him. As one they turned back to look at me.

"What are you needing, lass?" Alistair asked kindly. His eyes were tired, and he did not seem nearly as jovial as he'd been this morning.

"I'm so sorry about taking your horse and you having to ride with Ian," I said. "Perhaps we can trade the carriage for another horse, so you won't have to ride with Ian tomorrow."

"I *won't* ride with Ian tomorrow," Alistair said, his voice shaking with anger. "Won't make any other Campbell do it neither. Ian can ride by himself, and if the MacDonalds set a toe out of line they can be hanged." He removed a flask from the pouch at his hip, opened it, and took a long drink.

None of what he'd said made any sense, and I wondered if rattling around in the carriage over rough roads all day had addled his mind a bit, or if he'd earlier had to indulge in drinking whatever it was in his flask to endure Ian's company. "I'm so sorry," I said once more, feeling surprisingly upset that I'd let my newfound relatives down so quickly, and when they'd come so far to see me wed. "Nothing in my trunk is that important." I pushed the thought of my paints and canvas to the back of my mind. "We can go on without it, and then we won't even need the carriage." Maybe I could find a way to transport a few of my supplies on the back of a horse.

Alistair's eyes softened, and he beckoned me closer. The other Campbells, Quinn, Finlay and Donaid, as well as those I hadn't figured out how to keep straight yet, gathered around us.

"The carriage isn't really for you," Alistair confided.

"No matter what the MacDonald told you," Donaid added.

"He did think you'd be riding in it," Alistair continued. "But it's really a way for us to have our weapons nearby without displaying them to the world."

My gaze moved to his waist, and I realized his broadsword was missing, as was his pistol, though I supposed that might be hidden elsewhere. I glanced at the other Campbells and realized that they, too, had removed the weapons they'd been wearing this morning. *Have the MacDonalds taken theirs off as well?*

Alistair was watching me closely. "You'll not be knowing this, I'm guessing, but the Scots aren't allowed arms. If we're found with 'em, it's treason, and enough to land us in prison—or worse."

"But to travel unarmed is asking for trouble as well," Finlay said. "Especially in England. Bloody Dragoons don't need a reason to bring us in."

"Alistair's beard here is reason enough." Donaid tugged at a red, springy lock.

"So we've got to have the means to defend ourselves—without parading it afore the world," Alistair finished. "The carriage works nicely for that."

"The weapons are inside?" I wondered *where* exactly. Had I been sitting on a pile of loaded pistols? I hadn't seen any this morning, but then I had been trying to see as little of the inside of the carriage as possible.

He nodded. "Beneath the floor, behind the cushions and such."

"But if you were attacked, what good would that do? You'd not be able to reach them quick enough."

"A few of us have our pistols." After a quick glance over the heads of the others, Alistair peeled his vest back to reveal his. "And with Collin in the carriage, we knew we'd a pretty good chance for a fair fight."

Fair? Against whom or what? "Why is that?"

"He's the best aim," Donaid said.

"Now I don't know about that." Alistair looked slightly offended. "I've a fair hand, too—as does Ian, I hear."

"That's why you two were chosen." Now it made sense.

And here I'd feared that Collin had made Ian give me his horse because he'd been so surly toward me this morning. It was a relief to know I wasn't any part of the reason at all.

Except that I was. An enormous part of it.

"You can see what a risk this was, us coming here to get you." One of the younger, quieter Campbells spoke up.

"That's enough, Malcom," Alistair scolded him. To me he said, "'Course we'd come. Couldn't have you stuck in England forever. It's high time you were with your people again. We might not have much these days—but each other. We've got family, and so do you."

Such an eloquent speech from a tired, old man who'd had a difficult day brought tears to my eyes, and I only just checked the impulse to hug him. I'd needed my father so much these past months and still needed him now, but in Alistair I sensed a relative who might fill in nicely.

"You'd best get back now, lass," he said. "We're bedding down nearby, but Collin'll be waiting for you at the tavern. Don't want him thinking you've left him already, do you?"

Already? Did they think I'd ever leave him? I'd given my word. First silently, to Father to honor the promise he'd made, and then out loud to Collin—before God and witnesses. I did not imagine that I had Anna's situation and was in for a lifetime of bliss. Collin and I were strangers to one another, and I'd no doubt the days and weeks and months ahead of us were going to be difficult. But I'd made a commitment, and I'd keep it.

"I don't want him thinking anything of the sort," I said, standing up for—my husband? Our marriage? I wasn't sure what exactly, but I wanted the Campbells to know that though they were family, Collin was now, too—as much or more than they, as far as I was concerned.

"Go on with you, then," Alistair said, a hint of a smile in his voice that made me think he'd read and understood my thoughts. "Collin's a good man, to be sure. A MacDonald, but a good man. You've your grandfather to thank for that, I reckon."

This bit of information brought a dozen other questions to mind, but with a wave of my hand I bid the Campbells farewell, telling myself there would be time enough for answers later. For now . . . it was my wedding night, and my husband was waiting for me.

"Mercy would have been to help my father instead of turning him in, to show some respect for your fellow countrymen. Instead of working against them with the English." My heart brimmed with hatred for the man before me.

Laird Campbell's hand came down on mine forcefully, pinning me in place. "We've things to discuss; you'd best learn your place and to control your temper, or it will lead to great trouble."

"Perhaps you should gain a temper," I shouted. "You should feel something for your people, for Scotland, instead of allowing one of those English dogs to lie with your own daughter."

The bitter taste of blood filled my mouth before I even realized I'd been struck. Laird Campbell towered over me.

"You will learn to control your tongue. You will learn patience. And most importantly, you will, from this moment forward, never speak ill of any Campbell."

Chapter Five

Unfortunately it was not Collin I first encountered upon my return to the Black Lion Inn. Ian stood beneath the sign, a blade of straw clenched between his teeth, his dark eyes upon me, following my every move. I was going to have to walk past him to enter the building, and it was all I could do not to slow my steps.

Yesterday's PROMISE

As I approached, I spoke with what I hoped was a pleasant, confident voice. "I have just been thanking Alistair for taking my place in the carriage today. I extend that same gratitude to you." I reached for the handle and started to pull the heavy door open.

Ian's hand above mine pushed it shut. "You'll never be a MacDonald."

"I am Collin's wife," I said, my voice sounding less certain.

"Not for long," Ian hissed in my ear. His breath was hot and foul, and I couldn't help but grimace.

"Collin didn't want you." Ian's hand touched mine on the handle, and I jerked away, frightened and repulsed by everything about him.

He pulled the door open, a wicked smile curving his lips. "Didn't want you at all. Not likely he'll be keeping you, either." He held his other hand out, in mockery of gentlemanly behavior. I ducked beneath his arm and hurried inside without a backward glance, though the sounds of his quiet laughter followed me, as did the words he'd spoken.

My eyes blinked, attempting to adjust to the dark. *Collin didn't want you.*

"Over here, Katie."

The sound of his voice, and the name that sounded almost endearing or at the least friendly, felt like a spark of hope over Ian's declaration that I was unwanted. But I feared Ian was right. Beyond the awkward and falsely sentimental vows he had spoken, Collin had shown no inclination toward friendship with me. At best I felt I annoyed him. And at worst . . .

I am a Campbell and English. Doomed before we even met. No doubt my ridiculous behavior over the carriage had confirmed whatever suspicions he may have had about my character.

For my part, Collin and I were simply strangers. I had no ill feelings toward him, and I hoped that with time we might at least be friends, that our situation would be tolerable for us both.

The evening looming before us promised to be anything but tolerable.

Yet tolerate it I must.

With a smile of false courage, I turned in the direction of Collin's voice as he called to me again. The low light of dusk filtered through the tavern windows, casting an eerie glow over the cramped room. Collin sat alone at a table in the far corner. Between us stood a dozen other tables, all crammed with men engaged in the various stages of eating and drinking. It seemed at least half had turned to look at me.

Collin rose to greet me, and I felt a surge of gratitude at the small gesture as I walked toward him, taking care to pass between the tables that allowed the widest berth. Still, I felt eyes following my every move.

Have they never seen a woman before?

"Our food is almost ready," he said by way of greeting. Considering what Alistair had said about Collin thinking I was leaving him, and Ian's unnerving assessment that I would not be Collin's wife for long, talk of food seemed rather unexpected. I stood there dumbly for a few seconds, trying to think how to respond.

"Or would you rather go upstairs?" Collin asked,

misreading my lack of response for exhaustion. *Or other interests?* "Your trunk has already been taken up to the room."

This was enough to snap my mind back into focus. The *last* thing I wanted was to go upstairs with him. "I would prefer to eat down here, thank you." I walked past him and seated myself at the table before he could offer further suggestions.

If Collin thought my behavior odd, he did not comment on it, but seated himself opposite me and signaled the server that we were ready for our food.

"You did well today," he said, in a rather begrudging tone, as if he did not really wish to offer the compliment or could not quite believe it true. He glanced at me. "It was a long ride. No doubt you'll be feeling it tomorrow."

I was feeling it already but wasn't about to share that with him. "We sold my horse some months ago, and I have missed riding. It was a fine thing to be able to do so again. And even finer to be away from the carriage. I thank you."

"No thanks necessary." Collin took a sip of whatever was in his cup and indicated with his hand that I might do the same. "I had it filled for you earlier."

I brought the cup to my lips, hoping for cool water but found instead something considerably stronger—some sort of ale, I guessed, though I was not familiar with the taste. I took but a small sip, not trusting the drink or my ability to consume it without becoming intoxicated before the night even began.

Instead I attempted to start a conversation that I hoped would both last a while and answer some of my many questions. "About my father—"

"Mm-hm," Collin grunted, his gaze remaining fixed near the tavern door.

I pressed on. "Why do you believe he is responsible for my fear of carriages?" I'd been thinking on this throughout the day. There was my entire recently discovered past that I remembered nothing of. Any knowledge of previous events or relationships might help me better navigate a future vastly different from the one I'd imagined.

"You do not remember the day you left Scotland?" Collin said, finally pulling his gaze from the door to look at me. I wondered who he was watching for, then caught sight of Ian, lingering in the shadowy entrance.

"No." I shook my head. "I remember nothing of my life before England."

"*Nothing?*" His face seemed to pale, and his mouth gaped.

"No," I repeated. "Not my mother or my home in Scotland or—"

"Me?"

There seemed something vulnerable in Collin's expression as he asked the question. No longer did he appear quite so stern and foreboding as I had first believed. Or possibly it was only that he seemed less fierce compared to some of the other MacDonalds. *Compared to Ian.*

I thought that perhaps if Collin smiled, he might be pleasant to look at. I hoped it would be sooner rather than later that I would get to test that theory. I wished I could remember him and if he ever was prone to smiling. But in searching the deep brown of his eyes and the lines of his face, I found nothing even vaguely familiar. Still, there had been that feeling when I'd first seen him, a jolt of recollection when our eyes met. Or had I just imagined that? Had I wished it so?

"I don't remember you. I'm sorry."

He sat back in his chair and considered me as I had just done him. I squirmed uncomfortably beneath his gaze.

"If you don't remember, how is it that your father came to convince you to return to Scotland and marry me? What did he tell you?"

"Nothing." My answers were all starting to sound the same. And how had he come to be the one asking the questions when I was the one in need of answers? "Father never spoke of you. The only time he ever spoke of Scotland was when he stood up for her. He went to parliament to protest the Act of Proscription. He lost his commission because of that."

His commission. His will to live. His health. His life.

"If you think to convince me that he was a good man, you are sorely mistaken."

"He *was* a good man," I said, rushing to Father's defense. "How dare you say otherwise when you didn't even know him."

"I did know him," Collin said, his voice as quiet as mine had been raised. "You have forgotten; I have not."

I worked to reign in my temper. I'd had a lovely childhood in a fine home. Collin had seen none of that, none of Father's stories when tucking Anna and me in our beds. He'd seen none of our outings together, nor the way Father spoke kindly of all things, encouraging our curiosity about the world. Collin didn't know of Father's quiet and gentle temperament and the way he'd astonished everyone when he took up the fight for Scotland.

"It would seem I am at an unfair advantage," I said coolly

when at last I trusted myself to speak. "As are you," I added before Collin could jump in with further insults. "I have known the man one way; you knew him in quite another—during a time when he was enlisted in the fight against Prince Charles and his supporters."

Collin acknowledged my speech with the barest nod. He'd gone back to watching the doorway again.

"Will you tell me about my father during that time?" *Will you answer the question I first asked?* "Tell me what happened the day that we left for England. Let me hear the whole of it and judge for myself."

"Your father was good to you?" Collin asked. Something in his tone made it seem as if this was a new idea to him, as if he'd never considered that possibility before. "Or were you visiting his grave today out of duty?"

Had that only been today? It felt as if years had passed since then. "He was good to me. I loved him very much."

"Then we had best leave it," Collin said with finality. "The past is just that." His gaze traveled beyond me again, to some other distant point. To a time that I was not now, or would be, privy to.

With an inward sigh I conceded defeat—for the time being. But I knew I'd best come up with a longer-lasting topic, or I would find myself upstairs and alone with my husband within the half hour. I dared a glance at Collin and found him drumming his fingers on the table and looking with some agitation toward the door, where Ian still stood.

"Excuse me a moment." Collin stood and pushed back his chair, then strode across the room to Ian. I watched, uneasy, as they exchanged what appeared to be heated words.

After a few minutes, Ian turned his back on Collin but not before he'd swept his arm in front of him, beckoning fellow MacDonalds to rise from the surrounding tables. I'd not realized that nearly all of them seemed to be present in the smallish room. Once they'd filed out the front door, the tavern became decidedly more quiet.

On the way back to our table, Collin stopped by the bar and placed a handful of coins on the counter. I guessed these were to cover whatever drinks and food the other MacDonalds had consumed. He returned to his seat looking considerably less worried.

Would that I felt the same. We were as alone as we'd been all day, and I almost found myself wishing there were still a few more MacDonalds for company.

"They are not staying here?" I asked when Collin had taken a drink and leaned back in his chair.

He shook his head. "Too costly—in more ways than one. We don't want anyone to take notice of us. They weren't to be in here to begin with. "Ian's foolish idea. Wanting to stir up trouble, no doubt."

"He doesn't like me very much," I said, not particularly wanting to talk about Ian, but finding him as good a topic as any at the moment.

"Ian doesn't like anyone," Collin said.

Do you? "What an unpleasant way to go about life."

Collin grunted his agreement, then surprised me by speaking actual words on the subject. "When Ian was fourteen he was given over to the Munros. They hated the MacDonalds even more than the Campbells did and treated Ian cruelly. It was only two years ago that he gained his freedom. Until then I'd believed him dead."

I didn't see what this had to do with Ian hating me, but I kept my opinion to myself. Collin had just spoken more words—excepting his vows—than he had to me all day, something I was not about to discourage. "And now, where does he live?"

"At the MacDonald keep, of course. With me. We're brothers."

My eyes must have shown my distress at this, because Collin's mouth curved in what might have been a wry smile had he held onto it long enough. Instead the look came off as much more of a sneer—the same expression I'd seen on Ian just a short while before.

"Not exactly the family you were hoping to marry into?" Collin lifted his cup to his mouth.

"I wasn't hoping to marry into *any* family," I threw back, dismissing his sinister half-smile from my mind. I did not wish to draw parallels between the two brothers. "I hadn't plans to marry at all—until last night, when my mother told me you were on your way for that very purpose."

Collin choked on the drink he'd been in the process of swallowing. "*Last* night?"

I nodded. "At this time yesterday I had never heard of Collin MacDonald or Ian, or Alistair Campbell—or any of it—of you. I didn't even know I'd Scottish blood."

Disbelief, then anger paraded across Collin's face. "What did your mother mean to accomplish by that?" he demanded. "By waiting until we were almost upon your doorstep?"

I shrugged. "She insisted that it was Father who asked it of her. There was only his letter, telling me that he had promised long ago that I should marry you. He asked that I honor his promise." I held out my hands. "So here I am."

"You are either very courageous or extremely foolish," Collin said. "I'm not sure which."

"Courageous sounds so much better, don't you think?" I smiled, showing him how it was done and hoping he might follow my example. He glared at me instead.

A slow learner. I withheld another sigh. "What choice did I have?" I asked. "We were about to lose our home, and Father's letter led us to believe that if I wed you there would be a more substantial payment for my mother." I frowned. This still did not sit well with me. "Though without your funds my mother would not have even been able to get to London to stay with her family there." I said this to console myself more than anything, though it did not. *Have I given myself away for nothing? Might I still have been in my attic–perhaps counting out the pounds paid to me by Lady Gotties for my painting?*

"Some mother, trading you away like that," Collin said derisively. He'd drained his cup and took to refilling it again from the bottle on the table.

"That is oft the way of marriage in England," I said, wondering at my defense of Mother. Her behavior this morning *had* been rather wretched. "Fathers often trade their daughters away. Is it not so in Scotland?"

"Sometimes," Collin said absently. "Though nothing is as it used to be—as it was before the uprising. We're too consumed with having enough to eat and a roof over our heads to worry much over bloodlines and such. Many couples simply handfast in front of a witness. Then, after a year has passed, their marriage becomes official—if they both live that long." He muttered the last under his breath.

The picture he painted set me to worrying again. Yet were

we not at an inn, two bowls of steaming stew and a basket of fresh bread being delivered to our table this very minute? If Collin was truly that poor, how could he afford this meal and our lodging? I felt the need to apologize for the expense that I was.

"I am sorry it was so costly to come to England."

He waved away my regrets and concentrated on his food.

"Would it not have been simpler to send for me?" *One woman to make the journey instead of two dozen men from different clans?*

"And who should have been your traveling companion?" Collin did not wait for me to answer. "Not safe."

If he'd said the words in a different tone—one that didn't indicate I was, in fact, both an annoyance and a serious problem—I might have felt touched by his concern. Instead I felt frustrated with my new husband and his lack of compassion.

My stomach chose that moment to growl with hunger. I hadn't eaten all day, but I wasn't certain if I *could* eat, uptight as I was. I took a piece of bread from the basket and nibbled it.

"Should we be staying at an inn?" I asked. "Is it wise, if the others are not? Will they feel slighted?"

Collin's spoon stopped midair, and he looked up at me. "Would you prefer to sleep in the forest with Ian and the other men?"

In the midst of twenty or so strangers or alone in a room with Collin? Neither choice seemed particularly appealing.

"I don't want to be a burden."

"Don't worry about it." Collin shoveled another

spoonful into his mouth, eating as if it was his first meal in a very long time.

He hadn't denied that I was a burden. I nibbled my bread some more.

"Eat," Collin said, pointing at my nearly untouched plate. "I can pay for it. If you must know, your grandfather had set aside funds for when the time came that I was to fetch you."

"Oh." *So Collin was paid to marry me as well?* The situation grew more discouraging by the moment.

"Why did my grandfather not come himself?" I asked, feeling both anxious and excited to meet my real mother's father.

Collin's eyes darkened. "He's dead."

Of course. Just like my real mother, Father, his parents . . . I was surprised to feel disappointed. I should have known. I should not care.

"Why did you come to get me, then?" *If neither Grandfather nor my father were there to make you?* "Why did you marry me?" Surely there were women in Scotland who would love to marry a laird.

"Long ago I gave your grandfather my word."

"So we are both bound by promises made to another and by another long ago?"

Collin met my gaze. "We are bound by promises made by *us*. Long ago and today. My word was binding then, as it is now."

Don't even think you will get out of going upstairs with me tonight, is what he might have said.

"I am grateful, at least, that this is not at your expense."

You aren't paying for this meal or our room. I know I am legally your wife, but you are a stranger, and I do not feel as if I owe you anything—yet." I would have to behave as a wife sometime soon. I knew that much. *Thanks to Anna.* But did it have to be tonight?

Collin's gaze slid from mine, down to the table and his near-empty bowl.

Was that guilt I caught flickering in his eyes?

"You ought to know—" he began, and for all the world it sounded like he was about to make a confession of some sort. "You came with a dowry sizeable enough that my clan stood to benefit from it."

"Ah—" Hurt and shock competed at the forefront of my mind, followed by another, even more sobering realization.

If I'd felt trapped by my predicament last night, Collin must have felt—must still be feeling—the same ten times over. I'd needed to marry so that Mother and Timothy would be all right. Collin had an entire family—families, a clan—to worry over. His cause was that much larger, and the necessity of going through with the marriage that much greater if he stood to obtain funds for his starving people. *He might not have wanted me, but he needed me—or rather, my money.*

"Scotland is not so very different from England," I said.

"No," Collin agreed, his own voice sober. "In some ways not so different at all."

I forced myself to finish the meal, reasoning that I couldn't feel any worse than I did already, since Collin's revelation about the true nature of our marriage. It was clear now why so many Campbells were present this morning, escorting us on our journey. They'd not come to see me, but to ensure that the terms of the contract were carried out.

The same reason so many MacDonalds had lingered in the tavern? Keeping watch over me and, thereby, their investment? Ian's earlier words took on a new, chilling meaning. *Not likely he'll be keeping you . . .*

"What would you have done if I'd refused to marry you?" I asked Collin before I'd quite realized the direction of my thoughts and stopped them from being spoken aloud.

"I half-expected you *would* refuse," he said.

Half expected or half wished? "What would you have done?" I asked. *What will you do if I refuse to go upstairs with you now?*

He shrugged. "Ian would have been happy. He's not much for bargaining with the devil."

I laughed, a nervous giggle. "The Campbells are the devil, I suppose?"

Collin nodded. "Though were you to add horns to Ian's head, he'd be a good likeness himself."

My eyes widened, and I smiled. I thought, perhaps, that Collin almost did, too. Again, it did not last long enough to fully form. It was as if he was reluctant to have any sort of pleasant interaction with me. Every time I thought we'd made a little headway, he withdrew again, back to the morose quiet that led me to believe Ian had been absolutely right in his assessment of the situation.

Collin doesn't want you.

"You'd best get some sleep," he said, pushing back his chair and standing. "Tomorrow will be another long day."

Sleep? That I could be so fortunate. According to Anna, not much of that occurred on one's wedding night.

When Collin made no move to assist me I pushed back my own chair and stood, my movements stiff and awkward as my body protested the long hours of riding.

So much for similarities in culture. If my husband was lacking in such basic manners, what might I expect from him tonight? Would he show me any kindness or consideration at all?

He tossed a few more coins on the table and waited for me at the base of the stairs. Though the MacDonalds had vacated the tavern, I felt other eyes upon me as I crossed the room and imagined that each man here knew that Collin and I had just married and tonight was our wedding night.

He held his hand out, indicating I should go before him. I wished that he had taken my hand in his, or placed it upon his arm as I had seen Anna's husband do so many times. My trembling fingers were left with only the rickety railing to hold for support. I clung to it, my trepidation rising with each creaking step.

At the top we turned right and made our way down a long, narrow hall, to a door with peeling paint. *Away from the others so no one will hear if I scream? Curse you, Anna, for all your vast knowledge of things that ought not be known.*

Collin turned the knob and pushed the door open. He stepped inside, and after a few seconds' hesitation I followed. The room was stark—iron rail bed, smallish stand, a chipped washbasin, and along the far wall, my trunk. Plain curtains hung at the lone window.

"We leave at first light. Be ready." Collin stepped from the room, closing the door as he went.

"Wait." I put my hand out, grasping the knob. "You—you're not sleeping here?" As soon as I'd asked the question, I realized how foolish it was. Of course he'd be sleeping here. He was probably just giving me a moment to change and get into bed.

"I'll be in the next room over. Lock the door."

"But, Ian—the others—they weren't waiting downstairs to see that, to ensure—" I broke off quickly, my mind finally realizing what my mouth was saying. Heat crept up my face. *What is wrong with me? Do I want him thinking I expected to be intimate?*

"Good night," I muttered, not daring to look up. I released my grip on the door and expected it would close at once.

Instead, Collin continued to stand there with it partway open. "We've spoken vows, Katie." His voice sounded strained and weary. "No physical act will strengthen the truth of the promises I gave you. You have my word. We are well and truly married. Nothing further is required."

With that he was gone, and the door clicked shut behind him. I turned the lock, lest he change his mind, then sagged against the door in short-lived relief, as some other, completely foreign feeling raged inside.

He really doesn't want me. This final rejection hurt badly. I told myself that there were far worse things than having a husband who didn't care for me. I was safe—and free—if only for a little while.

Nothing further is required. I would be grateful for this respite.

For the first time all night, my stomach unclenched, and I anticipated a pleasant evening to myself. I ran to the window to look at my surroundings and saw that the forest grew right up to the back of the inn. I wrestled the window open and leaned out, close enough to touch the nearest tree. Glancing down, I caught sight of a light bobbing between the branches below. It swayed momentarily, then steadied, lifting in the air to reveal a set of eyes staring up at me.

Ian's mane of inky black hair didn't quite blend in with the night, and the white of his teeth when he flashed what could only be called a sinister smile sent chills up my spine. I backed away, slamming the window shut and letting the curtain fall into place. I would not be enjoying a cool breeze or the view tonight.

As I crossed to my trunk to fetch a nightdress, decidedly wicked laughter echoed up the wall from outside.

Ian was right about Collin, and he knew it. But worse, he knew that I did, too.

My mouth and cheek stung. I touched my lip and brought my fingers away bloody. Fury burned within me, but I kept silent.

Laird Campbell sat again and pulled his chair closer. "I mean to deal fairly with you, lad, but you must learn your place."

"I'll never have a place here. I'd rather die than be your servant."

"I don't want you for my servant." Laird Campbell leaned forward over the table, looking at me intently, searching my face. "I want you to grow up well and marry my Katie. You're to be a leader to your people and hers as well."

Chapter Six

Wanting to get my mind off the MacDonald brothers—both of them—I took a thorough assessment of the tiny room. I discovered the basin to be full of water, and beside it was a towel that appeared to be clean, to my delight. After some minutes of awkward wrestling with hands behind my back, I managed to get out of the grey silk and my corset and slips. Being free of such encumbrances lightened my mood considerably, and I grew cheerier yet when I had made good use of the water and towel.

Dressed in a clean shift from my trunk—the night and

tiny room being too stifling for a sleeping gown—I lay back on the bed, thinking over the day's events. While this tavern room wasn't my attic, I felt grateful for the privacy it afforded after such a trying day. A part of me, a tiny part, to be certain, felt a little bereft.

I had worried over tonight, but I certainly hadn't imagined spending it alone, in a roadside inn that appeared to be at least a century old, and with a husband as eager as I to avoid intimacy. It puzzled me and wounded my pride. I tried to dwell on the positives. By this arrangement, Collin had spared me a great deal of embarrassment, at the least. His words suggested that this reprieve was to last beyond tonight, indefinitely perhaps. This was fine with me, though I realized that I wanted him to like me, to know who I was beyond the heritage he found so offensive. Perhaps tomorrow would be better and we would start anew.

I could hope.

I could also think of little else. I did not enjoy being at odds with anyone, particularly the man I was now destined to spend my life with.

It was strange to realize that a little over twenty-four hours ago I'd been in my attic, my biggest worry getting a painting ready for Mrs. Gotties.

I'll never finish it now. Thinking of all the paintings I'd left behind soured my mood. Imagining my mother and Timothy and Anna all together—without me—made my heart ache. My evening alone was turning to self-torture.

Almost before I realized what I was doing, I was out of bed and rummaging through my trunk for my sketch pad and charcoals. Art had always soothed me; why should it not do so now? Time and my worries began to slip away as my hands sketched first broad and then more detailed lines. The image before me was starting to take shape when a sudden thumping from the next room over startled me.

I pressed my palm flat to the thin wall and listened. The sound of stretching rope came from the other side as the bed's occupant settled in.

I sat facing the wall, imagining Collin on the other side of it. *So close and yet . . .* It had been the same all day. Though I'd been able to see him then, it was as if he had built an invisible wall between us. Looking directly at me might have breached the wall, so he'd managed to avoid that as much as possible, looking through or past me instead. Touching of any sort was dangerous, too. *The reason he'd made certain I had my own horse to ride?* Talking too seriously or in any detail was also to be avoided, as was anything that might allow us to be at all close, to behave as husband and wife ought.

I let my hand slide from the wall and scooted away, returning to my drawing. Moonlight was just beginning to come through the curtains, and I remembered something Father had told me long ago whenever he had to go away for a time.

It's the same moon shining down on us always. When you miss me, look at the moon and know I'm looking at it, too, and thinking of you.

Was that true still? Could he still see it and think of me? Missing Father only made me sadder, so I forced my thoughts elsewhere, shading and reworking the sketch in front of me.

My mind still traveled the past, thinking of our family, specifically Anna. She was on her wedding trip, too, somewhere in Europe, with opportunities to see the cities and art and culture I'd always longed to. And at night . . . I'd no doubt that she did not sleep alone.

By contrast, I was heading to the forsaken north, to Scotland, land of barbarians—a term more believable than ever thanks to some of the acquaintances I'd made today. I envisioned a life of misery ahead of me unless I could unravel the mystery that was Laird Collin MacDonald.

At last, when the moon was nearing its zenith, light spilled through the faded curtains and came to rest on the picture in my hands. I set my charcoal aside and looked at the paper, into the deep-set and serious eyes of my husband.

We stared at one another for some time, while I silently asked him a dozen questions. Of course he did not answer, but looking at him helped nonetheless. I'd drawn a man who had not had an easy life. One who was faced with tough choices and who shouldered too much responsibility. Though the lines around his eyes were deep, those around his mouth were not. Collin did not smile much, if ever.

Does he laugh at all?

I set the sketch pad in the trunk and returned to bed, feeling that this time sleep would claim me. As I drifted off I made one more promise to myself and to my new husband.

I'll make you smile, Collin. I will.

"Marry a Campbell?" Lead them? The old man was more addled than I'd realized. I wondered that no one else in his clan had stepped forward to claim his position.

"The clans will never be what they were." He removed his hand from on top of mine, but his look remained hard, a silent threat that he wasn't as infirm as he appeared, and I'd do well to sit up and listen. For now I heeded the warning, biding my time for the perfect opportunity to escape.

"In coming years the clans will dissolve altogether," Laird Campbell continued.

"We've risen from beneath the English thumb for centuries," I argued. "We'll do so again." Or at least the MacDonalds would.

"It's not the English who'll destroy us," Laird Campbell said solemnly. "The clans will turn on their own. Lairds will forget their responsibility to look out for those under their care. Like the English, the Scotsmen will turn greedy and selfish, thinking only of power and gain."

It was the pot calling the kettle black, and I was sure the old laird could see the thought in my eyes.

Chapter Seven

I woke to the sound of someone beating down my door.

"Katie, are you ready? Are you *in* there?"

Who is Katie? I rolled over, opening one eye

briefly, trying to guess the time by the light coming through the window.

"Oh my!" I sat up quickly, hand to my pounding chest as I stared at the unfamiliar room. I'd been dreaming of home. *Only dreaming.*

A key turned in the lock, and the door swung open. Laird MacDonald—*Collin*—filled the doorway, ducking his head to enter beneath it. His mouth curved downward, and his eyes drew together as he looked at me pointedly.

"In Scotland it is customary to answer when called."

We are not yet in Scotland. "I was asleep."

"You're not ready?"

This much was obvious—to me, anyway, but he appeared so perplexed that I felt the need to laugh. Only the situation was not amusing. Not at all. Angering one's husband first thing in the morning on the second day of marriage was not good.

"We are all waiting for you." He could have been Ian, so cross was his face. How had I not seen their resemblance yesterday? Likely because I'd not wished to. Nor did I now.

"I'm sorry." *Apologizing already, and we're not even five minutes into our day.* "I'll hurry." Glancing down, I was mortified to realize that I still wore only a shift and had been sleeping on top of the covers. Without the window open last night, the air in this upstairs room had felt stifling.

Collin had already turned away. "I'll be back in ten minutes."

As soon as the door shut behind him I was up, stumbling across the room when my legs refused to carry me properly. The memory of yesterday's six-hour horseback ride was suddenly quite fresh in my mind—as well as in every other part of my body. With hands outstretched, lest I fall, I made my way toward the open trunk. Grabbing a lightweight petticoat and the first gown I came to—one of my black mourning frocks—I began dressing, only to discover that I had another significant problem.

Getting undressed had been difficult enough, but how was I to begin to go about lacing my corset? With an exasperated sigh, I set to doing everything else that I could—putting on petticoats and the corset over—without having it done up properly—pulling on my stockings, garters, and shoes, running a brush through my hair, hastily repacking my trunk. That I'd accomplished so much in only ten minutes seemed nothing short of a miracle, and when Collin knocked again, I gathered my cloak over the front of my petticoats and stays, then opened the door and met him with a smile.

"Good morning." *Let's do our best to make it good, shall we?*

"Let's go." Collin stepped aside so I might exit. "Alistair and I will get your trunk." My mother's cousin stood in the hall just behind Collin.

Oh dear. I'd believed Collin would come for me alone, or at the least that he would notice something amiss with my outfit. "Thank you," I said, then swallowed what little pride I had left, stepping backward into the room and beckoning Collin to follow. I lowered my voice. "I am in need of assistance. I cannot lace my corset." I felt a blush heat my face as I turned sideways, gathering my hair so he might see my predicament.

Instead of helping, he stepped quickly away—almost as if I had the pox—and muttered some oath in that Scot's brogue of his. He pulled the door closed so quickly it nearly hit me in the face.

I heard Alistair's admonishing voice in the hall, followed by Collin's terse reply, then two sets of footsteps marching swiftly toward the stairs.

Disconcerted and feeling an absurd desire to cry, I fell back on the bed, wondering if perhaps they would just leave me here and go on their way, one less troublesome Englishwoman in tow. The ceiling above me blurred, and I squeezed my eyes shut against it and the apparently fragile state of my emotions.

I pictured Ian's triumphant look, were he to see me now, and that was enough to cease my tears before they fell. I rose from the bed and looked around the room, contemplating what I must do next.

Collin is not used to being around women. That is all. He did not realize I would need help. I surprised him with my request. I did not particularly believe any of those rationales but kept repeating them as I splashed the last of the basin water on my face.

I wound my hair into a knot and put on a bonnet, then opened my trunk and withdrew a handkerchief to wipe my misting eyes. The sketch of Collin stared up at me. I slammed the lid on it with more force than necessary.

"Stare at that all day," I muttered, and somehow felt better for it.

Yet another knock came to my door—this one softer than the first two. I continued my pout as I opened the door to one of the tavern maids. "I've been sent up to assist you, Miss."

Mrs. He'd not even bothered to tell her I was a married

woman. "Thank you," I said. She followed me into the room, and I turned my back to her. I twisted the wedding band round my finger as she did up my laces. The ring had to have taken Collin a considerable amount of time. What had he been thinking as he made it? Had each link of the engraving only strengthened his resolve not to care for me? If so, why had he even bothered to give me a ring?

Because the Campbells expected it. It was a required part of the act.

"There now, Miss. You're together all right." The barmaid curtsied again, and I smiled my gratitude.

"Best not keep the gentlemen below waiting any longer," she suggested. "The one, especially, seems in a rare temper."

"A temper, to be sure," I agreed. I was starting to suspect, though, that it was not rare. We made our exit, and Alistair and Donaid headed up the stairs, presumably to fetch my trunk.

Collin waited near the tavern door, a basket held awkwardly in his hand. He thrust it toward me as I joined him. "You'll need to eat today."

Kind of you to think of that. I was about to ask him how I was to manage holding onto the basket, let alone eating, while riding a horse, when I caught sight of the carriage out front. It was the same we had started in yesterday—only it looked as if someone had taken an ax to it since then. I walked outside for a closer look.

The door had been chopped off just above the handle, so that a hole—easily large enough for a man to fit through— made up much of the one side. In addition to this, all of the glass windows were gone, the curtains and coverings pulled aside and secured at the corners inside the carriage. The seats were still intact, as were the floor and roof, but with the sides opened, it seemed almost an entirely different vehicle.

A strange lump had formed in my throat, but I willed it—and the accompanying emotion—away. This could not have been done for me as a kindness. Not *from this* husband. "What have you done to your carriage?" I asked when I had gathered my wits and trusted myself to speak.

"Ian did it, actually," Collin said. He'd come up behind me. "I thought a bit of hacking might be a good outlet for his anger. Altering the carriage was my idea."

"It's—brilliant." Standing close to the door as we were, I could feel the breeze blowing through from the other side. Sunlight spilled through the glassless windows, illuminating the seats and floor. The carriage had transformed from a dark tomb to something light and airy. I could ride in it without fear.

"You did this for me?" The lump in my throat returned. How many times had I attempted to ride in a coach over the years and met with disaster? Father had finally resigned himself that I should have to sit out with the driver, and we had always had to take great care when and how we made any sort of trip—with plenty of guards on well-traveled roads, and during the daylight only.

Those accommodations for my fear had been nice, necessary. But never had Father considered, or would he have, I knew, destroying a vehicle for my comfort. That Collin had done so, when it was perhaps the only carriage his people had use of, began a curious warmth deep within me.

"I thought you might be sore after yesterday's ride," he said.

I guessed this was as much of an admission of his thoughtfulness as I would get. I was starting to understand my husband, to realize that he did not want or expect gratitude from me—for some reason it made him uncomfortable—and he was not going to go about building our relationship or behaving toward me in any customary way.

I turned to him and lightly touched his hand. He pulled away as if I had burned him.

"Thank you," I said. "It was most kind."

He looked away with an unintelligible grunt. I smiled, not because I had discomfited him but because I had predicted he would react just as he had.

Progress. The first step in friendship was to understand the other person. Collin had understood me—or my fear, at least—and found a way to help me overcome it. And I was starting to comprehend him. He'd done a good turn; it was up to me to do the next.

"Is it safe?" I asked, peeking through the open window. "No glass or—"

"Alistair and I took care of that this morning." Collin opened the carriage door, and I climbed inside, unassisted, so he did not have to touch me. I slid to the far side and looked out the empty windows. I heard the door shut behind me and felt the familiar lurch of fear. Gripping the seat, I turned, my mind filled with thoughts of escape. But there was no need for that. I wasn't trapped. The lock was no longer in place, and the door came just barely to Collin's knees.

"You will have to be careful not to fall out," I observed.

"Aye." He followed my gaze to the low door. "But this will work for you?"

The carriage rolled forward, and I inhaled deeply, breathing in the fresh, country air and enjoying the nearly-unlimited view. My fear slipped away, and not into full-blown panic or a sense of despair or entrapment. A *miracle, if ever.* "It will do nicely, thank you."

"Good."

I let him enjoy the silence he seemed so bent on and watched as the inn faded from view. The forest came up on either side of the road, and I peered out, trying to see how far ahead the others were.

"Four men are out front—far enough from us to limit the dust and to scout out any trouble. The rest are in the rear."

"The roads are better here," I said, sticking my head out the window to look at the dark ruts worn into the earth.

"They'll be more bumpy, but the dust will be less." Collin kept his face averted, looking out his side, away from me. But at least he'd answered.

The ride did seem bumpier than yesterday. I recalled Alistair's information about the cache of weapons hidden inside the carriage and hoped our journey wouldn't get so rough as to send them jostling about.

"Am I sitting on a dozen loaded pistols or a stack of sharpened sabers?" I asked.

"Pistols," Collin said. "The swords are hidden in the cushion behind your head. Who told you?"

"Alistair." I wished he was riding with us today. Thus far he'd been far more open about answering questions than was Collin. "I was glad to know what is required of me when I am a passenger." I spoke with a confidence I did not truly feel when it came to weapons.

"Nothing is required of you," Collin said, deigning to look from the window long enough to scowl at me.

I ignored it. We would have a pleasant conversation today if it killed us both. "If I understood correctly, you are the best shot of this company—both among the Campbells and the MacDonalds. You are so good, in fact, that were we to be waylaid by thieves, you could easily defend this carriage and its occupants single handedly."

"Aye," Collin said.

And modest, too. I looked away so he would not see the roll of my eyes. "And what am *I* to do in such an event?"

"Get down on the floor, stay out of my way, and try not to get shot," he said tersely.

Words every girl dreams of hearing from her husband the second day of her marriage. *Oh, Anna, you have nothing on my circumstance, dear sister.*

"You're able to cover both windows at once?" Even with the glass already gone, I found this rather difficult to believe.

"More or less," Collin said.

"Well, which is it?" I demanded, giving him a pert look. "More sounds all right, but less might prove fatal."

"I'm not going to let you die," Collin said.

"Nor shall I let you perish," I declared. "You take the right side, and I shall defend the left."

It was Collin's turn to roll his eyes. "You know how to handle a pistol?"

"More or less." I did my best to match his surely Scotsman's tongue, then folded my arms across my chest and slumped a little in my seat for emphasis.

"It's no joking matter." He leaned forward so as to catch my eye. "Especially once we've crossed the border. You'll do as I say and keep to the floor if anything happens. Otherwise I cannot promise you protection."

That same prickle of fear I'd felt last night during my brief encounter with Ian flared to life again. Collin wasn't angry with me, but he was deadly serious.

"Promise me, Katie."

"I will—I do."

"And promise you'll not say another word about our weapons. What we've with us are near the sum total of what each clan has to defend itself—not much. And it's taken years to scrape these together."

"And if found with them . . ."

"It would not go well for any of us. I need your silence on the matter."

"Yes. Of course. I promise."

On that renewal of our vows, Collin leaned his head back and promptly fell asleep. I rummaged through the basket and found a dry bun and some overripe fruit and breakfasted by myself. The minutes and hours slipped by, and with no one to converse with, my eyelids drooped lower until I, too, was near sleep.

My last thoughts were of my mysterious husband, and so I dreamed of him—that he cared for me. I imagined him close beside me and his voice, not gruff but tender, whispering in my ear.

"I should never have come for you, Katie. Bad enough that I let you go, but bringing you back is unforgivable."

"In time you will understand," Laird Campbell predicted. Silently I disagreed.

"My actions—the actions of our clan—had naught to do with the English or taking sides, but everything to do with knowing what was coming in the future, and wanting to prevent it, or at the least to preserve what little of Scotland we could."

I scoffed. "Fighting against your own countrymen preserves Scotland?" I would never understand him, and certainly I would never wed his granddaughter. Though the part he'd said about me being a leader of his people and my own intrigued me.

"I thought to stop the rebellion," Laird Campbell confessed. "If your prince had not crossed the ocean and set foot on our soil, if he'd not rallied so many clans against King George, if more clans had refused their support . . ." His scarred face drooped with mournful longing. "Scotland might have had a chance."

Chapter Eight

The horses required rest, so at midday we stopped at the outskirts of Leeds. From what I could see from our vantage point overlooking the town, it appeared to be much larger than Nottingham, and I knew a moment of wistfulness, imagining walking the streets with my husband, looking in the different shops.

That is Anna's fate, not yours.

I told myself to quit thinking of my sister, to quit comparing our lives. There would be no comparison. Hers was everything a properly bred English girl hoped for. Mine— I glanced over my shoulder at Ian, standing a short distance away and openly glaring at me—mine bordered on nightmarish.

Turning my back on the men, I picked my way carefully down to the River Aire, wishing the bank was not so steep and I might remove my shoes and soak my feet in the cool depths. The day was hot, and notwithstanding the breeze I enjoyed in the glassless carriage, I felt sticky and dirty and longed for a cool bath.

Instead I crouched down and gathered several stones in the palm of my hand. Walking closer to the river, I lobbed the first one in a graceful arc and watched as it splashed in the stiller waters near the edge. Circles rippled out from the point of impact. *One, two, three—*

"You're not any better at that than you used to be." Alistair stood beside me, his arm drawn back. He brought it forward and, with a flick of his wrist, sent a stone skimming across the surface.

"I wasn't trying to skip it," I said and proceeded to do just that, my own rock traveling nearly as far as Alistair's had.

"Not bad." He nodded his approval. "You ken who taught you that?"

"You?" I sent another rock flying, though this one didn't go as far. I'd been able to skip rocks—a most unladylike skill— as long as I could remember, though I'd always preferred to watch the stones splash into the water and create ripples.

"Me? Hmpf." Alistair shook his head, as if I was a hopeless cause. "I hadn't time to be chasing my own wee'uns around, let alone entertaining another's lass."

"My father then," I guessed.

"Him? Not likely," Alistair said. "Nor your mother either."

"Father wasn't really the rock-skipping type," I agreed. He'd been wonderful to me in many regards, but he had never been the sort with any time for play or frivolity. I could no more imagine the two of us standing by the shore throwing rocks than I could imagine us dining together at the king's palace.

"You've your husband to thank for your skill." Alistair tilted his head in the direction of the MacDonalds.

"*Collin* taught me?"

"Aye." Alistair sat on the grass and began untying a cloth bag.

I settled beside him, eager for information about my past, especially anything having to do with my reclusive husband.

Alistair held an apple out to me.

"No, thank you," I said, the overripe fruit I'd eaten earlier still churning around in my stomach from our bumpy ride. "I remember nothing of my life before England. Will you tell me?"

"*Nothing?*" Alistair frowned, the creases on his forehead deepening as worry crept into his eyes. "Collin said as much this morning, but I didn't believe him." Alistair shook his head, as if discouraged. "Well, this complicates matters a bit."

"How so?" Even if I had remembered Collin, the

memories would have been those of a little girl, not a grown woman. I didn't see that it really mattered one way or another.

"Ne Obliviscaris."

"Forget not?" I translated. "I'm afraid it's a bit late for that."

"That's the Campbell motto," Alistair said. "You can start by remembering it."

"Ne Obliviscaris," I repeated, leaning forward to show I was an eager student. "How was it that Collin came to teach me something, to even know me at all?"

Alistair bit into the apple before answering. "Laird Campbell—your grandfather—gave Collin charge of you. Your mother had just died, and Collin's father had been killed. The laird figured the two of you might be good for each other."

I looked at Alistair skeptically. "Father told me I was four when my mother died." I didn't know how much older Collin was, but certainly much too old, even at that time, to find a four-year-old girl good company.

"You were just a wee thing," Alistair said. "Small for your age. And Collin got teased something fierce. The other lads used to call him nursemaid." He grinned. "I mighta said it a time or two myself."

"That seems a cruel task to place upon a boy," I said. But more than that was strange about this tale. "How was it that my grandfather came to be giving orders to a MacDonald boy?" I looked behind us at the two distinct groups of men, tending to their animals and eating. "Were the Campbells and MacDonalds friendly then?"

"Heavens no!" Alistair laughed so hard that when he slapped his knee, I wasn't certain if it was a gesture of amusement or if he was choking.

Yesterday's PROMISE

"The Campbells and MacDonalds were *not* on friendly terms," I said, when, after several seconds, it appeared he was still incapable of speech.

"Never," he gasped. "Enemies—since forever. No two clans loathe each other more."

"It might have been good to know that yesterday," I muttered.

"Collin was given o'er to the Campbells because his father knew of no other way to keep him alive."

"Wouldn't handing his son over to an enemy clan be the way to ensure his son's death?" Perhaps this somehow explained Collin's serious nature and the burdens I sensed he carried.

Alistair glanced toward the others as he seemed to consider my questions. "'Suppose I can tell you a piece of it. You've a lot to catch up on—quickly." He sounded worried. "After Culloden, Ian MacDonald—Collin's father—was a hunted man. He'd been key in aiding the prince's cause, and there was a price on his head—and on the heads of his sons." Alistair paused to take a drink from his water pouch. "The three of them managed to hide quite a while, but Ian was wise enough to know his luck wouldn't hold."

Alistair stopped again, taking another bite of apple and chewing slowly.

I glanced at the other men. A few Campbells had wandered closer to us, but the MacDonalds still stood in a bunch, engaged in some sort of serious discussion. I understood that Alistair needed to eat, but I wished he would hurry and finish this tale at least, before we had to leave.

"Brave man, Ian MacDonald," Alistair said, respect in his

voice. "Came to see your grandfather. Said he'd give himself up to your grandfather, who could turn him over to the English, if only he would promise to spare one of his sons and see him safely raised."

"Just one?"

"MacDonald had already given the other o'er to Isaac Munro. A mistake, if you ask me."

I silently agreed, recalling what Collin had told me about his brother the previous night.

"The man's ruthless. Kept his bargain to see the lad raised, but he showed him no mercy along the way. It was what Ian MacDonald had feared—and the reason he split the lads up. He hoped at least one would fare well."

"And did Collin? With my grandfather?" I wanted to believe so, to think that Grandfather had been a kind man.

"Depends on what you consider well," Alistair said. "Collin had plenty to eat and a place to lay his head. He wasn't subject to cruelty. Wasn't treated as a slave or even as a servant."

"How old was he when his father died?" *What is Collin's age?* Though his face was solemn, he did not necessarily appear *old*.

"Fourteen. The both of them. Twins, ye see."

"I do now," I said, not having realized it before. Though Ian carried an aura of danger, I would have guessed that Collin was the older of the two, by a few years at least. He might have been treated fairly with the Campbells, but something had happened to place the weight of the world upon his shoulders.

"They were tall enough to look like men and, as sons of the laird, old enough to have participated in most of the '45."

Yesterday's PROMISE

I leaned back, my hands supporting me, and looked out to the river, thinking on Alistair's revelations. If I understood him correctly, my grandfather had been at least partially responsible for Collin's life being spared. And in return, he had asked Collin to first watch over me, when I was a motherless child—and then to marry me when I was older?

"Supposing I was good company," I said, still doubting that at four years of age I had been anything close to a good companion for a fourteen-year-old boy, "why would my grandfather entrust me to the son of his enemy?"

"Good question." Alistair finished the apple and tossed the core away. "But I'm not the one to answer." He stood, and I gathered my skirts, scrambling to join him.

"You're the only one who will talk to me," I protested. "You have to tell me."

"The only one for now," Alistair corrected. "Give Collin some time. He'll tell your story."

My story or our *story?* I gave Alistair a last, pleading look, but he shook his head.

"The lad never betrayed your grandfather's trust. And he taught you to skip stones. Took him weeks and weeks. Someone less patient woulda gone mad with it. It's your turn to be patient now." Alistair looked past me, down the road we would soon travel. "I don't suspect you'll have to wait long. There are things you need to know and understand. Collin won't neglect to share them." Alistair lifted his hand in farewell and trudged off toward the Campbells.

Left alone once more, I faced the river and tossed another stone, watching the ripples appear. I imagined the moment of impact was my father arriving in Scotland. The first ripple was meeting my mother, the second the two of them marrying. I was the third—my marriage to Collin the fourth? The ripples widened after that, spreading thin and uncertain in a circumference around the spot where the stone had dropped. What did my future hold? What were the events of the past that contributed already?

I skipped the last of the rocks, then brushed the dirt from my hands. I turned to go and found Collin standing apart from the others, watching me, his arms crossed as if angry.

What are you thinking? I wondered. *And where is the boy who taught me how to play?*

It was full dark by the time we reached our lodging the second night. No light hung above the door, and only a few dim lamps lit the inside. Collin spoke to the innkeeper and had us shown directly to our rooms, promising a meal would be delivered shortly. I thanked him, closed the door, and collapsed on a piece of furniture that barely qualified as a bed. Straw poked from the tick beneath me, and the lamplight revealed bedding that appeared long overdue for washing. I shuddered and rose quickly, pacing the room until my trunk was delivered.

I opened it and found the previous night's sketch of Collin staring up at me.

"Hello again," I muttered. "Lovely place you've got here. No expense spared, I see." I withdrew my cloak from the trunk and spread it across the bed, feeling I'd sleep better knowing it was between me and whatever else might inhabit the sheets.

Yesterday's PROMISE

I straightened and stepped back from the bed, then nearly stepped from my skin as I caught sight of Collin standing in the doorway, two plates in his hand.

"Are you alone?" he asked, glancing about the room.

"Yes."

His eyes narrowed with suspicion. "I thought I heard you talking to someone."

"Only myself." I glanced behind to make sure that I had closed the trunk. What would he think if he saw the picture I drew? "Who else would I be talking to? No one speaks to me." Since my brief, midday chat with Alistair, not a dozen words had been spoken to me by anyone, least of all my husband.

Collin handed me a plate of food and turned to go without so much as a goodnight.

My annoyance surged to anger, along with an anxious desperation. "You're leaving? Just like that?"

He stopped but did not face me again. "Was there something else you needed?"

"Not at all." I set the plate on the night table. "I am in the middle of nowhere, traveling with two dozen men I don't know, most of whom only glare at me when they want to communicate. I've left behind my family and home—and soon, my country. I have no idea where we are going or what my life is to be like—what is expected of me." I walked away from Collin to stand at a window so filthy I could not have seen out of it in better light. "The man I married cannot stand to be in my presence. His brother loathes me." My voice cracked. "I am exhausted and sore and dirty, and the bed probably has fleas. My sister is on her wedding trip in Paris, visiting art museums with a husband who adores her, and I've never felt so wretched or alone in my entire life. But no, there is nothing else that I require."

I closed my eyes against the tears slipping down my cheeks. *Just go,* I silently ordered Collin, wishing I'd kept my mouth shut.

I heard the quiet chink of a plate being placed on the table, then felt him come up behind me—close enough that he might have touched me, had he wished.

"Do you want me to take you back?"

"To what?" My throat was swollen with the sob I held in. "My mother has left by now, and I am not welcome where she is going." I'd not before voiced that realization out loud, and declaring it stung anew. My mother had never felt like a stepmother. Anna had never felt like a step-sister—until recently. But she knew, somehow, that I was not her equal, and were we together again, she would not let me forget.

Silence filled the little room. I fought to restrain my tears and sensed that behind me Collin fought his own demons.

"Life in Scotland will be hard," he said. "I wish it was otherwise."

"I don't mind working," I said, wiping my cheek. "I'm not some spoiled English girl." No doubt my petulant outburst had sounded just that.

"I could see that when I met you yesterday," he said.

How? I wondered. Was it my simple clothing and our bare foyer, or did he sense that I was more than a girl who did embroidery and played the pianoforte nicely? Did he know I was the one who had cared for Father during his last year? Did he realize that it was I who took control of the household the first two months after Father's death, when Mother was incapable of managing herself, let alone the accounts and the selling of our property and dismissing of our staff? It had been my jewelry that had paid for Father's burial and prolonged our stay.

It was I who'd written letters of recommendation and found new positions for many of our servants. I had done the bulk of the work while Mother and Anna had dress fittings and attended tea parties and planned and purchased and played, all in preparation for her glorious wedding.

"I am accustomed to hard," I said, wondering if that was really true, wishing I did not feel as if my life had changed for the worse.

"I hope so," Collin whispered. He stepped nearer, not touching me but close enough that I could hear his breathing above me.

I sighed, feeling even more drained from my brief outburst. "I am weary."

His fingertips brushed my shoulders. I stood immobile, hardly daring to breathe. Slowly his palms came to rest, his touch light but warm. I closed my eyes, savoring the simple contact of another human. It was not much, but I sensed it was costing him, that he was giving all he was capable of.

Patience. Alistair had said. Collin had waited for me to be old enough to marry; surely I could wait for him to trust me—with whatever darkness haunted his soul.

We stood at the window, neither moving. His hands curved over my shoulders with gentle pressure, their weight comforting.

"Don't worry so, Katie."

"Because you do enough of that for both of us?"

"Aye." There was no humor in his tone. He did not promise me that all would be well, but he offered what he could.

For now, it was enough.

"I've seen the future, and it's bleak." The old laird bent low in his chair, as if weighed down. "Scotland's only hope is if her people unite." He grabbed my hand, still throbbing from when he'd pounded it earlier. "If we're to do that, if we're to work together, we've got to have peace between us."

Between the MacDonalds and Campbells? "Impossible. It will never happen."

Laird Campbell shook his head. "Perhaps not in the measure the clans need, but enough so that my posterity—and yours—will continue."

Chapter Nine

The next morning began better than the previous two. When Collin knocked, I was mostly ready, trunk packed, and my clothing in place, save for the cursed stays I could not lace on my own.

As before, I held my cloak up to shield my state of half dress as I opened the door.

Upon seeing me, Collin's mouth pressed together in a look of grim determination. "There is no woman here this morning—or none coherent enough to assist with your needs." He ducked, then stepped forward, voluntarily entering the room.

I moved back, out of his way, suddenly uncertain what he had in mind. Yesterday I had been prepared to allow him to help me; this morning I felt inexplicably shy in his presence. Last night I had let down my guard, sharing with him both my fear and despair. In return he had offered comfort—a simple act that had kept me awake a good hour after Collin left my room, pondering the tumult of emotion my new husband evoked within me.

He turned now and pushed the door shut behind him, so it was just the two of us alone in the tiny room. Sunlight struggled to stream through the filthy window, casting only broken bands of light across the stained floorboards.

In the near darkness, I raised my head and met Collin's stoic gaze, not distant as I'd seen in the past, but focused intently on me and on the task at hand. Slowly I turned away from him. I allowed the cloak to slide a little, then lifted my hair so he might have access to the corset.

"What do I do?" His breathing was labored, as if he'd just run up the stairs. Perhaps he had. I wished I had the same excuse as I looked down and noted the rapid rise and fall of my chest.

"Start with the laces at the middle," I instructed. "Pull them taut, then work down from the top, tightening those as well, moving down to the middle again and then the bottom."

"All right."

I felt a tug at my back and stood up straight, bracing myself for the process.

"Middle, top to bottom," Collin mumbled as his fingers worked, overly gentle and slow, being careful not to pull too hard.

"I won't break," I said. "And neither will the laces."

"I don't want to catch your hair." His fingers skimmed across the base of my neck as he brushed a few straying strands aside.

"I'm sorry. I meant to put it up but ran out of time." My skin tingled where he had touched me.

"You don't need to wear it up," Collin said, sounding as surprised as I was at this suggestion. "If you don't want to, that is. It looks fine when it is down, the way you wore it the day we wed." Again I felt his hand on my skin as he carefully moved another unruly curl out of the way, over my shoulder. "Soft." The word was so quiet I wasn't sure I was meant to hear. Yet I had, and I felt something within it.

I closed my eyes and worked to stay upright, when really I felt like sagging against the bed. *So this is what swooning feels like.* I'd always silently mocked young ladies given to such antics, but I could not deny that the sensation, *these* sensations, caused by his gentle touch and attentive words, were pleasant.

Collin had both mentioned our wedding day and acknowledged that he noticed and approved of something about me. Perhaps I was somewhat desperate for his praise after three days of near silence, but the words—along with his tender comfort the previous night—filled me with hope for our marriage.

"One of the Campbells—" I paused, regretting that I had just reminded him of my heritage, when it seemed he might be given to overlooking it after all.

"Yes?"

"One of them said my hair was like a field of dry heather. I wasn't sure what that meant—if it was a compliment or not."

He made a noise in the back of his throat, one I was becoming accustomed to, as it seemed all Scotsman used it. "Have you never been to a moor?"

"No. Fields near our home, but not a true moor. I've traveled very little, carriage rides being difficult for me."

"Ach." I felt him nod. "Heather is a flower that grows on the moorland. It's purple at bloom, then later turns more of a burnished gold. Not a bad likeness of your hair, though I always thought it more comparable to an amber stream of honey."

Always? He had thought of my hair before?

"There," Collin announced. "Does that feel like it will work?"

"Yes, thank you."

"I'll tie it then, here at the bottom?"

I nodded, unable to trust my voice as I felt his hands at my waist. *What is wrong with me? What is happening?* I felt both frightened and exhilarated by our nearness and conversation the last few minutes. A few kind words from my husband, and I was coming undone.

Collin finished with the laces as footsteps sounded in the hall outside. I turned to thank him just as the door burst open, and Ian's tall frame filled the doorway. Collin stepped between me and his brother, but not before Ian's gaze swept the room, took in my state of undress, and made several assumptions, I was certain, given the narrowing of his eyes and sneer on his lip.

"Didn't take you long to lose that battle." He glared at Collin. "Perhaps I should have wagered against you after all."

"Get out." Collin lurched forward, as if to enforce his command. "You knock at ladies' doors. And this isn't what you think."

Ian had already stepped into the hall. Collin followed, pulling the door closed behind him. I wasted no time, but hurriedly dropped my cloak on the bed and donned my gown, grateful that poverty had allowed for our mourning frocks to be only the simplest design.

From the hall Ian's angry voice and Collin's terse, hushed one carried through the flimsy door.

"You know what this means." Ian's voice.

"It means nothing," Collin insisted. "And if you think to harm so much as a hair on her head, you're mistaken. The Campbells are watching closer than you realize. Don't be a fool."

Ian snorted. Or at least, I assumed it was Ian.

"You're the fool, marrying a woman who is both English and Campbell. But perhaps not as foolish as I thought. Obviously you've no thought for her, if you've risked—"

"I've risked nothing," Collin said. "And you won't either if you've half a brain. We *need* her dowry, and it'll not be delivered until Katie is. To the Campbell keep, safe and sound."

He meant to take me to *my* former home and not his?

This realization, along with the reminder of the true reason Collin had married me, doused the warmth he'd kindled between us just moments ago.

"She'll be delivered all right." Ian's low chuckle sent a shiver down my spine. I stuffed my cloak into my trunk and secured the lid, then marched toward the door, intending to open it and discover just what this conversation was about. I was not some piece of baggage to be hauled about and deposited somewhere, left alone to—

"Mhairi will be none too pleased when she hears of this," Ian said.

I paused, my hand on the knob. *Mhairi?*

"She's no claim on me," Collin said. "She knew I was to be married."

"Hell hath no fury like a woman scorned," Ian said as I yanked open the door.

Our eyes met, and his lip curled in a mocking sneer.

Collin doesn't want you. I fought to hide my insecurities as I stepped into the hall, chin raised, eyes never leaving Ian's.

"I am impressed," I said in a voice as mockingly sweet as his expression was intentionally vile. "Quoting Congreve when I didn't take you for a man who read much—or one who could read at all. You *do* continue to surprise. Though the wording was not entirely accurate. Perhaps you should check your references." I sashayed quickly past, joining Collin at the top of the stairs.

Instead of offering his arm, he took mine in an unnecessarily firm grip, guiding me swiftly down the steps, pulling me almost. Without so much as a word of explanation he hurried us through the main floor room and out to the waiting carriage. Still holding my arm, Collin used his free hand to pull open what was left of the carriage door and hand me inside. But instead of joining me, he shut the door and leaned over it briefly, a warning in his eyes and on his lips.

"Ian doesn't need baiting. I've my hands full managing him already. I'll thank you not to make it worse." With that

Yesterday's PROMISE

Collin turned away, then stalked back inside the inn, leaving me wondering how a morning that had started so hopeful had gone so terribly wrong.

For some minutes I sat stiffly on the seat, arms folded and held close to my middle, lips pressed into a thin line, doing my best to contain the ache coursing through me. My arm hurt where Collin had grasped it, but that was nothing compared to the injury he'd caused to my soul. Ian had spoken cruelly concerning me, and Collin had taken his side.

Blood is thicker than water. A phrase I'd heard my mother use, often when referring to some doings with this or that family of society. The irony of this phrase coming from her lips struck me anew, adding to my distress. I was not of her blood—only Anna and Timothy were—and so I had been sold away for a pittance. *So they might all be together.*

The only true kin I had in this world were the Campbells. And while those I'd met seemed congenial enough—particularly when compared to the MacDonalds in our company—I did not feel a particular affinity toward any of them. Rather, the need to gain my husband's approval and affection grew with each passing hour. If I was being honest with myself, I had felt drawn to him from that first moment he made himself known to me.

But I did not feel particularly drawn to him now and scooted to the far side of the carriage, where I angled my body to face out the window so I would not have to look at Collin when he returned. He did so, shortly thereafter, rocking the carriage with more force than usual. I supposed he was still angry with me, and that incensed me even more. It was I who had been wronged, I who deserved an apology.

"Who is Mhairi?" I demanded in a bitter voice, warning him that he'd best answer my question and not even think of scolding me again.

"I've no idea, but jealousy doesn't become you, lass. Didn't then, and it doesn't now."

I turned toward the voice—not Collin's—and found Alistair seated across from me. His lips were turned down, and disapproval etched deeper the wrinkles beside his eyes.

"What do you mean *then*?" I asked, choosing, for the time being, to leave off the questions of who Mhairi was and why Alistair, and not Collin, was riding with me. My need to know of my forgotten past was nearly as great as the need I felt for my husband's approval.

"You wanted him all to yourself, even way back then," Alistair said. "And most of the time you had him. But once Collin had regular meals again, he grew into a handsome lad, and MacDonald or no, there were other Campbell lassies who took a fancy to him. You weren't too keen when that happened, would work yourself up into a tantrum the likes of which most people ain't never seen. Only Collin or your grandfather could calm you—and it weren't no easy task."

Ignoring Alistair's unpleasant recollection of my younger self, I pressed on with my present concerns. "Do you think Mhairi might be one of those other women who took an interest in Collin?" If she had been near Collin's age when I was just a small girl, she would be a woman now, too, and one far past what was considered marriageable age.

Alistair shook his head. "No Campbell lass by that name that I know of. Could be a MacDonald, though. Collin's been with his own clan a good six years now. It's not unheard of for a man his age to have had—uh—" Alistair's face brightened suddenly, coloring to a shade near the red of his beard. "I could be wrong of course. Usually am about female doings." He cleared his throat, as if uncomfortable, and looked out his window. "Right pleasant in here without the glass."

I recognized the poorly veiled attempt to change the subject. But I did not ask him to speak of it more. He had confirmed my suspicions. There was likely another woman in Collin's life. Ian had said as much already. And Collin's reticence toward me all but proved he was right.

This was a setback I'd not before considered, and the implications were sobering. Collin's avoidance of everything from conversation to the barest touch were because of his previous—continuous?—attachment to someone else. Someone he likely cared about. *More than me.* If I'd felt alone before now, that feeling multiplied, even as the hope I'd felt for my marriage shrank.

I stewed for probably another hour, feeling sorry for myself until the warming sun and the beauty of the passing scenery pulled me from complete despair. The world outside our carriage appeared utterly glorious, and again I found myself wishing for brush, canvas, and paints to capture all I was seeing. I took comfort that when we reached our destination I should have those again at least, and hoped they would provide me with some solace as they had the previous months since Father's death.

Recalling those months and that self pity would gain me

nothing; I buried my hurt and shook myself from melancholy. According to Collin and Ian I was shortly to be deposited—and presumably left—at the Campbell holding. I supposed then, if the Campbells were to be my only family, I had best learn all that I could about them.

"Alistair, why do the Campbells and MacDonalds dislike each other so much?" This seemed as safe a topic as any, and perhaps it might lead to more discoveries about my past. Though the most recent one—the recounting of my tantrum-throwing younger self—should have encouraged me to let my childhood go unremembered.

Alistair made the same noise in the back of his throat that Collin had earlier. "Dislike is too mild a word."

"But why?" I did not particularly care what he labeled it. "You're both Scotsmen, and Highlanders at that."

"Being a Highlander doesn't mean you get on with the other clans." Alistair turned from the window toward me, warming, I hoped, to the subject. "MacDonalds and Campbells been enemies since before anyone can remember."

"Do you know what started the feuding?" I asked, wanting much more of an explanation.

Alistair shrugged. "Hard to say. Though Mort Ghlinne Comhann made it lasting."

At my puzzled expression, Alistair reverted to English again. "Glencoe in '92."

I still didn't understand and so said nothing to this, but gave him what I hoped was a look encouraging him to continue.

"Don't suppose you'd know about that." Alistair rubbed his beard. "The MacDonalds of Glen Coe waited to pledge their fealty to the new king, you see. And William wasn't particularly patient. For their reluctance, he ordered that all under age seventy be killed."

"That's terrible," I exclaimed, imagining innocent women and especially children suffering a brutal death.

"Aye," Alistair agreed. "Can't say it's Campbell history I'm fond of."

"What had the Campbells to do with it?" I leaned forward in my seat, both eager for and dreading the answer.

"Campbells had been guests of the MacDonalds, staying a piece and getting on well—or so it seemed. But it was an act, and Sir Robert Campbell was the one who gave the order and led in the slaughter."

"And were they—successful?"

Alistair nodded. "Near eighty dead—some from the sword; others froze after their homes were burned. Happened in February, and winter in the Highlands is no time to be without shelter."

The bleak hopelessness I'd been able to fight off returned with vengeance. These Campbells—these barbarians—were whom I was going to live with. *Whom I've descended from.*

"Don't go thinking we're all bad," Alistair said, as if he'd read my thoughts. "MacDonalds have done their fair share as well. And it's them who are always stirring up the pot."

"What do you mean?" I asked warily, fearing another bloody tale.

"Well—" Alistair paused, tugging on his beard this time, as if considering a great deal. "It's like this. MacDonalds are known for their independence. They don't want anyone telling them what to do. In ancient times, that worked well.

They were the leaders, and respected at that. But when times changed and Scotland formed as one—and England wanted her—that fierce MacDonald independence became costly. For everyone."

"The English kings punished everyone when some disobeyed." I'd had enough history from my tutors to understand that much.

"That's the crux of it," Alistair said. "The MacDonalds would not give, whereas the Campbells—thinking of the good of all—have cooperated with the ruling powers. And at times, we've helped them, too. Probably more than we ought," he added beneath his breath.

"You're part of the Black Watch," I said, recalling that tidbit from my lessons as well.

"Not now so much, but yes," Alistair said. "Between that and Glencoe, we've made a powerful lot of enemies. Yet we've survived more than most because of our alliance with the king."

"You sided with King George during the uprising?"

"Aye," Alistair said. "We supported the side your grandfather knew would win."

That seemed rather a lot to boast of, but I did not argue his point. The English *had* won. "I see." Or I was starting to, anyway. My father's conviction that the Highlanders should not be punished so severely and should be given back some of their rights was making more and more sense. As was the mystery surrounding my parents' union. If the Campbells had been working with the English, was it not possible that some of the English soldiers might have visited with them, or stayed with them even, while stationed in the Highlands?

Yesterday's PROMISE

"Be time to stop and eat soon," Alistair said, alerting me to the possibility that I might have the opportunity—wanted or not—to speak with my husband.

"Remember," he continued, his voice kind and not stern. "Jealousy does not become you. And all is often not as it seems."

He was speaking about the lass and me marrying. A grander delusion I could not imagine. She peeked around the corner again, then entered the great hall, vacant now, save for the laird and myself, sitting alone at the high table, the candle between us sputtering low.

"Come, Katie," he said. Though he was facing away from her, and though she made no sound, he had somehow known she was there. Perhaps he had noted my gaze straying to her. Was it I who had given her presence away?

Chapter Ten

My jealousy had abated somewhat by the following afternoon, replaced by an acute loneliness that would not subside. With each passing hour it seemed the literal ache in my heart grew stronger. I wanted to believe this was caused by each mile traveled farther from my home. But I feared the reason otherwise.

Surly as he was, I longed for the companionship of my husband. But Collin had not spoken to me since yesterday morning. He had not ridden with me, nor even been anywhere near me. And though I feared it was Ian's reminder of Mhairi that kept Collin away, I missed him and the hope I'd had for our companionship.

Yesterday's PROMISE

Alistair had not deemed it wise to impart any more of the past to me, but instead sat stiff and alert on the seat, ever wary of some unseen enemy. For the first time since our journey began, the Campbell party had become separated by considerable distance from the MacDonalds. Alistair said this was for our added safety, as we neared the border. If an English patrol were to happen upon us and choose to detain us, the MacDonalds would be in the rear, able to come to our rescue if need be.

I had my doubts that they would actually choose to do that—if need be—but kept those to myself. Ian had vowed that he would not spend another night on English soil, so it seemed that any delay, particularly one involving Campbells, was not likely to be tolerated.

As this was to be our longest day of travel, having begun well before dawn and set to end well after dark, with our crossing into Scotland, I'd slept in my gown, petticoats, and stays the night before, correct in my assumption that no assistance would be offered me at our early morning departure.

Before first light we'd left Newcastle behind and the thrilling glimpse of Hadrian's Wall. How I would have loved to walk beside it, to touch the ancient stone and to see and feel the history I'd only heard from my tutors. But there was to be no stopping for such frivolity, no stopping at all. A bourdaloue sat on the floor in one corner of the carriage, having been provided for me—should I have need to relieve myself, Alistair had explained, his face heating to crimson. In other words, I was not to request that we stop today—for any reason.

Aside from this practicality, for the most part, I did not mind the long day. The rolling green hills and endless sky were enough to keep my mind occupied, imagining the landscapes I might paint. I finally saw a moor, rife with the purple Collin had described. I turned to the other side of the carriage, eager to point it out, only to recall that he was not there and would possibly never speak to me of moors or honey or the color of my hair ever again.

The hours crawled by, our progress good. The sun was now on my side of the carriage, forcing me to turn away from it and face Alistair, who'd today been nearly as silent as my husband.

"That'll be trouble," he said suddenly, scooting to the edge of the seat. His eyes flickered to mine, then to the bench beneath me as the carriage started to slow. I leaned out my window to see the cause of our delay, but Alistair pulled me back. "Keep your head. Stay calm."

"I am," I said even as a sea of redcoats surrounded us. Being both English and having grown up around soldiers, I felt at once that I should be the one to talk with them. We came to a complete stop. I stood, leaning over Alistair to reach the door.

He grabbed my wrist. "What do you think—"

His hand fell away as a soldier appeared in front of what was left of the door. I gave Alistair a brief smile, imparting confidence, I hoped, before the door swung open, and I accepted the soldier's outstretched hand.

"Thank you, sir." I turned my smile upon him and descended the carriage. "What a relief it shall be to stretch my legs for a few moments after such a long and tiresome ride."

Yesterday's PROMISE

Alistair appeared directly behind me, his expression troubled. I sensed his dilemma at once—stay with me or with the weapons, which might ultimately save us, were we to find ourselves in trouble.

"No need to get out, cousin," I said lightly. "I am certain this gentleman will behave."

"You'll remain in my sight," Alistair said gruffly, his Scots' brogue as evident as my English accent. I was going to have some explaining to do.

"Very well." I stepped aside, and the soldier shut the carriage door. A dozen other redcoats were out in front of the carriage, circled around the Campbell riders. I didn't need to wonder what had roused the interest of the soldiers to our group. Though no outlawed kilts would be found among them, something about the Campbells—the combination of their proud stance and poor clothing perhaps—proclaimed them Highlanders.

"Good day, Miss." The soldier had kept my hand this entire time and now raised it to his puckered lips.

I returned his greeting as I tugged my hand away, noting that it was more evening now than day. I guessed the man to be somewhere between my age and Collin's. Tall, clean shaven, and with his light hair tied back in a queue, he was quite handsome.

"What brings you and your—cousin—to the border road?"

"I'm afraid it is a rather long story." One, at present, I was still fabricating.

"We have time." He took my arm leading me several paces from the carriage, but still in its view. "Now, then, you may speak freely here, Miss—"

"Mercer. Perhaps you have heard of my father, William. He was an officer for many years." Mentioning Father was a risk, but I could think of no other explanation for my travels, other than a tale as close to the truth as possible.

The soldier's mouth tightened. "If you mean William Mercer, the former lieutenant colonel, I have heard nothing good."

I waved a hand dismissively and in so doing somehow encouraged a second redcoat to join our conversation. "I expected as much. Father's last days in the military were not so glorious as those that came before. He was a lieutenant during the uprising of '45, you see." I pressed on, not allowing them a chance to agree or not. "Well known for searching out and capturing those who supported the prince." My own statement gave me pause. This was a history I'd heard many times, yet I had never before connected it to names or people. *The MacDonalds?* A chill passed through me. Collin despised my father; that much he'd made clear the day we wed. What if his feelings were not without cause?

"*Former* Lieutenant-Colonel Mercer publicly denounced the king," the first soldier said.

"Not the king himself," I corrected. "But his policy."

"They are one and the same," the second soldier said gravely. He was shorter than the first, and stockier, his close stance suggesting he was eager for a fight.

I felt quite sober now, though for a different reason than he might have imagined. Collin was a laird, which meant his father had also been a laird—who'd sided with the prince during the war, and who'd had a price on his head afterward. He had given himself up to the Campbells, who in turn had given him to the English. *To my father?* I pressed a hand to my stomach, feeling ill.

"My father died six months ago, and he was quite unwell for some time before that. But his actions during the previous two decades of service should not be forgotten." Collin would not be able to forget them—or forgive—if they were as I feared. "He was a hero of the war, a restorer of peace after. And I believe, in his last days, he thought he was doing what was best to try and maintain that peace, to prevent another rebellion."

"Another?" The second soldier's brow perked up, and he stepped closer. "What do you know of that?"

"Nothing." I'd misspoken. One word, terribly misplaced. Clasping my hands together in front of me, I forged ahead. "I was simply trying to explain to you my purpose here today. I gave a promise to my father, upon his death bed, that I would honor his wish that I travel to Scotland. And while he might have been mad with illness when he extracted such a promise from me, I do not wish to trifle with an oath given to one now dead. Tell me, is that something either of you gentlemen would wish to do?" I was banking on them being somewhat church-going, God-fearing, superstitious, or having otherworldly beliefs of some sort. Most folks did, fear being the great enforcer of morals.

"But why send you to Scotland?" the second soldier asked. I could see that he was going to be the harder of the two to persuade.

"That's simple." My smile returned. "My mother was Scottish. A Campbell. You'll recall that the Campbells allied with the English during the rebellion. Their help proved invaluable in defeating the Jacobites." I wasn't certain of the amount of truth in my statement, but both men appeared young enough that hopefully their detailed knowledge of recent history was as sketchy as mine.

"You're Scottish." The second soldier's lip curled. From the corner of my eye, I saw Alistair's hands upon the door, ready to leap from the carriage if need be. *And to his death.* Easily fifteen redcoats surrounded us, each armed and ready to fire. I had to keep talking.

"And English," I said, lifting my chin proudly. "Both lines faithful to the crown. I've spent my life in England and now journey to Scotland at my father's request. These kind gentlemen—Campbells, all of them—are my relatives and escort, to see me safely there." With their scruffy beards, worn clothing, and fierce expressions they hardly looked the part of gentlemen.

"Escort?" The first soldier snorted. "One woman with a dozen men? No proper lady would dream of traveling thus."

"They are my *relatives*." Of course I ought to have had a female escort or a maid or something—if either my mother or Collin had been able to afford such. "They're honorable men, all of them."

"Ludicrous." The second soldier spat on the ground near my feet. "No Scot's a good Scot."

"My father disagreed, and as he lived and fought beside them, it would seem he might have been correct."

"You'll not mind if we check your trunk and carriage then?" the first soldier asked.

"Of course not." *The carriage.* I tried to push the panic from my mind. What would happen when they discovered the weapons?

Yesterday's PROMISE

"Wait here," they instructed and strode toward our pathetic-looking vehicle. I stood stiffly, watching as my trunk was untied and brought to the ground. While I wasn't particularly eager to have my belongings rifled through, I was not overly worried either. There was nothing inside that would condemn us.

The carriage, on the other hand . . .

"Where is your plaid?" The whispered words nearly caused me to jump. But it was Collin's voice at my ear, not a soldier's. He'd come out of the forest behind me and stood as close as he'd been in my room two night's past.

"Safe," I assured him, my lips hardly moving as I spoke. I treasured both gifts Collin had given me, my wedding ring and the joined square of our clans' tartans. The cloth I wore tucked inside my bodice over my heart, though it did not ease the ache I felt there or the void of knowing I was not loved or even tolerated by my husband.

"It's not in your trunk?" Collin asked.

I gave a slight shake of my head. Did he take me for a fool?

My trunk had been opened now, and my cloak spread on the ground for the other contents to be piled upon as they were removed. I tried not to care as the men callously lifted each worn garment, made derogatory remarks, then tossed them aside. They barely glanced through the sketchbook before adding it to the pile, and I said a silent prayer of gratitude. The last thing I wished—aside from being detained further—was for Collin to see the drawing I'd made of him. It was bad enough that he did not want me for his wife and, in all probability, loved another. I didn't need him realizing the depth of my yearning, the inexplicable pull I felt toward him, the emotion he so easily roused. To have him believe that I, too, did not care seemed infinitely better.

It did not take long to empty the trunk, and soon the only things left were the canvases I'd placed at the bottom, wrapped carefully in my winter shawls. I'd brought only my two favorite paintings, each with a sky and landscape of my imagination—nothing like the countryside near Alverton. The shawls were removed, thrown atop the pile of petticoats and underclothes laid out for all to see. One of the soldiers held up the first painting, and the others gathered round it, talking amongst themselves, sending furtive glances my direction.

"What is it?" I dared to ask Collin. Were they all critics of art?

"I don't know." He sounded worried.

Finally the second soldier, the more callous of the two I'd spoken with, strode over to us. Collin did not abandon me, but stood at my side.

"Have you ever been to Scotland, Miss Mercer?"

"Not since I was a child," I replied absently, even as I worried over what Collin would think of the soldier's use of my maiden name.

"And you are the artist of these?" The soldier pointed at my canvases, held up by his comrade who had joined us.

"I am," I said proudly, uncertain where this line of questioning was leading. I glanced toward Collin for guidance, but he had moved away from me, closer to the paintings, eyes narrowed with—displeasure?

"How is it, then?" the soldier questioned. "That you were able to capture in such vivid detail—"

Yesterday's PROMISE

"Bealach Druim Uachdair." Collin reached out, not quite touching the canvas but running his finger along the twisting road I'd painted until it disappeared between two mountains, near the top and beneath the bluest sky filled with the most glorious clouds. I always named each of my paintings, and this one I had dubbed "Top of the World." I imagined that one could see forever, in all directions, if he followed the path I'd created.

Collin turned to me, question in his eyes. "You said you didn't remember Scotland."

"I don't." My voice rose in pitch at his frown. "I am telling the truth." I looked from Collin to the soldiers, then back again. "This place is from my imagination."

"No, lass." Alistair had joined us. "It's from the Highlands."

"Similar, you mean? Mere coincidence, I am sure." My heart beat wildly as I stared at the partially hidden path. I had always wanted to see what was beyond, to journey to the top of that mountain, but of course I'd known I couldn't. It wasn't real. The idea that it might be, or something similar, was almost too joyous to contain.

"A blight on the cursed land." The soldier grabbed my painting and thrust his foot through it.

I gasped. "How dare you!" I stepped forward to wrest what was left of the painting away from him, but Collin's firm hand on my arm restrained me.

"I'll dare that and what e're else I please," the soldier spat. "You're a traitor like your father. Jacobites hid in the crags of those mountains, ambushed a group of English soldiers as they came through that pass, killed them all. But I'm sure you know that already. Perhaps this painting was the trophy from that attack, meant to hang over the fireplace while the tale is shared over and over again." He broke the frame and continued to rip at the canvas until there was nothing left but scraps blowing about on the ground.

"She was a child then," Collin said quietly. "She'll know nothing of it."

"Her father, then." The soldier began destruction on my second painting—an ancient castle perched on the edge of a bluff—while I stood paralyzed with grief and fear.

"One of their own had betrayed them—a Campbell perhaps?" The soldier scrutinized all three of us.

"No," Alistair insisted, feet planted firmly and standing proud. "Check your history, and you'll find we had men killed that day as well."

The wind picked up a piece of the torn painting and carried it skyward. I snatched it from the air and held it tight in my clenched fist. The beautiful place I'd imagined wasn't a blight. It was my refuge from the world when I wished to escape the troubles around me. I'd never thought it might be real. And now it was simply gone.

I closed my eyes but not before silent tears escaped to slide down my cheeks.

I was starting to understand what it meant to be Scottish.

After much discussion the English soldiers chose not to detain us, but decided it best to accompany our group to the border, escorting us safely out of *their* country. No longer mine. Though the soldiers were angry about the painting, it appeared they still believed enough of my story to let us pass.

"Good riddance it is," the cruel redcoat said. "Don't expect to be coming back."

Collin knelt beside me on the ground, handing me items as I repacked my trunk. He said not a word when he reached the sketchbook, but placed it in my hands, along with my other possessions. I still shook with anger, though the bitter tears had dried on my cheeks. I tried to be grateful that the soldiers had not confiscated my paints and brushes. At least I still had the possibility of painting something new. I could recreate what they had destroyed, and this time I would have the real landscape to draw from.

When we had placed the last of my possessions in the trunk, Collin offered me his hand and helped me rise.

"Are you all right?" His dark eyes reflected sincere concern, which for some reason brought a fresh wave of tender emotion. If only he truly did care about me. I battled to keep more tears at bay.

"Well enough," I said, looking at the ground, as that felt less painful. "I am sorry to have caused trouble. I meant to keep us from it."

Collin touched my chin, lifting it gently so I was forced to look at him. "Alistair's told me what you did, what you said. It was wise—and brave. You couldn't have known about the painting."

"I didn't," I said, desperate for him to believe me.

"I know." His hand fell away from my face, though his other still held the tips of my fingers. "I'm glad to have seen them—your paintings—before they were gone. Since we took you from your home I've felt I shouldn't have, that it was a mistake to bring you back. But now . . ."

"Yes?" Silently I begged him to keep talking.

Collin shrugged. "Scotland, the Highlands, they're in your blood, too—whether you realized it or not, whether either of us wished it. It's your destiny to be there."

With you?

Perhaps he might have said that, but three redcoats were approaching. Collin dropped my hand and stepped away. "I'm your cousin, aye?" His mouth quirked in that near smile of his. "Best be behaving like one, then. And not the man who stole you from home."

"Get that trunk on there, or it'll be left," one of the soldiers ordered. Quinn and Moireach came forward to help, while Collin and Alistair accompanied me to the coach.

I was pleased to realize Collin intended to ride with us, though I had a dozen questions swirling around in my mind. What of Alistair's horse? Where were the other MacDonalds? How had they not discovered the weapons? I dared not say anything within the confines of the carriage. As it was, I worried what might happen were the soldiers to discover even one MacDonald among them.

We started again, our progress slow this time, restrained by the pace of the redcoat riders surrounding us. As full dark descended, my agitation proved no match for the sleepiness threatening. I did my best to sit upright and as far from Collin as possible, but as evening's chill descended I found my eyelids heavy and the open carriage less than delightful.

"Rest your head against me, Katie," Collin said when mine had bobbed abruptly in sleep for the second time.

For a moment I battled within myself—resolve to protect myself from Collin, versus the appeal of being able to sleep, being warmer, and being close to him. The latter won out, though I knew there would be consequences later. But Collin felt like gravity, and I an autumn leaf falling from the tree above. I couldn't help myself, couldn't stay away from the ground, though I realized it would cost me and I would become first brittle and then crushed.

But oh, how thrilling the fall would be.

I scooted closer to him on the seat. In a slow, awkward movement, I leaned toward him, then rested the side of my head against his arm. With a sigh of both longing and contentment I closed my eyes.

The little lass came to stand before him, an outlawed plaid wrapped around her and trailing behind. Perhaps, for their loyalty to England, the Campbells had been allowed to keep their tartan.

"You wanted to see me, Grandpa?"

He had? When? The two of us had been here for the better part of an hour, during which time we had spoken only to each other.

"Aye, lass. You're listening well." The laird smiled at her but lifted his gaze to mine. "She has the Campbell gift, you ken. She's able to hear without being told and able to see what is coming."

This made no sense, but then I'd already determined the old man was mad.

He was also worried. "This gift puts her life in grave danger."

Chapter Eleven

"Katie, wake up." Someone gave my shoulder a gentle squeeze, then a firmer one, then finally a shake.

I opened groggy eyes and found my head tucked next to Collin's chest and his arm around me, the weight of which was both warm and comforting. The beat of his heart reassured me. I felt safe and cared for. This was how I'd imagined marriage to be.

He helped me sit up, but his arm lingered. "Did you sleep well?"

"Yes, actually." Better than I had any night since we'd wed. I was surprised to note that we had been inside the carriage the entire night. The sun was already up and forcing its way through the trees, and Alistair no longer sat in the seat across from us. "How long have we been stopped?"

"Only a short while." Collin's arm slid away, and he stretched. "Wanted to put some distance between us and the friendly English at the border, so we kept going. Sorry to wake you, but I've got to help with the horses and see to Ian."

The absence of Collin's arm, or perhaps the mention of his brother made me shiver. Collin leaned close, retrieving a blanket I'd not noticed before from the seat beside me. He pulled the cloth over my shoulders, pinning it in front with his hand.

"What happened to all the weapons?" I asked as the prior evening's events made their way to the forefront of my mind.

"They're still here." Collin brought his other hand up and began tying the ends of the blanket in a knot. "When the seat is lifted, an empty compartment is revealed—on purpose. But within the seat itself is a padded case, and beneath the false floorboard as well. Easy to open, but difficult to find if you don't know it is there."

"Clever," I said.

"Necessary." Collin finished with the knot and turned as if to go.

I was reluctant to let him. I reached out, touching his sleeve. "I am doubly sorry now that you've ruined your carriage for me when it is so useful."

"Don't be." He shook his head as if it wasn't important. "We've no need for a carriage in the Highlands. The roads are too poor, and we're not much for social calls and tea parties."

"And you believe that is how I spent my days, prior to your arrival?" I raised my chin, challenge in my eyes, refuting his ridiculous assumptions.

"I did not say that." He met my gaze and held it with one equally stubborn. "Given your dislike for carriage rides, I should assume you attended very few social calls."

He was right. It was Anna who had gone out with Mother, before our circumstances had changed and invitations had ceased. I begged off going anywhere that wasn't absolutely necessary and so was left at home with the servants, and later Timothy, to come up with my own means of amusement. I'd never minded. "You are correct," I said, my voice softer. "Still, I *am* sorry about the damage to your carriage."

Collin grasped the door handle. "Better a carriage than any of us. I believe its poor state encouraged the dragoons to be careless in their search. To them it likely didn't appear we'd be able to afford one weapon, let alone a carriage full. All is not always as it seems."

Had Alistair not said the same to me two days ago? I sensed that both he and Collin were hinting at something, but I'd no idea what.

Collin opened the door and jumped from the carriage. "Rest in here as long as you'd like. We'll be on our way again at midday. Everyone is eager to be home."

Was he eager as well? To be back on MacDonald land with Mhairi as his companion instead of me? "And where is my home to be?" I pulled the blanket tighter around me.

"With the Campbells, of course," Collin said without hesitation.

"Not the MacDonalds—with you? I've taken your name, but I won't live with your clan?"

"It would not be safe for you." He closed the door firmly.

"You might have told me," I said, forgetting my resolve not to let him know that I cared. "When a woman is married, there is an assumption that she will live with her husband."

"Who says you'll not?"

"You." Exasperated, I leaned out the glassless window. "You've just told me I'm to be left with the Campbells. While you return to the MacDonalds—and Mhairi." It seemed impossible that, as laird of his clan, he could live elsewhere.

Collin's face registered surprise, and he stiffened, even as he stepped back from the door. "Who told you such lies?"

"You," I repeated. "And Ian. I heard your conversation at the inn two days ago. You said I was to be deposited with the Campbells in exchange for my dowry. And Ian said Mhairi would be angry with you for marrying me. And then, not a minute later, you scolded me for defending myself against Ian."

Collin's jaw tensed, and a flicker of anger sparked in his eyes. He stepped forward again, nearer the carriage, and bent his head close to mine as he spoke in a harsh whisper. "Provoking Ian was not defending yourself. It's taken me the better part of two days, keeping him away from you, to calm his temper."

This was why Collin had been avoiding me? I felt myself shrinking into the seat.

"And that you would think I would just leave you and take up with another woman—does my word mean so little? We've spoken vows, Katie."

He almost sounded hurt. The anger in his eyes dissipated to something else—sorrow, uncertainty? The emotion I felt was far clearer. Guilt washed over me. How could I have been so wrong? Had I spent the past two days in a haze of jealousy, needlessly despairing? But Collin still hadn't explained Mhairi. And now I dared not ask.

Perhaps if he had spoken more to me, or had refuted his brother's criticism, then something other than Ian's *Collin doesn't want you* might have taken root in my mind during the four days since we'd wed.

"I'm sorry." I looked at him directly, hoping he might see that I meant it.

"As am I," Collin said, staring at me a long moment before he left, leaving me still wondering if he really did regret our marriage.

While I lingered in the coach berating myself for the better part of an hour, the men gathered wood, tossing the logs into a large pile. By the time I found enough courage to leave my seclusion and face Collin again, a fire was roaring in the center of our temporary camp.

By some taciturn agreement, two of the Campbells and two MacDonalds worked around each other, preparing food for the men in their parties. Until now I had taken my meals in the coach or with Collin at whatever inn we happened to be staying at. As I strolled about the edges of our camp, attempting to look both occupied and useful, I wondered which party—if either—would offer me something. I'd eaten nothing since noon the previous day and felt ravenous, so much so that the smells from the campfire started my stomach grumbling.

Some minutes later the Campbells finished their cooking first and beckoned me over to join them. I started towards Alistair's outstretched hand only to have Collin grasp mine and pull me back.

"We'll eat with the MacDonalds." He dropped my hand as quickly as he had taken it.

Why does it matter who we eat with? I knew better than to ask. The past few days had taught me that every word and action that happened between the Campbells and MacDonalds mattered a great deal.

I nodded, then sent an apologetic glance over my shoulder at Alistair. He was scowling at us—or rather at Collin—but when he saw me looking at him, he smiled quick enough and waved me away as if my refusal to dine with my mother's clan was not the insult it likely was.

Breakfast—on our side of the camp, anyway—proved to be a solemn affair. The meal consisted of burnt meat—the origins of which were rather suspect—moldy cheese, and crusty bread. The MacDonald men ate quickly and in silence, devouring their food as Collin did—as if it were either their last meal or the first they'd had in a very long time. I wondered if any of them worried this *might* be their last meal. Where were we to obtain food henceforth? Only a day across the border, and already I'd seen the differences. Though the countryside was beautiful, abandoned crofts, surrounded by fallow fields, dotted the landscape. I wondered what had happened to make so many families leave their homes. Was the land really cursed, as I'd heard some of Father's friends say before? The entire country couldn't be this way, *could it?* Would it be worse or better when we reached the Highlands?

"Do the MacDonalds farm much?" I asked, after choking down a particularly tough piece of meat.

"How else do you think we eat?" Ian said.

"What do you grow?" I asked, ignoring both his rude tone and the sniggers coming from the others around the circle. Collin hadn't joined them; neither did he rise to my defense.

"Barley," another Macdonald said. "Makes a good mash for whisky."

"That sounds like a fine crop, certainly something one can live off." I'd spoken with sarcasm, but the others nodded their heads in agreement.

"It's the one thing the other clans will always trade for," Collin said. "There are always sorrows to be drowned."

"And what of the bodies that need to be nourished?" I asked.

"Whisky's as good for the stomach as it is for the mind," Ian said. "Soothes 'em both."

"I see." I glanced around the circle, trying to look past the fierce eyes and scraggly appearance of most of the men. Collin's face was still discernible beneath the few days' growth, but many of the others were hidden behind thick beards. If they ever did smile, I'd never know. Though given our conversation, that possibility seemed less and less likely.

What were the sorrows they endured that made their

whisky so popular? They'd lost the war, but what differences had that really brought about? George II had been king before the uprising, and he'd retained his throne after crushing it. How much had he done to crush the clans? I wished I'd listened closer to Father's arguments against the crown and for Scotland. If he'd taken up their cause, he'd had to believe it just.

He had to have been worried about what he was sending me to. I tried, unsuccessfully, to shrug off my own concerns and ate in silence.

After the meal was over, the Campbells stayed to their side, abrupt barks of laughter and an occasional burst of song reaching our ears. The MacDonalds did not sing, or even talk much. They were an even more sullen lot than I'd first thought them to be, and I determined that on the morrow I would eat with the Campbells. Collin wished me to stay away from Ian, and I would happily oblige.

Eager for any excuse to be away from the men—exchanging covert glances with one another and staring at me with what I imagined to be shifty eyes—I excused myself to prepare to travel again. Collin rose and left with me as well, escorting me to the carriage.

"Did I mind my tongue well enough this time?" I asked when we were well away from the group.

"Aye," Collin said. "And unless I'm with you, mind your distance, too. Stay clear of Ian."

"I will," I promised, only too eager to follow my husband's counsel.

Part Two

Danger and delight grow on one stalk.

"How is she in danger?" I didn't want to care but found the thought of anyone hurting the lass concerned me.

"Knowing the future is a power most men can only dream of," Laird Campbell said. "Many would kill—or worse—for it."

I thought I understood. He was afraid someone would take his granddaughter and force her to use her . . . gift. If that's what it really was. I wasn't convinced that her coming into the hall just now was anything more than coincidence.

Chapter Twelve

The evening meal was both sparse and later than usual that night. We had resorted to sleeping in the forest and eating around a campfire. There were to be no more inns or taverns. Our days of travel would be longer, Quinn explained. The men had been gone too many days and needed to get home to their families and crops.

I felt both apprehensive and excited at the idea of spending the night out in the open. It was certainly not something any properly bred English woman did, yet it seemed with each mile I traveled from home—to home?—everything about me that had been proper slipped further and further away. Leaving my hair down to blow about wildly had seemed a scandalous freedom; sleeping in an open meadow with twenty men nearby was almost too much to contemplate.

A trickle of a brook meandered through the middle of the camp, naturally and effectively dividing the Campbells from the MacDonalds. The rivulet was an offshoot, Collin said, of the river that cut through the mountains to the north and ran swiftly in the valley just below our camp. I'd thought England beautiful, but the piece we'd traveled yesterday and today took my breath away. The distant mountains reached skyward, their peaks both majestic and threatening. The rolling hills leading to them boasted color as I'd never seen it before. The grasses were greener, the wildflowers deeper purples and blues and yellows, the sky darker and more intense. My fingers itched for a canvas and my paints to capture it all.

As usual, Collin and everyone else largely ignored me. Instead of feeling hurt by this or complaining, I recognized that all were busy at some task and so went about my business quietly and avoided the MacDonald side of camp and Ian as much as possible. It soon felt wrong to meander or sit about doing nothing, when all around me men were busy gathering wood, tending to the animals, preparing what I guessed would be tomorrow's breakfast, and repairing the wheels on the carriage—a daily task—yet again.

My repeated offers of help had all been politely refused when Malcom—the youngest of the Campbells traveling with us, a shy youth who kept mostly to himself—took up his water pouch and announced he was heading to the river to fill it, only to be ordered to some other task by Ruaridh. Seeing an opportunity to do something useful, I determined to fetch the water myself. The river was not far, just across a short meadow and down a slope from our camp. With Malcom's pouch in hand, I forged a trail through the tall grass, then picked my way carefully down the hill.

The river ran swift and cold, and before filling the pouch I knelt on the bank and took a moment to wash my hands and face. Though the freezing water stung, I persisted, knowing this was likely all the grooming I would be allowed tonight. My trunk had not been taken down from the carriage, and I was reluctant to ask anyone for such a favor. I had now gone three days in the same dress and dearly wished for a change, but without the privacy of an inn it did not seem that I would have the opportunity to either bathe or change my clothing anytime soon. Collin had said life in the Highlands would be hard, but I hoped it would not always be this dirty.

When I'd filled the pouch, with some reluctance I left the peace and solitude of the river and started up the bank. Holding my skirts and looking down to avoid any missteps on the uneven ground, I hurried along, suddenly conscious of the near dark. Fear prickled along the back of my neck, along with the feeling that I was being watched. I glanced behind me, but the only movement was the rushing water below.

Nothing. No one was following me. The feeling of unease persisted. Telling myself to quit being so foolish, I trudged on, crested the hill, and came face to face with Ian and another equally menacing MacDonald I did not know. Their cold eyes narrowed at me, and a victorious sneer curled Ian's lips.

"Too easy," he said beneath his breath.

His companion gave a short laugh.

I took a step backward and struggled to find my footing as they advanced. I was a fair distance from our campsite.

Alone. At twilight. And worse, I had not told anyone where I was going.

"Good evening." I forced my lips into a smile, hopeful my quavering voice did not betray my fear.

Instead of returning my greeting, Ian took another step toward me, forcing me back again. No matter, I could walk through the grasses and go around. I veered off course, only to have him follow, blocking my way once more. All of Collin's warnings about Ian rushed through my mind. His intent to harm was clear, clearer still when his accomplice withdrew the knife from his belt.

I had the fleeting thought that this was not my destiny. Grandfather had not planned for me to return to Scotland to meet my end at Ian's cruel hand.

I stopped and craned my neck up at Ian, pressing the water pouch to my chest to hide my pounding heart. "Yes? Was there something you wished—to discuss?"

He came even nearer. I held my ground. The other knife-wielding MacDonald stepped up beside him, blocking the last bit of light from the fire at our camp. The river had seemed so close when I'd wandered down here, but now I realized how foolish I was to have ventured this far alone.

"Last night, because of you, I spent three hours surrounded by Englishmen and pretending to be a Campbell." Ian's words were slow and deliberate, as if he'd spent those three hours imagining this meeting and his revenge.

"I didn't think you were nearby when we were detained." I assumed the MacDonalds had gone around or ahead of us, or at the least were well hidden in the forest. I wished I was well hidden now. My eyes darted about, attempting to peer around Ian, searching for a way—any way—I might escape. But the last of the light had fled, and I could no more see a place to run than I could see anyone coming to help me.

Ian chuckled. He was enjoying this, a predator amusing himself with his prey before pouncing. His hair hung down his back, melting in with the darkness behind him, so that I could not tell where he ended and the night began. For the first time in my life I felt afraid of the dark.

"I'd ridden with Collin and was waiting for him," Ian explained, continuing in that painfully slow voice. "Watching to see if he'd get himself in trouble looking out for you." Ian's tone was bitter.

"A redcoat found our horses. I'd crept behind him and was about to slit his throat when that Campbell lad found me."

He had to mean Malcom. He was the only Campbell traveling with us young enough to be considered a lad.

"He called out to me, greeted me as *cousin*, and alerted a half dozen other redcoats to my presence. I ended up the tail end of your happy little caravan, surrounded by English. I'm no Campbell. Bloody traitors," Ian spat.

"I'm sorry," I said, the words thick in my throat. "But we are all here safely now, are we not?" He might have spent a few discomfiting hours, but no real harm had come of it—whereas, if Ian had killed the English soldier, there was a good chance we all would have paid, perhaps with our very lives.

"I can look out for myself." Ian took another step toward me. "I don't need anyone's help."

"I didn't—"

"I fight my own battles." Ian was now close enough that he could reach out and grab me if he wished. I stepped back and felt frigid water pool at my ankles.

A sinister smile curved Ian's lips upward. "It would be a pity, if—after all the trouble we've gone to retrieving you—you had a careless accident in the river."

"If you harm me, you'll not have my dowry."

He shook his head. "It won't be my fault you drowned in the river. Don't worry. The MacDonalds will keep their part of the bargain. You'll be delivered to the Campbells as promised. I'll fetch you out of the river myself—all pale and bloated, fingers and toes nibbled by the fish." He laughed again. "And I'll have that money."

"The Campbells aren't fools. They'll never give you anything if I'm—" *Dead.*

Ian crouched slowly, never taking his eyes off me, and retrieved a dagger from his boot. I could barely see its gleaming blade in the dark. The other MacDonald moved closer, so that one of them stood on either side of me.

"I'll scream."

"Aye." Ian nodded, encouraging me it seemed. "And poor Collin will rush to your rescue."

"They'll know it's you. You'll never—"

"*You'll* be downriver. And we'll be waiting when Collin comes at your bidding. Two birds with one stone—or with two knives, as that may be." He touched the tip of his with his finger.

Not Collin. I squeezed the pouch so tight against me that water began to bubble over the top, wetting the front of my gown. I would not scream. I could not let them harm Collin.

"Niall." Ian motioned to his companion.

Niall grabbed my arm, dragging me farther into the river.

"Go ahead. Call for him." Ian's blade was suddenly at my throat, the tip sharp against my skin when I tried to swallow. I pressed my lips together to keep from crying out.

A twig snapped somewhere above us, followed at once by the sound of footsteps and voices. I recognized Finlay's lilting speech.

"Don't—"

Ian's forceful shove cut off my warning and sent me plunging backward into the icy river.

"Give me your hand, Katie." The old laird held his out.

She hesitated, one hand clutching her wrap, the other stiff at her side. "Brann says I'll get warts if I touch the MacDonald."

She *was* worried? I was the one likely to be infected with something, surrounded by Campbells as I was.

The laird frowned, stretching his scar in a most frightening manner. "You're not to believe anything Brann tells you—ever. Do you understand?" He took her hand and then mine before I'd realized what he intended. He joined them together, placing her tiny one in my large.

She looked up at me with wide, frightened eyes, but it was I who felt suddenly afraid—chained and burdened. I snatched my hand away, worried over far greater matters than warts.

Chapter Thirteen

A thousand knives pierced my skin. I pushed to the surface, gasping for breath the bitter cold and Ian's blow to my chest had stolen. My arms flailed on top of the water while my legs thrashed uselessly below, heavy and tangled in the weight of my petticoat and skirt. I managed only one other word.

"Ian!" Let them know he'd done this. Let Collin be safe. The river pulled me under again, sweeping me along in the swift current. I tried to move toward shore but had barely the strength to push my head above the water. I came up at last, coughing up the river, desperately sucking in air.

Men were shouting and running in all directions. But they were so far away, and I was too tired to cry out, and the current carried me off again.

Float. I heeded the thought, arching my back, straining to keep my face free of the water. My legs refused to rise. Still I forced my head aloft, arms out, feet uselessly kicking. The river rose suddenly, thrusting me forward, dashing the back of my head against a rock. Sharp pain exploded along the top of my skull. My throat and chest burned as I sank again.

Water flooded my lungs. *Collin. Grandfather. Father. Collin. Mother. Anna. Timothy. Collin.* I lifted a feeble hand and struck something solid. A second later my forehead bumped it.

I curved my fingers, searching for purchase on mossy wood. My other hand joined the first, and I pulled myself up, chin level with the river, coughing up water as I tried to take in air.

"Katie!" A man stood on the bluff above. A lantern swung from his hand as he scrambled down the hill, rocks skittering to the river's edge. "Hold on."

Collin. I dug my fingers in deeper, pressing my face against the partly submerged branch.

With a great splash, he entered the river, his silhouette visible from the light left on shore. Stroking with one arm, Collin swam closer. His other held tight to the tree that had fallen and somewhat blocked the river's path. My arms burned from holding on, and I felt the pull below, sucking my legs and sodden clothing beneath the log, trying to sweep me away for good.

"Hold on," Collin shouted above the roar.

I will. I am. Hurry. I'd no breath for words.

He reached me at last, placed an arm on either side, then half climbed over me, so that he was behind now, between me and the center of the river. Collin wrapped one leg around mine, anchoring me to him, and placed one hand on top of mine, twining our fingers together.

"Slide one hand at a time along the log. I'll push from behind."

I followed his lead, leaning forward, pulling with what little strength I had left. Below the surface, Collin pushed my useless legs along until we'd reached the shallows and I could touch the bottom.

"Keep going," he warned, tightening his grip. "There's an eddy here that will pull us right back out."

Another step and I felt it, strong and powerful, made more so when the floor of the river dropped away again. We continued our labored progress until at last we reached the bank. Collin grasped my waist and hauled me onto the shore, out of harm's way.

I lay face down, heaving and coughing and still searching for breath, but alive.

"Over here," Collin shouted, waving an arm and holding the lantern as he stood above me.

Behind us the river roared, angrily swirling around the fallen log that had been my savior. *No.* The log had merely delayed my drowning. It was Collin who had pulled me from the river, Collin who had saved me, literally shielding me from the dangerous current.

I shall be a shield for your back . . . Just one of his many promises—and I'd judged our vows as overly dramatic.

Alistair scrambled down the hill toward us.

"Get up, Katie." Collin grasped my arms, pulling me to a standing position. My legs, exhausted from their fight, wanted to buckle.

"Lean against me, lass." Alistair stopped in front of me, and I leaned into him gratefully, resting my head on a blanket slung over his shoulder. I felt a tug at my back.

"We've got to get you out of these wet clothes," was followed by the sound of tearing fabric. "Can you help me, Katie?"

"Y-yes," I stammered, guessing the alternative was that Collin and Alistair would undress me here and now.

"Hold up that blanket," Collin ordered.

With one hand out to steady me, Alistair used the other to pass my temporary pillow to Collin.

"We're going to hold this around you," he explained. "Take off your dress and underthings. I've cut the fabric."

The blanket wrapped around me from the nose down. I peeked over it to see Collin replacing the knife in his belt.

I wanted to change out of this dress. The fleeting thought, laden with irony, was replaced almost instantly by necessary concentration as I attempted to force trembling, cold-stiff fingers into peeling back layers of wet clothing.

I tugged at my sleeves, all the while shivering so violently that my teeth chattered. What had been a decent mourning gown fell to the ground. I stepped from it, then leaned forward, freeing my corset to follow.

Ruined. The back had been slashed, not only through the strings but the fabric as well.

I peeled the square of tartan away from the stays but kept it in my hand while I continued to disrobe.

The petticoats came next and finally my shift. The vulnerability I felt was only rivaled by the terrible cold. Gooseflesh covered my arms and legs, and I couldn't control my shaking.

"Done now?" Collin asked, his face, and Alistair's, carefully averted.

"Yes."

Collin kept hold of both sides of the blanket and wrapped them tightly around me before handing me the edges.

"Can you walk?" he asked. "I'd carry you, but I'm soaked myself."

He's freezing, too. I'd thought only of my own misery the past several minutes, but now I looked on him with gratitude—and concern.

"Ian means to kill you," I blurted. Where was he now? Had anyone else been hurt?

"Ian and Niall went the other direction," Alistair said. "Finlay and Moireach saw them leave on their horses. Probably long gone by now."

"But if he comes back—"

"We'll talk about it later," Collin said. "It's cold that will get us now if we don't get dry and warm."

I listened to him, or perhaps my chattering teeth, and began trudging up the slope between Alistair and Collin, blanket clutched tight and my shoes sloshing with each step. I'd not discarded those. I hadn't another pair this practical.

Yesterday's PROMISE

Collin steered me toward the carriage, where my trunk had already been taken down by a few other concerned-looking Campbells. He insisted I change inside with the curtains closed across the glassless windows.

Only when I'd donned dry stockings and slippers, a clean shift and the grey dress I'd married in—the cleanest of my gowns, and still smelling very much like Ian's horse—did Collin see to his own needs. Then we made our way solemnly to the Campbells' fire.

"Give her a swig of this. It'll warm her." Malcom passed a flask to the man seated next to him, and I watched—teeth still chattering—as it made its way around the circle of men surrounding the fire. Though the night was not particularly cold, I had my doubts as to whether or not I'd ever feel warm again. The long, terrifying minutes I'd spent fighting for my life in the river had left me chilled to the bone.

The flask reached Collin. "Bit of whisky for you, Katie. Drink it slow." He held it to my trembling lips.

"*Uisge-beatha*. Breath of life," Finlay said, ever ready to wax eloquent.

Collin tipped the flask, and I took a sip, then almost immediately coughed most of it back out, much to the amusement of our companions. What remained in my mouth burned a path down my throat.

"Good, ain't it?" Quinn grinned broadly, what teeth he still possessed gleaming in the firelight. "That stock's been said to burn the hair off a man's—"

"Quinn!" Collin made what I'd come to think of as the Scot's sound in the back of his throat. "You're speaking to a lady."

"Aye, but a Scottish one, a Campbell. So she'd best become accustomed to our ways," Ruaridh said.

"Perhaps not all at once," Alistair suggested kindly.

My head swam, and I could not entirely blame the small bit of drink. I'd not felt right since Collin pulled me from the river. I tucked the blanket tighter around me and suppressed a shiver.

"Tell us what happened, lass," Alistair encouraged.

I didn't want to recount it but knew I must. Especially for Collin's sake. He, at least, was still in danger. I began with my foolish trip to fetch water and apologized to Malcom for losing his pouch.

"Not a bother," he assured, though his frown and furrowed brow said otherwise. "Drink up the whisky in the flask, and I can use that to store water in until we're home."

Knowing the drink would only make me feel worse, I allowed it to pass by me as it made its way around the circle again. Instead I continued my story. I told them how Ian and Niall had prevented me from returning to camp, forcing me to the river's edge.

"You ought to have called for help," Quinn said. "I was just in the meadow."

"That was what Ian wished. Had Collin—or any of you—come to my rescue, Ian and Niall meant to slit a throat." Recalling the prick of Ian's knife, my hand went involuntarily to my own neck.

Collin had remained silent throughout my recitation, and I looked at him now, wondering what he was feeling. Was he surprised? Hurt? Did he feel betrayed by his brother, or had he sensed this coming?

"We were fortunate tonight," Alistair said. "But let us be all the more wary now."

"No MacDonald is a good MacDonald," Malcom muttered from the other side of the fire.

Ruaridh shoved him, so hard that Malcom fell backward off the log.

"Watch your tongue, whelp. Have you forgotten who sits at our fire? Who had the blessing and trust of our laird and spent years among us?"

"He doesn't have the blessing of our laird now," Malcom grumbled as he pulled himself up and retook his seat.

Silence descended on the group, save for the crackling of the fire. All eyes, mine included, were on Malcom. What had he meant about the Campbell laird *now*? Was Collin not welcome there? Was that why he and Ian had spoken of delivering me to the Campbells, as if I was to remain there alone? But Collin had refuted that worry—hadn't he?

"Sorry," Malcom said at last, glancing around the fire at everyone except for Collin and me. "He's not a Campbell is all."

He spoke of Collin as if he was not sitting right among us, as if he was somehow less than the other men in our company. A few of them responded with their usual guttural noises, which I took, in this instance, to mean all was forgiven—for now at least. Prejudice on both sides had been building for centuries and did not seem likely to go away anytime soon.

The fire had taken the worst of the chill away, and now I longed only for sleep. "I'm warm enough. May I rest now, please?" I addressed my question to Collin, having determined somewhere between leaving the river and sitting beside him at the fire, that I would endeavor from now on to be a more obedient wife. I had not disobeyed him exactly, with my visit alone to get water, but neither had I taken his warnings about Ian seriously—something that could have cost our lives.

Collin took my hands in his and held them tight a moment. "I wouldn't say you're warm, but better than you were. I suppose sleep won't hurt." He stood, then helped me rise.

I mumbled a goodnight and again expressed my gratitude to everyone. Finlay and Quinn's timely arrival had saved at least one life tonight, for even had I managed to avoid crying out, it was likely Collin would have come looking for me. And Ian and Niall would have been waiting. That we had both come away mostly unscathed seemed no small miracle.

"Don't worry yourself over Ian," Alistair called after us. "We've arranged the watch. Should he be fool enough to show his head here, we'll be ready."

"Do you think Ian *will* come back tonight?" I asked Collin. His arm was around my waist, supporting me as we left the others and walked through the dark over uneven terrain.

"Perhaps—or not," Collin said. "I've no doubt he'll have to be reckoned with at some point."

I shuddered, not wanting to think about such a confrontation, while at the same time feeling so exhausted that I could scarcely care about anything beyond sleep and warmth. So much so that everything else—even Ian's threat—almost paled in comparison. "Wouldn't it be warmer to make our beds near the fire?" I glanced over my shoulder at the cheery glow we'd left behind.

"It would," Collin confirmed. "But not as safe. That fire will burn for some time yet, illuminating all around it. I don't want anyone coming into camp to be able to see you."

So he did think it possible that Ian would return this night. This ought to have terrified me awake. Instead I felt my steps slowing, my body dragging. *I'm so cold and so tired.*

"What of the other MacDonalds?" My eyes flickered to their fire, some distance from the one we'd warmed ourselves at with the Campbells.

"They'll do us no harm," Collin said. "I'm still their laird—perhaps even beyond this journey's end. I've their fealty."

"What do you mean *perhaps*?" Did a laird not hold his position until his death? Collin wasn't expecting to die, was he?

"Ian was shortly to take my place as laird." Collin stopped us as we reached the carriage. He retrieved blankets from inside while I leaned against it, eyes closed.

"But why would you allow that?" I asked. Was it possible to sleep standing up?

"It's Ian's right. He's eldest."

"He's reckless." Only this evening had I begun to appreciate the difficulty Collin faced in keeping Ian from doing harm to me or anyone else.

"Dangerous and temperamental, too." Collin's sigh sounded as tired as I felt. He jumped down from the carriage, blankets in hand.

"Why then? Aren't you afraid of what Ian might do to

your people?" I threaded my fingers through my hair, attempting to comb out at least some of the tangles before I lay down.

"I am concerned," Collin admitted. "But I cannot be two places at once, and I need to be with you."

My hands stilled. I watched as he shook out a blanket, spreading it carefully across the ground. This was my fault. The ruin of the MacDonald clan could be as well, if Ian was allowed to take over. I could not allow Collin to do such a thing.

"If you had not married me, you wouldn't be considering this, would you? Ian wouldn't be taking your place as laird, putting your people in danger of—who knows what?"

"But I did marry you." Collin's voice held no regret, yet I wondered how he could not resent me, and again why he had gone through with our marriage in the first place.

"Is my dowry that much to make it worth it?" I asked, unable to come up with another, logical explanation.

Darkness enveloped us, but as he turned to look up at me, I almost imagined a corner of his mouth lifting in a brief smile. "I would have married you without the dowry."

His quiet admission shocked me, warmed me considerably, and confused me more.

"Come, Katie." He stood, then tugged on my hand, pulling me away from the side of the carriage. Gratefully I sank onto the blanket he'd spread on the ground. While Collin continued bustling about I savored his words and continued running fingers through my hair, in a likely futile attempt to reduce the hideous tangles I knew would be present come morning.

Yesterday's PROMISE

"You'll sleep warmer if you plait it," he suggested.

"Aye." My first Scottish one-syllable answer. Next thing I'd probably be making that noise in my throat to save opening my mouth altogether. "I haven't my brush right now, and even if I did, I'm just too tired to work a braid." I leaned sideways, intending to lie down and sleep, wet, tousled hair and all.

"Wait." A peculiar expression crossed Collin's face. His brow furrowed in a look of recollection perhaps, then wry amusement. This time I was certain a corner of his mouth lifted.

"What?" I asked warily, my arm supporting me in the awkward position of being half way between sitting and lying down.

"I'll do it." Collin crouched in front of me and tucked a blanket over my lap. "I'll braid your hair."

"You?" I'd never heard of a man plaiting hair.

"Me." There was a smile to his voice. He came around and sat behind me, allowing me to lean into him. "I'll even tell you a story while I do." Gently his hands took over, his fingers combing through my hair with a tenderness and skill I'd not expected.

His ministrations quickly set my heart to racing and alternately left me feeling like a bowl of pudding at the same time. Heaven help me if he ever realized what power he could wield over me with such a simple touch.

Perhaps he did realize.

"You've done this before." *Mhairi.* There was hurt in my voice.

"Years ago," Collin confirmed. "Let's see if I remember."

Not Mhairi then. I felt myself relax, releasing the last of my jealousy. I had every reason to believe Collin took our wedding vows seriously. *I will trust him. Even with my heart?*

His words had warmed me, but his touch felt like fire, waking me fully—arousing new feelings. Slowly his fingers separated the strands of hair, taking care with each, bringing me under his spell completely.

He finished with my tangles, or those he could, and separated my hair into two sections. The first I pulled over my shoulder and held out of his way.

"If I remember correctly, the secret to a good braid is three equally divided sections."

"That, and you must weave it tight," I said.

"Ah, but that is not always well-received. As with the story I share."

I waited as he separated the hair and began plaiting one side. I hadn't worn my hair in two braids since I was a little girl, but he was taking such care with me, I wasn't about to tell him that a single braid, down my back, would have been more preferable.

"There was once a little lass," Collin began. "Quite bossy and quite certain she knew all there was to know about everything."

"She sounds dreadful." No doubt this was a tale about the younger me. Since I could not go back in time to correct my apparently poor behavior, at least I would not condone it now.

"She might have been an unpleasant child," Collin agreed, "had she not other qualities that made her likeable. But this story is about her bossiness and determination. One day the lass told me I must learn to plait her hair. And that I must do a proper job of it, too, or there would be grave consequences."

"But why you?" The answer came to me as soon as I'd asked the question. Collin had been assigned by my grandfather to watch over me, both an unusual and perhaps precarious assignment—if my displeasure at something made its way back to Grandfather's ears.

Recalling Alistair's less-than-favorable descriptions of me as a child, I braced myself for more far-from-complimentary truths.

"That was what I asked." Collin tugged a bit too hard, and my head tilted to the side with his effort. "But the lass insisted that one day her life would be in danger, and I should be the only one around who could plait her hair. And doing so would save her." He finished with the first braid and placed it carefully over my shoulder. "Hold this while I come up with a tie."

My eyes followed Collin as he got up and disappeared around the other side of the carriage. A few minutes later he returned, something clenched in his fist.

"A bit of the laces. From your corset. They're wet but should work fine."

Somehow I'd missed my sodden clothing being brought up to the carriage. I hadn't given it a second thought since taking it off. The garments were ruined—or so I'd believed. But I had a feeling Collin felt otherwise. In the past year I'd learned that poverty makes for thrift. I wondered if I should soon be appreciating that principle far beyond what I'd experienced already.

"So you plaited my hair when I was a child," I said, bringing him back to the story when he'd tied off my first braid and started on the second.

"I did. Took many a try for me to get it to your liking. How you carried on when I pulled your hair too tight, and how you complained that it looked messy when I did not. Once, when I had done a particularly fine job and the weave was extra tight, you complained and complained of a headache. Your grandfather finally dismissed you from the table and sent you to your room, and I enjoyed a nice evening, free of whining."

"I'm sorry I was such a wretched child."

Collin laughed—actually laughed—the sound so pleasant that I didn't mind at all that it was at my expense.

"You said that, not I," he insisted. "Let me tell the rest."

"There's more?" I winced, not from his braiding but from the discomfort of hearing about my past misdeeds.

"*Much* more," Collin said. "The tales I could tell." He spoke with more animation than I'd ever heard from him, and I decided that if recalling my horrific behavior got him talking, then I would endure listening. Penance for wrongs committed long ago, I supposed.

"The meal finished; evening turned to night," Collin continued. "I had not seen you since your banishment. Your grandfather took me aside and spoke to me a while. All in all it had been a pleasant few hours, free of worry over my charge. I went to my place to sleep for the night and had just made myself comfortable when a terrible, high-pitched scream rent the air. I jumped to my feet and found myself face to face with a spirit. All white and ghostly, it floated from the ceiling, arms outstretched, and hair—" Collin paused and cleared his throat. I turned to look at him and caught him struggling against laughter.

"Hair out to here." He held his hands wide on either side of his head and then above it.

"The spirit was me, wasn't it?" My voice lacked the humor his held, but I could not deny that the story was amusing. And I knew what he meant about my hair. Anna used to make fun of me after taking out my plaits each morning. Her hair often hung in soft waves down her back, whereas mine tended to fluff and stick out at all angles. "How did I manage to float from the ceiling?"

"You'd climbed up to a beam and tied yourself there with some cloth. You'd been sitting up there, waiting to scare me—who knows how long—when I came up." He held the second, completed braid out for me to see. "But I learned to braid and do it well. And here we are. Me saving you—from catching your death of cold, no doubt."

"I couldn't have known this would happen." While I believed the story of the mischievous ghost girl easily enough, I didn't for one minute think I might have foreseen this night ahead of me, all those years ago.

"That is the question now, isn't it?" Collin's voice quieted. "It's said the Campbell leaders know the future. Your grandfather certainly did. Your mother as well, I've been told. And you . . ." His voice trailed off to a long moment of silence between us. "There are those who would use such a gift for their own purposes. You must be careful, Katie." Collin wrapped both braids around the top of my head, then bound them together. "There. No wet hair to chill you—or less so, anyway. Now off to bed with you."

He spoke to me as if I was still that little girl he'd tended. For tonight, at least, I didn't correct him—about that or the fact that I had no gift of predicting what was to come. My childish premonition had likely been nothing more than a ploy designed to make Collin pay me some attention by plaiting my hair. I could not see the future then or now. If so, I certainly would have seen Ian coming tonight. I would have seen Collin coming to marry me as well. And I had seen neither.

"Lie down, and I'll cover you up."

Too tired and cold to protest, I followed Collin's suggestion. He pulled first one blanket, then a second up to my chin. He reached behind him for a third, from his own pile, and began to spread it over me.

"You keep that one."

"I'm used to the cold and did not get as wet as you."

I disagreed. He'd been in the river, too, and one minute or ten, wet was wet. "We can share it," I offered. "Spread half over the top of your other quilt."

Collin hesitated, then shifted his own bedding closer to mine. "All right."

"Thank you," I said, feeling my eyes water from something other than pain or cold. I wanted to have him close. I was still scared, as much or more for him as I was for myself.

I was also falling into some sort of trance, the plunge every bit as surprising as my spill into the river, the current of emotion sweeping me along just as swift. Every minute in Collin's presence, every word he spoke to me, his slightest touch—all combined within me, stirring to life new and exhilarating and tender feelings. I kept reminding myself that I'd not even known Collin a week yet and could not possibly care for him so deeply. But that argument was quickly losing ground. He was my past, though I could not remember, my present—saving me, caring for me, patient with me. And he was my future and had given up his own as laird for me. *For us?*

My only experience with romantic love had been watching Anna's courtship and marriage. After only a few days with Collin, I knew that what we had—or had the potential to have together—went far beyond anything my sister had experienced. There was something more to us than romance or even friendship. It was as if we had been together forever already and had the strength of that bond, yet a newness of feeling, for me, anyway.

I cared for Collin. I needed him. I didn't understand how, exactly, I could feel this, but these emotions came from within and ran deep. The vows I'd judged dramatic seemed beautiful now, and I meant every one of them. I cared more for his life—that no harm came to him—than for my own. And that terrified me.

Since pulling me from the river, Collin had been the epitome of a caring husband. I lamented that it had taken my near death to garner such concern and wondered if his attentiveness would continue after I recovered. After tonight I didn't think I could bear going back to the silence of our first days together and hoped Ian's disappearance meant we wouldn't have to. I wanted to be near Collin always, to talk with him, to laugh, to plan and dream. If only the rest of the world would fall away and leave us alone.

He lay down beside me, wrapping himself in his own blanket, then covering us both with the shared one.

I closed my eyes, and though sleep beckoned, I did not give into it yet. Something—many things—from this evening and our conversation troubled me.

Ian tried to kill me. First I'd been hated, and now I felt hunted. How could someone hate a person so much simply because of her name? Ian didn't even know me. He'd made his decision before even meeting me it seemed.

What kind of man did that? Certainly not one who might soon be leading others.

I turned toward Collin. "Did Ian know you intended him to be laird?"

Collin grunted. "Aye. We agreed to it when your father's letter came. Ian had wanted the position for a while, but he wasn't stable enough when he finally rejoined the MacDonalds. He'd been abused those many years, and it had left him less than whole."

I tried but could not muster any sympathy for Ian. I couldn't see anything in him except a bloodthirsty, ruthless man, out to get gain any way he could. Even if that meant murdering his own brother.

"The Munros did not treat him well." Collin's hands were behind his head, cradling it while he looked up at a night sky filled with more stars than I'd ever imagined. The creamy path of the Milky Way glittered above, like hundreds of jewels clustered together. I'd never seen it so clearly or felt its pull, beckoning me to follow, to find its end and discover the real treasure there.

North, it seemed to say. *That is the place for you.* I could only wonder at what I would find there, in my mother's homeland and the place Collin and I had begun.

Had it not been such a trying day and terrifying night, were I not so tired and still shivering, sleeping beside him beneath the starry night would have been enjoyable. As it was now, I felt the cold and discomfort entirely worth our conversation and this new closeness.

Collin continued his excuses for Ian. "Whereas I was given a place to lay my head within the very walls of your grandfather's castle, given plenty of food to eat, and even a task that turned pleasant enough—" He glanced over at me with another of his near smiles that warmed me while at the same time making me feel strangely lightheaded—"Ian was near-starved, frequently beaten, worked like a slave, and led to believe our father had sold him to the Munros for a bit of silver."

"Wasn't he old enough to remember the truth?" It was one thing for me to forget my four-year-old self. But it seemed entirely impossible that Ian should not remember the events of his fourteenth year.

"Truth can be blurry," Collin said. "Ian's remembrance of the night the Munros took him was that Da pushed him down the hill and left him for dead. Myself, I did not see the fall, as it may be, only Ian lying limp at the bottom of the ravine. I wanted to go to him, but Da held me back. Told me he was dead and we must leave him or be caught ourselves." Collin paused, his voice gruff. "I'd never seen Da weep before then. Never saw it after. Even when he left me behind and went to face the English and their rifles."

There it was again, that mention of his father and the

English. I wanted to ask if *my* father had been one of those pointing a rifle at Collin's father's heart. I would have to ask that question someday, as it stood between us—but I hadn't the courage tonight and didn't want to risk what progress we'd made.

While my mind had been with our fathers, Collin's was still upon his brother.

"Ian has gradually been getting better—more able to think of consequences, to act rationally. I thought him ready. And with the time come to bring you home, I knew he must be."

"Because you could not marry me and still be laird of the MacDonalds—even were we to live among them?"

"Even then," Collin confirmed, further stunning me. "Intermarriage between clans happens, but not between MacDonalds and Campbells. *Never.* What I have done amounts to treason, and it is only that I renounced my lairdship before going to England, and only the promised wealth my marriage offered the clan, that has allowed me continued association."

My knowledge of the workings of Scottish clans was limited, but I guessed enough to know that a lairdship was not something oft given up—without a fight, at least.

"You truly planned to leave your people, what family you'd left, to give up living among them and being their leader—for me?" Those did not seem the actions of a man who did not want his wife. I leaned up on my elbow, searching through the dark to meet Collin's gaze as he turned his head toward me.

"That was my intent," Collin said. "Though just now I don't know what to do. If Ian is not fit to take charge, I cannot simply leave the MacDonalds without a leader."

"What, exactly, does a Scottish laird do?" I asked.

Collin made a noise in the back of his throat. "He works. He cares for his people—who oft expect him to solve their problems, be they sick animals, an unfaithful wife, or a disobedient child, crops that fail, a house unfit to live in. To be a laird is to worry constantly over the affairs and welfare of many. It means providing for a great many and deciding what is best for the whole, even if that will mean a few suffer."

I thought of the sketch I had drawn on our wedding night. These were the burdens I had read in his face—or some of them, anyway.

"It is a powerful lot of work and worry," Collin said. "Not unlike being a husband," he added with a low chuckle.

"What do you mean?" Feeling indignant, I pushed up further, leaning on my arm.

"To be a husband is to worry constantly over the welfare of one's wife—be that altering a carriage for her comfort, finding someone to lace her corset or to do it for her when no one can be found, to cool my brother's ire when she has insulted him, to pluck her from the river when she has fallen in—"

"I didn't fall. I was pushed."

"To see that she is warm, to plait her hair—"

"Since I am such a bother, I'll just go sleep elsewhere." I leaned forward, intent on removing myself and my blankets, but Collin's hand stopped me.

"Let me finish." His eyes held mine. "Being a husband *is* a heavy burden—because of the fear of what may be lost. Marriage is the promise of having a friend—someone to stand at my side, to counsel with and confide in." He waited a heartbeat—a few of them. Mine were fast and erratic at his simple suggestion that he might confide in me, might consider me his friend.

Collin lifted my hand and turned it over, slowly tracing the thin scar along my palm. "Being a husband is to not be lonely for the first time in a very long time."

"Oh." *He has been lonely.* I'd not expected that. I ought to have recognized the emotion in my sketch as well. My heart ached for him, *with* him. Had I not felt the same, first with Father's decline, then with his passing and my being left out of Mother and Anna's preparations for the wedding?

And had it not started years before—my own fault, I supposed—with my preference for staying at home instead of going out? I had not minded—much. Safe at home had been better than terrified while traveling. Or so I had told myself while watching the carriage conveying my family away. I'd spent those silent days and nights lost in painting, imagining myself alone on a mountain that overlooked the world. But hidden in my art and deep within myself, I longed for company.

"I want to be your friend, Collin." In that moment I wanted it more than I'd ever wanted anything.

"Long ago you were. I've missed you, Katie."

I've missed you, too. Had I, without even realizing it? I slid beneath the blankets and lay on my side again, facing him. "I'm here now."

"It's different." He shifted our hands so that our palms pressed together, fingers entwined. "You don't remember."

"I want to. You can help me. I'll try not to be such a bother."

Yesterday's PROMISE

"You always were."

I caught his lopsided smile—every bit as beautiful as I'd imagined—and felt a catch in my heart.

"Kept me on my toes, kept life interesting, kept me from drowning in the sorrow of my losses. Whether you were looking like a specter, hanging from a sheet by a rafter, or causing me to get my fingers rapped by cook for stealing your favorite tarts from the kitchens—"

"I didn't—"

"*Frequently.*" He nodded. "I don't want you to change. I just want you to be safe, to be mine."

"I am," I promised and meant it more than I had meant any of my wedding vows five days earlier. I squeezed his hand reassuringly, both thrilled and concerned with this side of my husband. "But I cannot ask you to abandon your family. Ian cannot lead them." I didn't want to talk about Ian right now or Collin's status as laird of the MacDonalds. He had opened up a conversation about *us*, and I dearly wanted to continue that, to explore more on the topics of our past and present friendship. But it felt almost as if the weight of the MacDonald clan had somehow shifted from his shoulders to mine, and I could not let that subject go, no matter how much I wished to.

"As he is *now*, Ian cannot lead them—anywhere but to disaster." Collin gave a weary sigh. "If he seeks power he will think of none but himself. And the people will suffer for it. To be a laird is to provide for others, to be fair and just and continuously concerned with each and every man, woman, and child under your care. One's own needs and wants oft come last, or not at all."

Was marrying me—and acquiring my dowry—simply

another duty to his people, or had Collin thought of his own needs and wants? I wanted to believe the latter, but one night of attentive care and intimate conversation was not enough that I trusted him completely yet.

"The MacDonalds are fortunate to have you." I doubted very much that the English lords I knew were even aware of every man, woman, and child residing on their lands, let alone that they cared sincerely for their welfare. "It all sounds very contrary to the life of an English lord," I said. "He sits in his manor all day or rides his horse or visits friends. He goes to his townhome in London for the season, where he is free to play billiards and attend parties and musicales. He has servants to do every menial task. And he collects rents—or rather, his steward collects them for him—from all those living on and working his land. "

"And how do those working his land feel about this arrangement?" Collin asked. "What are they provided in exchange for their rent?"

"Provided?" I thought of the tenants I'd seen, the rickety cottages, their children who not only were uneducated but were sent to work in the fields almost as soon as they could walk—or so it seemed. "They are allowed to work the land and try to provide for their own. I imagine they feel rather poorly about their status." I would have.

"I should think so," Collin said. "And yet, in recent years, I see some of the lairds turning to this. They have forgotten their responsibility to the people and are coming to feel instead that they are somehow better than those who live on and farm the land. When really, those are the lifeblood of a clan. I should know," Collin said bitterly. "We've precious few of them left."

Yesterday's PROMISE

"What do you mean?"

"The rebellion cost the MacDonalds dearly. Those men who did not die in battle were hunted down after and imprisoned, killed, or expelled from Scotland. Nearly all our cattle were stolen, driven from our land and sold to lowlanders for a pittance. We've little more than the barley crop to support us, and widows and bairns cannot harvest a field like a man, though many are trying. It will be all I can do to keep everyone fed another winter."

"That is what my dowry is to be used for?" I could only feel glad of it.

"Aye. God willing, it will get us through another year."

"But Ian was willing to risk losing it. Killing me would have hurt your people as well."

Collin gave a solemn nod. "He was not thinking of the whole, of anyone but himself."

"It is well that I lived, then."

"For more reasons than your dowry." Collin held my hand close to his heart. My own leaped in response.

"Now we need only figure out how to live among the MacDonalds so you can continue as their laird."

He shook his head. "It would be too dangerous. Ian—"

"Must not be allowed to dictate our future," I said with more bravery than I felt. His knife at my throat had been real. His hands had nearly sent me to my death. But I could not allow that knife or those hands to harm others, not when Collin had it in his power to protect them.

"We need not solve it tonight."

"No," I agreed, recalling how tired I'd been an hour hence when we'd staggered to the carriage. Nothing would be resolved tonight. But a confrontation loomed in the near future. How long was it before the road we journeyed separated the Campbells from the MacDonalds, each to return to their own land? Which direction would I go? Who would I join? What would Collin do?

"We should sleep now," Collin said. "Tomorrow will be another long day."

I suspected that every day promised to be long. Instead of feeling discouraged about this, I took heart. Collin's hand remained over mine, warm and comforting. So long as he was at my side, I felt I could endure whatever hardship lay ahead. And more than that, I wanted to help him endure it as well. I felt an almost overwhelming desire to make his life better, to bear him up as he bore the weight of his failing clan.

"Sleep well, Collin," I said, wishing him a peaceful rest.

"Sleep well, Katie," he returned.

"I will," I promised.

But I did not.

"Now son—" Laird Campbell paused to clear his throat.

"I'm not your son, and I'll thank you to quit calling me that."

"I'm the closest thing you've got to a father, and as yours gave you into my care, I mean to take that responsibility seriously." Laird Campbell reached forward, pulling my hand from my side. I started to resist, only to feel his grip turn surprisingly firm. He placed Katie's hand in mine again, then wrapped his own around the both of ours.

He needn't have. I felt the inexplicable pull toward her as I had before, and this time I gave into it, clasping her tiny hand firmly, holding on as if our very lives depended upon it.

Chapter Fourteen

The moon had trekked halfway across the sky when I woke with both a sense of urgency and a feeling of imminent dread. I turned toward Collin and found him gone.

Hurry. A chill brushed against my shoulders as I sat up. I glanced around to see what or who had caused it but met only darkness. The necessity of leaving, of finding Collin intensified. I stood, discarding my blankets, and began walking toward a light so distant that at first I wondered if it might be a star. My steps were quiet, my stockinged feet stealing softly through the tall grasses of our camp.

Gradually the light grew brighter and closer, and upon cresting a hill I saw that it was not one light, but several, all streaming from the windows of an immense castle perched on top of the cliff before me. A thrill of anticipation shivered down my spine. The light was for me, beckoning me close to discover some wonderful secret.

I will not be alone for long. Collin is there—waiting. I ran as fast as my feet would carry me, tripping and sliding up the steep slope, ignoring the jagged rocks that scraped my shins when I fell and the burning in my lungs as I climbed higher.

Hurry.

I arrived, breathless, upon the doorstep, and the great iron doors unfolded, swinging inward, inviting. Light spilled from within, warming me, drawing me in.

Just inside I stopped in a vast hall, arched high with timber and stone. A circular dais stood in the center, upon which a singular casket resided, surrounded at the head by the flame of a hundred candles. My excitement fled. I reeled backward, clutching my middle against a sudden, crippling sorrow. My back bumped against the doors, and I turned to them, pulling the handles in a vain attempt to flee.

"Let me out!" I cried, beating my fists upon the doors. I begged and pounded until my knuckles were raw and bloodied, but the doors would not open. I leaned my head against them and wept.

"Oh, Collin." I whispered his name and knew it was he in the casket. With every breath my heart broke more. I had not known I cared so much, but the grief encompassing me surpassed even that which I had felt for my father. Instead of being mystified at it, I suffered under the worst kind of anguish, of a love forever lost. I pressed my hands to my chest, a feeble attempt against the physical ache crushing me.

"Please," I begged at the doors once more. *Release me from this.*

Come.

Against my wishes I heeded the demand, facing the center of the room once more and stumbling toward the dais. I stood before the box that held my Collin, then fell to my knees, laying my hands and face to the smooth wood as tears streamed down my cheeks.

Collin, the man I loved more than it seemed anyone ought or should or could love, was dead.

A terrible creaking came from within, shaking the casket, causing the candles to flicker. I stood and backed away as the lid crashed open. Inside I saw not Collin, but a woman who could only be my real mother—with a delicate and kind face and grey eyes that mirrored mine. She raised her arms, inviting me closer. Still crying, I climbed onto the platform, then leaned into her as she put her arms around me.

"It's all right, my little lass. All will be well. Courage, Katie. I am with you now."

I nodded into her shoulder but instead of softness and warmth felt only cold and the brittleness of bones long laid to rest. I fell backwards, screaming as her skeleton rose up, leering at me.

"Remember . . . all is not always as it seems."

My eyes flew open and the face, those black holes where eyes ought to have been, vanished. No creature of the dead towered over me. Beneath me I felt only grass—not the cold stone floor of a castle. The only lights were those of the moon and stars overhead.

A dream? It had seemed far too real. My rapid heartbeat pounded in my ears, trying to banish the all-too-lifelike images. I brought a hand to my mouth to quiet my heavy breathing.

A man standing a few paces away whirled to face me. I dropped my hand to my chest, scrunched my eyes closed, and feigned sleep, though not before identifying him as a Campbell, the youngest one. Malcom, whose water pouch I had lost in the river.

What is he doing here?

I peeked through one eye, daring another look, and saw his back to me, arms crossed as he gazed about the camp. He gave a low, peculiar whistle, and somewhere, from the other side of the meadow, it was returned.

The night watch. That is all. I strove for calm. Never had I experienced a dream so real—so tangible. I'd seen my mother's face. What did it mean? And even more disturbing, what of the casket I'd believed to be Collin's? I turned my head and saw that he was indeed gone from his sleeping place.

The sense of dread returned. I needed to see him, to know he was well. The meadow that earlier had seemed so quaint and lovely now felt only dark and threatening. Malcom had wandered off, to another part of camp, and I did not want to be alone.

I sat up slowly, pushed my blanket aside, and began groping about for my shoes. I'd found the first when strained voices reached my ears.

"I'm doing you a favor." Ian's harsh whisper cut through the dark.

"Keep telling yourself that lie, Ian. All the way to your grave."

Collin. I leaned my head back against the wheel in relief. *He is all right. It was just a dream—a ghastly one.*

"Won't be my grave tonight," Ian said. "But yours might be another matter." The click of a pistol being cocked followed this threat. "Be a part of it, or get out of my way."

The shoe slipped from my fingers as I rose up on my knees, peering around the back of the carriage. My heart jumped to my throat as I stared at Collin and Ian, facing one another in the clearing, Ian pointing a gun at Collin.

Collin held his hands out in supplication. "You know I can't do either." His voice sounded calm but insistent. "If you've any brains in that thick head of yours, you'll see why. Start a war with the Campbells, and they'll wipe out what little we've left. If you want the MacDonalds completely off the map of Scotland, this madness is the way."

I glanced behind me, fervently wishing Malcom was still nearby. Had he seen them and signaled for help?

Hurry. The same whispering I'd heard in my dream spoke to me now. I felt a breeze against my back, once more urging me to move, prompting me.

I looked toward Collin again. His lips were pressed tight, and his gaze locked on Ian's. Their profiles, silhouetted in the moonlight, were nearly identical, save for Ian's long hair, rustling behind him with the breeze.

"Don't do this, Ian," Collin said. "*Please.*"

"I don't want to kill you," Ian said, though the evil in his tone led me to believe otherwise. "It's them I'm wanting revenge on. And what more perfect way than to take away their chosen one, the prophetess who's going to restore the Campbells to their former glory."

What is he talking about? My peculiar dream rang fresh in my mind, but I dismissed it. *I could not be the one they spoke of.*

"You shouldn't believe everything you hear," Collin said. "Superstition. That's all it is. She didn't exactly predict we'd be met by an English patrol, did she?"

They *were* talking about me. I touched a trembling hand to the back of my head and the braids wound there as Collin's earlier warning rang through my mind. *It's said the Campbell leaders know the future. There are those who would use such a gift for their own purposes.* If Ian wanted me dead, then who were those others Collin spoke of? Who else believed I possessed such an ability?

"As for revenge," Collin said. "Don't confuse the Munros with the Campbells. I married to pay a debt," Collin said. "I owe Liam Campbell my life."

Hurry.

I stood, reaching up through the open carriage window. Bracing my hands on the frame, I placed one foot on the wheel and hoisted myself up, crawling carefully inside, fortunate the curtains were still closed, keeping me from view.

"Not to mention Katie's dowry comes at a crucial time for us," Collin continued.

I crouched on the floor, then reached beneath the seat cushion, attempting to pry it from the frame.

The cushion wouldn't budge. There had to be a latch. I ran my fingers along the top of the frame, earning a sliver before I felt the well-concealed lever.

"As for the rumors—" Collin said.

The seat lifted. I thrust my hand inside and felt nothing. Collin had said there was a second latch somewhere that would separate the seat entirely and reveal an additional, hidden compartment.

"—she's nothing but an ordinary woman."

Who knows very little of secret panels and the weapons within. Precious seconds ticked by as my hands fumbled along the bottom of the seat, searching. At last I found a bar, nearly hidden within the hinge at the back. I pulled, and the cushioned top sprang up, revealing a half dozen pistols. My hand reached in and closed around cold steel. *Please be loaded.*

"An *English*woman, and a Campbell," Ian hissed. "You couldn't have wed a lower form. Get rid of her and you're free to do as you like, to have Mhairi warming your bed."

I thrust the name from my mind. God willing, there would be time enough later to discuss that subject with Collin. But only if his brother didn't kill him first. I parted the curtain and eased the pistol through the glassless window, then took aim at Ian's hand.

"What I want ceased to matter years ago," Collin said. "I did what I must."

"As I do what I must." Ian's voice rang with finality.

Hurry! The trigger was slow to budge, though I held the gun in both hands.

Help me. I called upon whatever force had prompted me to act. The metal bit into my finger. I squeezed harder. A shot went off, ringing in my ears and sending me sprawling backward onto the carriage floor.

Alarmed at the strange sensation overtaking me, I looked to the old laird. "I feel—"

"Bound?" he suggested, even as he removed his hand covering ours. I wished to let go of his granddaughter and found I could not, as if some unseen force held us there.

"It is not I who has brought you together," Laird Campbell said. "Not my hand that joins yours today and again in the future. A far greater power is at play here and intends to work through you both."

In that moment he sounded and looked far more like a wizard, his grey beard touching his knees as he bent forward, close to us.

Chapter Fifteen

Jarring pain shot up my shoulder as my elbow smacked the edge of the open seat. I winced but clawed my way back to my knees to peer out the window.

Chaos reigned where only Ian and Collin had stood just seconds earlier. Campbells and MacDonalds alike had risen, alert and ready-to-battle. My eyes scanned the men, searching for Collin and not seeing him.

I took too long. Ian fired first.

"Coll—" The door opened, and a hand grasped me, interrupting my cry. I raised my arms, attempting to fight off my captor.

"Shh." Malcom appeared in the doorway, a finger to his lips. I nodded, and he released me. I followed him from the carriage and crouched behind it, all the while my eyes searching through the dark for Collin.

"Come," Malcom said.

"I've got to find Collin."

"Hold your fire! Ian's had an accident. It isn't serious." Collin's voice carried across the clearing as I finally caught sight of him kneeling next to someone I guessed to be his brother.

"Thank goodness," I whispered.

"It was *not* a Campbell," Collin shouted at the approaching line of armed MacDonalds.

"Oh yes it was," Malcom muttered. "Come on." He grabbed my wrist. "We've got to get you out of here."

"Put your weapons down!" Collin shouted, turning his head to and fro at both Campbells and MacDonalds, moving in to surround him on either side.

"Got to get you to safety. Laird's orders," Malcom said.

"Which laird?" Dragging Malcom with me, I crawled around on the grass, searching for my shoes. Collin had said nothing about fleeing to safety in the event of a fight. I'd been, in fact, right where he had instructed me to be—on the floor of the carriage, doing my best to stay out of the way.

"Campbell. MacDonald. Both," Malcom sputtered. "I'm charged with your safety."

"My shoes," I pled as he pulled me to my feet and hauled me away from the carriage in the opposite direction from Collin, Ian, and the crowd gathering around them.

"They'll bring 'em later. Hurry."

It was the same word I'd been hearing all night, and with the shouting and arguing going on behind me, I deemed it prudent to listen once more.

I shot Ian. It isn't serious. My hands felt clammy, and I swayed on my feet a second. Malcom swore, then stopped and scooped me up, showing more strength than I'd imagined him to have as he dumped me over his shoulders like a sack of grain.

"I've never shot anyone before," I said as we bounced along, my face at his back.

"Picked a good one to start with," he muttered as he jogged past the bit of earth the Campbells had lain claim to for the night. It was deserted now, save for a bedroll or two scattered about the remnants of the earlier fire. Malcom was proving surprisingly strong for one who appeared so slight in stature. I supposed the urgency of the situation spurred him to greater strength. It caused me to feel like vomiting.

When we reached the horses he leaned forward, nearly dropping me. Though panting heavily, he did not stop to rest but with nimble fingers untethered the closest horse. "You ride in front," he ordered, pulling me over to the animal.

"Ride where?" I attempted to step from his grasp, but Malcom tightened his grip on my arm.

"Away," he whispered fiercely. "You don't think you'll be safe here, do you? As soon as they sort out the tussle they'll realize who shot Ian. You've seen that the MacDonalds have no love for you, and now you've gone and shot the man who should be their rightful laird."

"Who was about to kill his brother!"

"Ach." Malcom clucked his tongue. "Most of the

MacDonalds would have taken more kindly to that than to what you've done. It's Ian they wish to follow."

"Up," Malcom ordered, hoisting me so that I had no choice but to mount if I did not want his hands on me. He pulled himself up next, grasped the reins, and we were off.

I looked over my shoulder, trying to tamp down the panic I felt at being separated from Collin. "Where are we going?"

"Away." Malcom's voice was terse.

The cool night air stung my cheeks. Gooseflesh sprang up along my arms, prickling from both cold and fear. What would happen to Collin? When would I see him again?

Once we were a distance from camp, Malcom ordered the horse to a full gallop. I jostled along in front of him, feeling more alone than I had since leaving home.

"Aren't we far enough away now?" I asked.

Malcom didn't answer but tightened his grip at my waist, as if he feared I might leap from the horse. I wasn't that foolish, though my unease grew with each minute.

"Where are you taking me?" I demanded, twisting to look at him.

"To the Campbell holding—eventually. There's a cave an hour or so from here that will do for shelter tonight."

An hour. "Will Collin know to meet us there?" I didn't want to be so far from him. Why hadn't he told me of this plan to keep me safe?

Malcom shrugged. "Perhaps not, but he knows the way well enough to Campbell land."

This brought little comfort, but there was nothing I could do, aside from risking Malcom's ire with my repeated questions. I wished it was Collin seated behind me, or even

Alistair. Why had they chosen the Campbell who seemed the least capable to protect me? Was it because the MacDonalds paid him little attention because of his youth and stature? When they realized that I had shot Ian and fled, would they even know with whom I'd gone?

The minutes rushed by like the cold air stinging my eyes. I lowered my head and closed them, then must have dozed, for suddenly Malcom was insisting that I wake and dismount. He jumped down before me, then lifted his hands to help me slide from the horse. We stood beneath the moon's light at the mouth of a cave.

"Go on." He nodded his head toward the cave. I'll see to the horse."

Still half asleep I stumbled my way inside, the palm of my hand feeling along the rough stone of the wall. It wasn't a particularly deep cave that I could tell, perhaps twenty or thirty paces before the wall curved to what I believed and hoped to be the end. Behind me I could still hear Malcom and the horse. When I turned to look at them I couldn't make out more than the barest shapes, shadowed in the faint light from the entrance. The tunnel must have curved more than I realized.

I slid to the floor, knees to my chest with my skirt pulled over them. *Collin*, I thought wearily. When would I see him again? What if he didn't come for me at the Campbells'? What if it was he who paid the price for my actions tonight? He'd said Ian's wound was not serious, but what if that wasn't true? I'd not heard Ian's voice again after I fired.

My eyes closed on these worrisome thoughts, and I welcomed sleep. Before it could entirely claim me I heard voices coming from outside.

"Go for Brann. Tell him I've got her and no one followed."

The voice answered in thick brogue, and I could not make out the garbled words.

"I can't take her farther and risk being caught in the daylight," Malcom said. "We'll be safer here. Brann should be at the pass already, so an hour or two at best and another two back here. That will see him here before morning."

What time is it? This night had seemed forever already, between my conversation with Collin, the nightmare, and then shooting Ian. Our escape on horseback had to have taken some time as well.

Malcom did not re-enter the cave, staying near the entrance to stand guard, I guessed. I wondered which other Campbell he had been talking to, who Brann was and why he must come. The name felt familiar somehow, though I could not conjure a face or any memory to go with it. I guessed he must be another Campbell and would see us safely to my grandfather's home.

It would be good to have another with us. Malcom did not exactly inspire confidence. Were we to meet with one or more angry MacDonalds, I feared the outcome would not be good. But perhaps this Brann would even the odds in our favor.

Or maybe Collin would come before then and I would not have to be escorted by Campbells. On that hopeful thought I again attempted sleep and then for the third time that night was woken abruptly. A heavy weight pressed on my chest, and hot, foul breath huffed in my face. I froze, imagining a bear or some other creature that resided in the cave.

"Malcom," I cried.

"Right here." It was *his* hot breath above me.

"What are you doing?" I made to push him off, but he clasped my hands together and held them tight.

"There now, Katie—that's what your husband calls you, isn't it? Don't fight me, and this'll be over in a minute." His knee pressed between my legs, making his intentions clear. I screamed. His mouth crushed mine, cutting off my airway. I sank my teeth into his lip. He jerked back and flung me away.

My head hit the floor a second before Malcom's hand struck my face. Tears sprang to my eyes, and shock silenced my screams, though I still struggled to get out from beneath him.

He clamped my hands together again, this time pinning them above my head on the cave floor. Once more I was surprised at his strength.

"We all know Collin's not had you," Malcom said. "Is this why? You're too much for the MacDonald?"

I spit in his face, then fought harder as Malcom reached a hand down to lift my skirts.

"Why are you doing this," I cried, changing tactics swiftly. "We are kin. I'm a Campbell, too."

"Only part," Malcom said. "*English.*" He spoke the word with loathing. "Brann intended to claim you as his in spite of that, but he's not come, and it's almost light. And if he's unable, he's offered a reward to any man who steals you from the MacDonald and ruins ye for him."

Instead of being more frightened, I felt outraged at this. I slammed my forehead into Malcom's chin, then freed one hand to claw at his face. With a surge of strength I pushed him off of me and rolled out from under him.

Yesterday's PROMISE

Malcom reached out, only just missing my head. I scrambled to my feet, too late realizing he stood between me and the cave entrance. I'd rolled the wrong direction to escape.

I backed up as far as I could. He laughed, then lunged forward, grabbing my arm and jerking me toward him. He struck me again. My eyes smarted, blurring his face and the look of determination I saw there.

"Don't do this," I begged. "Please. Think of my grandfather." I couldn't stop the tears flooding my eyes.

"Your grandfather's dead." Malcom grabbed the front of my dress and ripped the bodice down the middle. "Proof," he said. "So when they find you, they'll know what's happened."

When they find me—dead? Fear pounded in my ears. I stopped fighting and used my free hand to try to cover myself. "Please don't," I pled once more.

In answer Malcom pushed me against the wall and reached again for my skirts. He stopped suddenly, head angled toward the cave opening, listening. A horse nickered.

Footsteps.

Someone was out there, but I could not feel relief. *Don't let it be Brann.* I screamed louder than I had before and shoved Malcom from me.

He hauled me in front of him, a knife pressed to my throat. "Who's there?"

"Alistair." The man I'd thought of affectionately appeared at the cave entrance looking as grim and grey as the morning light behind him. "Brann's almost here. He'll have your head if you've harmed the lass. He wants her for himself."

You, too, Alistair. I tried to meet his gaze, but he wouldn't look at me. My heart broke a little more. Collin had trusted Alistair. I was sure of it. Had Alistair betrayed that trust before coming here? Had something happened to Collin?

Behind me Malcom stiffened. "It's almost morning, and Brann *isn't* here. Better she's ruined by a Campbell than to let the MacDonald have her. I'm just following the laird's orders."

Alistair shook his head slowly. "He said to bring the lass to him untouched, so he could take her to wife. You ken she's too good for the likes of you—granddaughter of a laird herself."

"One who betrothed her to a MacDonald!" Malcom's shouts reverberated through the cave. "I can have her as well as the next man."

Alistair shrugged and started to turn around. "It's your neck." Hoofbeats sounded outside. "That'll be Brann."

"Fine." Malcom held his ground, knife to my neck, but I sensed his hesitation and felt his hand tremble.

Alistair left the cave, and urgent, clipped Scots' brogue could be heard outside. I increased my breathing, feigning panic that wasn't far from the truth. "Brann," I whispered, fear unfurling inside of me. A tawny-haired bully of a youth appeared in my mind.

Never believe anything Brann says. Never trust him. Someone had once told me those things. Brann would have taken from me already what Malcom had attempted. "Not him." *Anyone but him.*

"You remember our laird?" Malcom asked.

I do. I gave the slightest nod and felt his blade against my neck.

Footsteps crunched over the rocky floor. A man's broad frame crowded the entrance, blocking what light we had. My heart leapt as a dark head ducked at the low ceiling. *Collin.*

Get down.

My knees buckled, and I sank to the floor in a pretend faint. Malcom tried to catch me as I fell, his hand with the knife moving from my throat. Another dirk sliced through the air, only just clearing my head and striking Malcom's shoulder. With a cry he released me. I sprang forward, crawling toward the entrance.

Collin held his hand out. I reached to take it when another shadow appeared.

"Behind you," I cried, my warning barely in time for him to whirl and face Alistair.

Malcom seized my foot, pulling me toward him. I flipped over and kicked at his jaw.

Collin leapt over me and drove a knife through Malcom's chest. Malcom's scream died out. His grip went slack, and he fell backward.

I scooted away. From behind someone lifted me beneath my arms, pulling me.

"Let go." I struck out at Alistair. He held his hands up and stepped from my reach.

"You're all right now, lass. It's over." His brows drew together, and compassion swam in the depths of his own, watery eyes. He wiped at them with the back of his sleeve.

"It's all right, Katie." Collin led me out of the cave. "Alistair's on our side."

"Are you sure?"

"Positive. It was he who realized you'd been taken and followed so quickly. If not for him, I wouldn't have been able to find you. He went into the cave first, to assess the situation so we had the best chance of rescuing you."

I turned my face into Collin's shoulder and sobbed. He held me tightly in his arms, whispering soothing words. A blanket was placed around my shoulders, and Alistair mumbled something about taking care of the body.

Collin led me a short distance from the cave and continued to hold me while I wept like a child. After some minutes my tears at last subsided, and my head cleared enough that I could begin to think of something other than the night's terrors.

"It's Brann, isn't it?" I raised my head to look at Collin. "He's the one you warned me about when you said there were those who believed I'd a gift and would use it for their own purposes."

"Aye," Collin said solemnly. He held me away from him, hands braced on each of my arms as he looked at me with concern. "Ian wishes you dead, while Brann wishes me dead and you his to control."

I shuddered, and Collin pulled me back into his embrace, wrapping his arms around me comfortingly.

"How are we to live among the Campbells if Brann intends us harm?" My earlier fears were confirmed. Collin was at risk, too, having married me.

"It is why I'll not leave you there alone," Collin said. "There are many Campbells, like Alistair, who remain faithful to your grandfather and his wishes. But there are some, particularly those younger men like Malcom, who give their allegiance to Brann."

"How are we to know who is to be trusted and who isn't?" The homecoming I'd envisioned was not to be.

"I was rather hoping you might be able to help with that." Collin stroked my back, his touch soothing away at least some of my worry.

It was my grandfather's abilities he was speaking of again. "And if I cannot?"

He shrugged. "It will be as it was when you were a child. It was a rare occasion I ever left your side."

But he could not be at my side and also be laird of the MacDonalds. We'd returned to the same problem we'd been discussing last night, which brought to mind his brother.

"Will Ian be all right?" I asked. "I only meant to shoot his hand."

"It was *you*." Collin looked down at me, his brows arched, incredulity slowly replaced with consternation. "I thought he'd accidentally misfired upon himself, but then a pistol was found on the carriage floor, and you'd gone missing. I thought it was Malcom who'd fired the shot to cause a distraction."

"Ian was pointing a gun at you," I said. "What else was I to do?"

Collin shook his head, and a corner of his mouth lifted. "Nothing else. It would seem we're even now. I saved you last night, and you repaid the favor."

He failed to mention he'd just acted a second time on my behalf.

"A shield for your back as you are for mine." I'd never

imagined our vows would be tested within the first week of marriage.

"Don't forget. 'Your name I cry out in the night—'" Collin quoted. "Had you but called for me last night, perhaps some of this might have been avoided."

That was not exactly the meaning I'd derived from that particular vow, but I didn't argue. He wasn't scolding exactly, but his expression appeared stern as we stood, toe to toe, his head bent close to mine.

"Never go away with anyone again—man or woman—unless I direct you otherwise."

I drew in a shaky breath and nodded. "I won't." Lesson learned. Trust no one, excepting Collin and perhaps Alistair. The latter joined us, leading three horses, his expression grim.

"I'm sorry I misjudged you, Alistair." He'd been so kind to me, and I had repaid him poorly.

He gave a little nod. "You weren't to know."

"Alistair has long been our ally," Collin said. "And a good one to have. He may not have the Campbell ability to see the future, but his tracking skills are astounding in their own right. There's not another man I'd rather have on my side."

Beneath such praise, Alistair's face turned near to the shade of his beard. "We'd best be off, in case Brann does show up here." He pulled a knife from the belt at his waist and held it out to Collin. "Cleaned it as best I could. Laid him out proper in the cave. We dare not take the time to bury him."

His tone was matter of fact, as if taking care of a dead body and cleaning the weapon with which it had been killed was ordinary, day-to-day business. I felt lightheaded as I had last night, after shooting Ian.

Yesterday's PROMISE

"Leave Malcom's horse behind," Collin instructed. "If we reach the Campbell keep before it does, we can watch to see who returns it. And even if we arrive after, with a bit of searching we could probably find out who brought it in. Someone else was helping Malcom, and I want to know who." Collin took the reins of Ian's horse from Alistair. "Katie will ride with me."

At my questioning gaze, he shrugged.

"Ian won't mind overmuch that I've borrowed it. He isn't going to be fit for riding for a while. He'll be taking the carriage home."

"His injury—"

"Is a bit lower than his hand." Collin looked away instead of meeting my eye.

Alistair chuckled. "Too bad she didn't have a pistol with her just now."

Collin's gaze flickered downward, to my torn gown. The tartan square, placed between my breasts when I'd dressed the night before, was the only thing left keeping me reasonably modest.

Embarrassed, I clutched the blanket tighter around me. Alistair had the grace to look away, while Collin stepped forward and tied the corners, then settled it around me like a temporary cloak. "I'd kill Malcom if he wasn't already dead."

Dead. By Collin's hand. I should have felt shocked or sorrowful—something other than the relief that had swept through me when Collin's knife had struck true. Was violence like that to be a part of my life here?

"How many men have you killed?" I asked, not at all certain I wanted to know the answer.

"Since the war, one. Today," Collin said. "It's not a practice I relish."

This both relieved me and made me sorrowful. *He killed a man for me.* "You fought during the rebellion? But you were just a boy."

"The prince wasn't particular about who stood up for him, so long as you could hold a musket steady. My first battle was at Prestopans. We won. I didn't celebrate with the others, but threw up afterward."

"I feel a little like that now," I admitted, though I thought it still more from what might have been than from knowing the end Malcom had met.

"As well you should," Collin said. "I don't imagine violence and death have been a part of your life."

"No." I prayed they wouldn't be now. "I'm sorry I was the cause of you taking a man's life."

"You weren't," Alistair said.

"True," Collin agreed. "Malcom made his own trouble." Collin helped me mount Ian's horse, then swung up behind me, leaning forward to study my face, as if to make certain I was well enough to ride.

"I'm glad you are safe, Katie. And if I've got to kill a man to see to that, or journey to the very center of hell and back to protect you, I will do it."

A slow smile grew on the old laird's face. "If you knew what a gift I'm giving you both with this betrothal, you'd be eager instead of hesitant."

Hesitant wasn't the half of it. My heart throbbed in my chest as I fought against the unseen forces holding me in place.

"I'm frightened," Katie said, her eyes large and round. From head to toe she trembled, shivering in her bare feet and night rail, her plaid having fallen to the floor. I squeezed her hand and shuffled closer, wanting to offer comfort from the storm encircling us.

"That's right, Collin." Laird Campbell nodded his approval, as if he understood the direction of my thoughts. "You are to protect Katie so she can fulfill her destiny. Henceforth you will feel drawn to her as a moth to a flame. Only you'll not catch fire with the effort." His look grew thoughtful. "Not for some time yet, anyway. Though there will come a time when you will burn for her . . ."

Chapter Sixteen

Our morning ride was vastly different than the previous night's, the pace steady instead of breakneck, with daylight instead of moonlight illuminating our path. With my back against Collin's chest and his arm securely around me, I felt safer than I had since leaving home, and might have found it the most enjoyable travel yet, if not for the turmoil within me.

We did not speak much. Exhaustion and tension kept me silent, and I suspected Collin had many matters occupying his mind. The one at the forefront of mine was where we should go from here; it seemed neither clan would welcome us.

I questioned aloud why we needed to go either place, why we were even considering it with the dangers awaiting us.

"We're not considering joining the MacDonalds," Collin answered in a surly tone. "And it's not up for discussion."

Fine. Allow your family to suffer under Ian's leadership. I stiffened my back, keeping as far from him as possible to show my displeasure at his curt and entirely unsatisfactory answer. "I don't see that living with the Campbells is any better," I argued. "Brann seems at least as dangerous as Ian."

"Aye," Alistair confirmed.

"Then why go where he is?" I looked to Alistair for an answer, but he sat straight and faced forward on his horse.

"Because it was your grandfather's wish," Collin said.

"He wished us to be killed?" My voice rose in pitch. Being shoved in the river by Ian had been terrifying, but what Malcom had attempted last night seemed worse. I wouldn't soon forget his hands on me or the feeling of his knife at my throat.

Brann's orders, he'd said. How many more Campbell men were there, willing and ready to carry out their leader's wishes?

Alistair exchanged a knowing look with Collin over my head, turning some of my fear to anger. There was something they weren't telling me. Many things, perhaps.

"Let's rest the horses a while," Collin said. "We can spare a few minutes." He guided Ian's stallion to a stop, then dismounted and held his hands out to me. I hesitated, half of a mind to continue on without him.

"Katie." His voice held a warning.

I glared as I allowed him to help me down.

Alistair joined us in a tight circle. Both men looked at one another again, a sort of uneasiness in their eyes. Alistair shrugged, as if to say, *she's your wife.*

"I'll make this simple." I put my hands on my hips and looked to both of them. "I'll ask the questions, and if I point to you, you answer."

Alistair tugged at his beard. "Nothing simple about this, lass."

"I hadn't thought or planned—" Collin rubbed the back of his neck. "We believed you'd remember—that you'd know what you've come from . . . and who you are," he clarified.

"I was *five* when I left Scotland. What was I supposed to remember? The names of my dolls?"

Collin's mouth twitched. "You never cared much for dolls."

"You're sounding much more like the lass we knew then," Alistair added. "A good sign, I think."

I assumed he referred to my flaring temper—rarely displayed without good cause. Perhaps my poor behavior as a child was justifiable after all, if I'd lived under similar stress as I had the past few days. "A good sign for what?"

"That you're up for the task ahead," Alistair said, eliciting a scowl from Collin.

"What task would that be?" Somehow I doubted they meant running a household or raising babies or any of the usual responsibilities associated with being a wife.

Neither man replied, and their shadowed looks returned. I tried a different, more direct question.

"Who else would like to see me dead?" After two attempts on my life in the past day, surely I was at least justified to know who or what might be after me.

"No one," Collin said. "Though as you've seen, neither Brann nor Ian works alone."

In other words, at anytime, anywhere, we might be attacked. I spun away. Tears stung my eyes, and I already had a headache from my earlier breakdown. *I can't live like this.*

Based on the previous day's events, I might not have to for long.

I pressed my lips together and squeezed my eyes shut, wishing that when I opened them again I'd find myself back in my attic, where my biggest concern was having to leave my paintings behind when we moved. How trite a worry that now seemed. I no longer had anything resembling a home, and my belongings had been reduced to a torn gown and stockings with holes. I stood alone in a strange forest in a foreign country, with nothing between me and death but two men I'd not even known one week.

"Alistair, give us a moment, please," Collin said.

"I'll see about getting the horses some water."

I remained where I was, facing away from them, and listened as the older man and animals moved a distance off.

"Katie." Collin's voice was gentle—and close. Why had he stayed? What did he think to say to me that couldn't be said in front of Alistair?

"May I—touch you?" He came up behind me as he had that night at the inn.

Yesterday's PROMISE

I hesitated, then gave a single nod. "Yes." *Please.* As much as I still felt angry with him, I needed his strength and comfort more.

Instead of resting his hands on my shoulders, Collin wrapped his arms around me, pulling me against him. He bent his head low, near to mine. "I should never have brought you back. I'm so sorry."

The words were the same I'd heard in the carriage, and I wondered now if that moment had been more than a dream.

"Why did you, then?" Was it only because my grandfather had asked it of him?

He took several seconds to answer. "Because I wanted you back." His arms tightened around me. "I waited so long—years spent dreaming of you. I needed you."

"That isn't what you said last night." I'd caught him in a lie, and a hurtful one at that. He probably hadn't realized I'd overheard his conversation with Ian. "You said you married me to pay the debt to my grandfather—and for my dowry, of course."

"That's what I need Ian to believe." Collin turned me toward him, keeping his hands upon my arms. "If he—or any of the MacDonalds—believed our marriage was about anything more than financial gain, if they had any inkling of your potential to change the fate of our clans, if they knew how I care for you—" Collin's eyes, soulful and brimming with truth and concern, met mine. "If they knew any of that, we couldn't have wed. Ian suspects even now. It's why he wants to kill you—and me as well."

I might have reeled backward if Collin hadn't been holding me. Questions swirled inside my mind. I wanted to ask them, to demand answers, to know what it was he believed I could do for our families. But none of that seemed as pressing after his declaration. *If that's even what it was.* He hadn't said it outright, but had inserted an *if they knew* in front of words I wasn't certain I would ever hear from him. Certainly I hadn't expected to so soon. *I care for you.*

I love you, Katie.

My eyes searched his face. His lips hadn't moved. It was only my imagination hearing such an endearment. The dark pools of brown in his expressive eyes, however, seemed to be speaking all on their own.

Collin's hands slid down my arms to take my fingers in a grasp somewhere between gentle and desperate.

"Do you have any idea what it was like for me on our wedding day? You burst into the house, eyes alight with expectation, a brave smile—which I saw right through—pasted on your face, dirt on your gown, and those curls of yours . . ." Collin released one of my hands long enough to brush aside a curl that had escaped from my braids. "You looked and acted just as I'd imagined you would. It was all I could do not to cross the room and take you in my arms right then and there."

"You didn't even make yourself known to me," I reminded him, remembering how bewildered and overwhelmed I'd felt that morning.

"I couldn't." He took both my hands again and lifted them near his heart, gently pulling me closer. "I had to pretend indifference if it killed me—or it could have killed you. The Campbells who'd come, those loyal to your grandfather, thought I was there to keep the commitment I'd made to him long ago. The MacDonalds had come believing that I was making a calculated decision, a sacrifice even, for the benefit of our clan. Really, I was there because I wanted to be, because I'd spent fourteen years dreaming of the day I'd see you again, when you would be mine." Collin squeezed my fingertips lightly, then brought them to his lips. "Believe me, Katie."

I wanted to. His impassioned speech stirred that something within me once more, lightening the burden on my heart.

Collin had seemed both aloof and distressed when we'd spoken our wedding vows. *But then that kiss.* I remembered the sweet promise of it, even as his lips lingered on the back of my hand now, over the ring he'd so painstakingly made for me.

I'd forgotten that when counting my few possessions. But it *was* mine, along with the man who'd crafted it. Certainly that meant more than the attic full of paintings and other possessions I'd left behind. To be loved by Collin suddenly seemed far better and more important than any other possibility for my future. But was it enough to overcome the danger we faced?

I waited so long. He was still waiting for my response.

I wasn't certain what to say.

"What a delicate line you've been walking." Pretending in front of Ian could not have been easy.

"Aye." Collin stared at me, expectation in his gaze as one corner of his mouth lifted hopefully.

I curled my fingers into his, returning the gentle pressure as I looked at him. "You don't have to walk it alone anymore."

Though my questions weren't close to being answered, Collin had once again managed to soothe my mind and heart. I forgave him—for now—and we continued our ride several more hours into the afternoon. After his sincere admission as to the real reason for our marriage, I promised myself I would trust that he would tell me all as soon as he could. Until then I would be patient. Or try at least.

I did my best to push worry aside and instead to enjoy a few of the rare, peaceful hours of our journey. Birdsong and the sound of a rushing creek filled the air. The sun shone warm and bright, and for the first time since our wedding, I felt the prospect for real happiness with my husband. Our uncertain future and the terrors of the previous night aside, I felt more hopeful than I had in a very long time.

As the afternoon progressed, I noted that Collin had turned Ian's horse west, and we could no longer hear the creek. The forest was not as dense here, with a vast moor opening up ahead of us.

A feeling of acute unease stole over me at the idea of being out in the open. "Where are we going?"

"Still headed toward home—your home. Campbell land," Collin corrected. "We'll see if they allow me to stay," he added darkly.

"If they don't, we shall find a better place." I thought again of Brann. He had a face in my mind now, with a lip permanently curled and beady eyes that followed me wherever I went. It seemed that any place he wasn't would be better.

"Agreed," Collin said. "But we have to at least try first."

Try what? We continued toward the open meadow.

"Straightaway will get us there quickest," Collin said.

The hair on the back of my neck prickled. There was something about crossing that moor . . .

"You intend to go through Murray lands?" Alistair shook his head as he rode up alongside us. "Thank you, no. I've a wife to get home to."

"MacDonalds have an old alliance. We'll be fine," Collin said.

"You, perhaps, and possibly even your Campbell bride, but no male Campbell in his right mind would dare set a toe on Murray land, leastwise when he's alone."

"You're not alone," Collin argued.

Alistair shook his head defiantly. "I'm not a fool. You can't promise me safety in such circumstances, and I'd not ask you to."

"What do you suggest, then?" Collin said, exasperation and impatience heavy in his voice.

"We could go by way of the Stewarts. No one will trouble us there."

"Unless Brann expects us to do just that," Collin said.

Alistair shrugged. "More likely he'll think like you and be waiting on the Murray's north border."

"Stewarts way will add a good day or more to our journey," Collin argued.

"A small price to keep my neck," Alistair said.

"No," I interrupted. "We mustn't take either route. We should *not* cross that moor." I snapped my mouth shut, shocked at my own words.

"What is it, lass?" Alistair stopped his horse, and Collin followed, then dismounted and helped me to do the same.

"I—" I glanced at Collin, expecting to see annoyance, or at the least amusement in his expression. Instead he leaned forward, watching me expectantly, as if I actually had experience and reason guiding my words.

"Go on, Katie. We're listening." He tethered Ian's horse then stepped nearer to me.

I shook my head and backed away, frightened by the myriad of images—people and places—stampeding through my mind. "What's happening to me?" I bent over, hands wrapped around my pounding head. "How do I make it stop?" Scene after scene converged in my mind, flashing from one location to another, Ian to Brann to other men I did not know and didn't wish to. They all spoke and acted at once, each demanding my attention. I feared missing something important and turned to and fro in a frantic effort to keep up. I stumbled, falling—

When I came to, Collin sat on the ground, holding me in his lap.

I lifted confused, weary eyes to his. "What happened?"

"You fell. I caught you—almost didn't. It was easier when you were five. Though holding you like this wasn't nearly as enjoyable then." His concerned expression gave way to a cryptic smile.

"Bit of advice," Alistair offered, chuckling. "Just sit yourself down next time. Save this poor fellow's heart from jumping out of his skin."

"You find this amusing?" I looked from one to the other.

Yesterday's PROMISE

Alistair appeared downright pleased at my ailment, while Collin at least attempted a look of chagrin.

"We're not amused," he assured me.

"Just relieved," Alistair said. "Forgive us if we seem a bit giddy. You've had us both worried. But it seems that was for naught. All is well."

I lifted a hand to my head and groaned, feeling anything but well. "How do I make it go away?" I squeezed my eyes shut against the replaying scenes, coming at me slower now, though they remained, each vying for the premier position.

"You don't," Alistair said. "And you shouldn't wish it so. The sight is in your blood, lass—a gift, just as surely as God blessed me with the finest hair color." He stroked his auburn beard with affection.

"Some gift," I scoffed. Hearing voices, seeing things . . . this wasn't good. "In England they lock away people with broken minds."

"Nothing about you is broken." Collin cradled my head to his chest, as if attempting to ease the ache. It did a little.

"Don't fight it," he advised. "The longer you hold the vision in, the more you'll hurt."

Alistair squatted beside us. "You've both a blessing and a burden to bear, one and the same, lass. To have the sight is to have power. And with that comes responsibility."

"I don't have the sight. I *can't*." Such a thing was impossible, wasn't it? "I've never had it before." Ian's angry face appeared in my mind again. It hardly seemed a gift, but rather something to get both me and Collin into a great deal of trouble.

"You had extraordinary visions when you were a child,"

Collin said. "Back then you bragged about it—leastwise so far as you were able to use it to get Brann or me into trouble. Your abilities were well known."

"They went away, then," I said, still denying the tremors of warning pulsing through me.

"Perhaps you are only able to see in the Highlands," Alistair suggested. "I don't know of any Campbell lairds who've tested their sight beyond that."

"Her sight has been working just fine in England," Collin said. "You saw her paintings."

"What about them?" I pushed away from him and sat up straight.

"The two you brought with you were both scenes in the Highlands—places I'm certain you've never been. If your other paintings were similar, I think it's possible you've been predicting your future without even realizing it."

Another shiver passed through me, this one filled with peculiar truth. Had I been painting my future? Even my mother had suggested as much when we parted, telling me that my art spoke of a longing for adventure. And the other night in the river I'd remembered a painting I'd done, of a woman floating upon her back. It had prompted me to do the same, a distinct thought of direction as I panicked and flailed helplessly. I tried to recall the details from the original canvas. The woman's hair had been about the color of mine, a shade darker perhaps, but the water would have made it so. She had been wearing a black gown, and I remember imagining that the scene was about a woman who had lost her husband and was so overcome with grief that she'd attempted to take her own life by jumping in the river—only to change her mind and wish to live. I'd painted her floating on her back for that reason. The similarities in detail were eerie. Had I painted myself?

"The other landscape I brought with me—the ruined castle. Do you know such a place?" I looked to Collin for an answer.

"Aye." He gave a brief nod but did not elaborate. As easily as the unwanted scenes had appeared in my mind, I saw also his reluctance to tell me. *Another aspect of the gift of sight?*

"Well, where is it?" I scrambled to my feet, gratefully accepting Alistair's hand as I rose.

Collin joined us, brushing the dirt from his breeches as he stood. "It's the old keep on MacDonald land, the one destroyed in the first uprising."

MacDonald. Land. So we would be going there at some point. This knowledge passed between us without a word.

"But first, to the Campbells," Collin reminded me.

"Painting, eh? I've never heard of the sight being used like that." Alistair stroked his beard thoughtfully. "Though I seem to recall your mother had a fair hand at portraits. Shortly before you were taken by your father, old Liam warned you not to let others know about your gift. Maybe it was more than a warning. Maybe he had it within him to alter your abilities for a time."

Collin scoffed. "Campbells are no sorcerers. Liam himself told me that. No magical skills or talents come with the sight. It's merely another sense, passed directly from generation to generation in her line. It grants no strength beyond that of an ordinary man, no means to stop someone doing something. Only the opportunity to see what is to come and to make wise judgments based upon that knowledge."

How was I to make any sort of wise judgment, given what little I knew of my home or people, the land or customs? Even my husband and I were still little more than strangers to one another, with much left unsaid and unknown between us. "Whatever it is, I wish it would go away again." I crossed my arms beneath the makeshift cloak and rubbed them briskly. Here in the shade of the trees, it wasn't as warm as when we'd been riding with the sun at our backs. Worse than that, the shadows of men and their deeds filtering through my mind chilled and frightened me. *I don't want to know.* About Ian or Brann or the harm they wished us.

Yet I did know.

"The only way it gets better is to heed it," Collin said. "I remember that much. Your head used to throb with it sometimes."

I had a brief vision of myself as a little girl, curled up on the floor, my head in Collin's lap. His hand stroked the hair back from my face, his words gentle as he tried to soothe away my agony.

"Tell us," Collin urged, as if he'd followed me into that same memory. "Don't allow it to become so bad."

"I'll try." I remembered why I'd refused to tell—so long ago—what I had foreseen. I had known Collin and I were to be separated, and had been so tormented by that and so desperate to keep it from happening that I had held the knowledge inside, believing that if I did not speak of what I saw, it would not come to pass.

Also in memory I could see my grandfather shaking his

head at my foolishness. I would have smiled at that glimpse of him, at the connection I was beginning to feel to my past, but the severity of the future demanded all my attention and gravity. I stepped forward, reached for Collin's hand, and looked to him in earnest, as I began to explain what had burst to the front of my mind moments before.

"Ian guesses you'll keep to Alistair's counsel, and he's overheard Finlay and Donaid predicting Alistair will choose the Stewart pass. Ian and the other MacDonalds will split with the Campbells, telling them they're going through Murray lands—as you suggested," I said. "But really they'll just let the Campbells get an hour or so ahead, while they enter the pass later and lay in wait for us." I looked from Collin to Alistair. "We won't have a chance."

Alistair let out a long breath, while Collin muttered beneath his.

"Some brother you've got there," Alistair observed.

"We're a close family," Collin said, a bitter edge to his voice. "What about Brann?" he asked me.

"He isn't that far away. And he isn't alone. There are other men with him." I paused, biting my lip as I concentrated. I was pulling this information from thin air, it seemed, yet it was also a near tangible thing. "Four, I think." In my mind I watched them conversing near a fire. "Brann didn't trust Malcom enough to come all the way to the cave last night. Instead Brann has men strung out all along our most likely route between here and Campbell land. He wants to stop me before I can get there."

"He's waiting for Malcom to join him," Alistair guessed.

I nodded. "Yes. I think you're right. If we keep heading

toward Murray or Stewart lands—across that moor—we'll meet up. It won't go well."

"Fine, friendly laird you've got," Collin returned to Alistair.

"The best sort," Alistair agreed with false heartiness. "Burn you in your own bed if you're not careful."

"Truly?" I asked.

"Aye," Alistair answered, his face drooping with soberness. "He wants the land for himself, for sheep. The Campbell families who have been farming that land and raising families there for generations are no longer welcome. But Brann doesn't just ask them to leave. No." Alistair shook his head. "He's set dozens of crofts on fire in the past two years, leaving the folks who do survive with nothing more than the clothes on their backs and a real desire to flee. Others he's sold off to the English as indentured servants to the colonies."

"That's horrible." I pressed my free hand to my stomach, feeling ill. Collin held tight to the other, as if to steady me. Images of burning homes, and families being torn apart flashed through my mind. Who knew, but that I was seeing real people whose lives had been forever harmed or even taken from them.

"Time later for those tales," Alistair said. "It's enough for now that you understand the Campbells need a change in leadership. There are many eagerly awaiting your return."

"And some not as much," Collin added, his expression grim.

"Brann does not wish—" I broke off, understanding—through those same wisps, vague snatches of both past and future—what both Collin and Alistair meant. I was a laird's granddaughter. The clan was split, with some believing Brann had the right to lead while at least half felt it was I who should have succeeded my grandfather. *Oh my.*

I tugged free from Collin's grasp and clutched my hands over my pounding heart. "But I'm a woman."

"So was Mary, Queen of Scots," Alistair said.

"And look at the terrible end she met!" I stepped back and shook my head. I wanted nothing to do with such a preposterous idea as being the leader of Clan Campbell. I turned away from them. Folding my arms across my middle, I hugged myself against the many worries I felt, the immense pressure suddenly coming to rest on *my* shoulders. What was happening to Scotland, to the clans? Lairds did not abdicate their authority to brothers less than fit to rule. And I'd never heard of a female taking over a lairdship. *Especially a female whose blood is half English.*

"Which way should we go, Katie?" Collin asked, bringing the subject round again to our more immediate problem.

"Back to England," I said, only half joking. The life I'd lived there seemed a fairy tale now, idyllic and peaceful, where I'd spent my days eating crumpets and drinking tea, riding my horse, and sitting in the yard with paintbrush and easel. I longed for those days suddenly, for my father and mother and siblings. For the home and comforts that had been mine.

"I'll take you back—if that is what you wish." Collin's voice was quiet and sorrowful. I turned to him, but he would not meet my gaze.

He doesn't want me—to leave. Whatever I'd lost in material possessions and security in the last twenty-four hours had been more than made up for by Collin's admissions last night and this morning. He had married me because he wanted to. He planned to leave his clan for me.

Being married is the promise of having a friend . . . the possibility of not being lonely . . .

Even if I had truly wanted to return, I could never leave him. With each passing hour I understood that more. The vows we had spoken in my foyer were not our first. Our bond spanned not five days but fifteen years.

And they weren't just vows of marriage. They were promises made to our families—past, present, and future. No wonder Collin appeared so serious and weary. While I'd been growing up in a home of privilege, he had been laboring alone. The years of my carefree childhood had been years of toil and trouble for him.

"I ought to take you right back where you came from." Collin spoke with conviction. "You'd have a chance at a normal life."

"Bah," Alistair swatted at the air. "Lass like this wasn't made for ordinary." He placed a heavy hand on my shoulder. "She was born for more'n that. As were you." He sent a pointed look at Collin.

Meant . . . for more. Father had told me that after it became apparent I would have no season, no real chance at suitors as other girls my age did. I remembered that conversation as if it were yesterday. At the time I thought he'd been referring to my paintings, my art, and that I should make something of it. Perhaps I still would. In a way I had never considered.

Somehow feeling that Father had known who I was and

what was intended for me helped immensely. He had believed I was meant for more. He had believed in *me*.

Pushing back my fears, I raised my chin and stared directly at Collin. "I expect you to take me right back where I came from—my grandfather's castle."

"*Your* castle, you mean?" Alistair grinned. "Your grandfather left it to you."

More responsibility. "Lovely." I tried to sound appreciative. It wasn't every day a girl inherited a castle.

"You're starting to realize what that means now." Collin stepped near to me. "Are you certain, Katie?"

"Yes." I nodded, feeling both rational and calm with the decision. The inner turmoil I'd been fighting settled, and it was almost as if I could hear my ancestors sighing their relief. I was not only on my way home but had accepted what I was supposed to do. *What we are supposed to do.* There was no I to the equation. Without Collin we would not succeed.

All this standing around was not going to accomplish anything either. I searched my mind, hoping for some clue of what we were to do next.

"I'm not sure which way we should go." I took a moment, pacing in front of them, trying to collect my thoughts and wondering where the previous ones had come from. I'd envisioned the whole thing so clearly, like a scene from a play unfolding before my eyes. Still, I couldn't quite believe that Collin and Alistair were paying me such heed. Had I ever dared to suggest strategy to Father or his military comrades I would have been laughed out of the room—had I even been permitted there in the first place. But my husband and cousin both appeared in earnest with their requests for more information.

"There has been some delay." I pictured the previous night's camp in my mind, men from both clans clustered around the carriage. "Ian insisted he must have the carriage to ride in." My eyes flashed to Collin's, remembering what he had said of his brother's injury. "But the Campbells felt they needed it to bring my trunk." I saw it opened on the ground, the contents more scattered than when the English soldiers had gone through them. Ian seemed to be at the center of both the argument and the crowd. When at last it parted, I saw him clearly, leaning against the carriage, my sketchbook in his hand.

Oh no. I watched as he discovered the picture of Collin, tore it from the book, and stuffed it in his pocket. More unease stole over me. The sketch all but confirmed what Ian might have only suspected—that I had feelings for his brother. I didn't know how he would accomplish it, but I had no doubt Ian planned to use that knowledge to his advantage.

"I'll be leaving you now," Alistair said suddenly. He swung onto his horse before we could object, though Collin reached up and held onto the reins.

"What are you up to?" he asked, mirroring my thoughts entirely.

"Just want to get home to my family. Can't stand around here talking all day."

"Alistair." I looked up at him. "You're going to meet up with Brann?"

His mouth twisted. "Didn't take you long to get that extra sense working again. I'd hoped to get ahead of it." He tried to take the reins, but Collin held them fast as he looked to me for an explanation.

"It's not my extra sense that gave him away, but his guilty, sly expression." I tilted my head back, looking up at Alistair. "You're thinking to mislead Brann about the way we've gone and who we're traveling with."

"Are you now?" Collin retained his grip.

"You have a better suggestion?" Alistair's brows knit together as he looked down on me with clear exasperation. "You're not the only ones with an interest in preserving the Campbells. And you won't be able to do it alone. First thing we have to do is get you there safely. And if Brann can't find you . . ."

"It's a dangerous game you're proposing," Collin said.

"Bit more at stake than a chess piece or two," Alistair agreed.

I've a wife to get home to, he'd said. I didn't want the responsibility for his safe return, yet—absurdly—I felt it. "I wish I could see the future and your safe return to your family."

Alistair shook his head. "Sight doesn't work that way. You can't choose what you want to see. It chooses what it wants to show you."

"What will you tell Brann about Malcom?" Collin asked.

"The truth," Alistair said. "That you've killed him and sworn to do the same to anyone else who threatens your wife."

"Take care, friend." Collin released the reins.

"You as well," Alistair said.

"We'll be all right," I said, still enjoying the aura of peace that had accompanied my acceptance.

"No doubt you'll do fine," Alistair said. "Now that you've

each other again." He nodded his head at us. "It was a pleasure to be at your wedding."

"Thank you," Collin and I both said at once.

"Don't worry if it's a week or more before you see us again," Collin added.

"Oh?" Alistair said.

"Katie deserves some time before she has to confront Brann," Collin said. "Not remembering, not knowing beforehand any of this or *us*—" He glanced at me. "I'd take longer if I thought we dared, but Ian will come searching out her dowry if I don't get it to him soon."

A fleeting look of discomfort flashed in Alistair's eyes.

At the prospect of a visit from Ian? Or was there some issue with my dowry?

"God speed, friend," Collin said.

"Thank you for everything, Alistair." I felt a swell of affection for the older man.

"Least I could do." He waved away my gratitude even as his face colored again.

Collin put his arm around me as if we were a couple long acquainted and familiar with one another. Almost feeling we were, and liking it immensely, I leaned into him and allowed my own hand to slide around his waist. We stood thus, watching Alistair ride off toward the moor until we could see him no longer. Even then we did not move.

The forest around us silenced, as if it, too, was in awe of this moment. I closed my eyes, savoring our closeness, the weight of Collin's arm across my shoulder both comforting and exhilarating.

Beneath my cheek his heartbeat sounded steadily, if not

a little quick. My own pulsed rapidly in my ears as well, hastened by our contact. His touch provided a physical warmth as well as something that went much deeper. We were alone in a Scotland forest, with nearly nothing with which to survive and multiple parties seeking our destruction, yet suddenly my worries were gone. *Alone but not lonely. In danger, yet safe.*

Somewhere I had heard such a sentiment before. What, moments ago, I would have rejected as utter nonsense now seemed perfectly logical.

Feeling bold, I tilted my face towards Collin, looking up at him. "What have you just done?"

He didn't avoid my question or pretend he thought I was speaking of Alistair leaving us. "What I am supposed to, Katie." He gave my shoulder a gentle squeeze, then released me.

I looked at him expectantly, hoping for more of an explanation as we stood facing each other.

Collin reached out and brushed his fingers against my cheek. "What I am sworn to do."

If he had sworn to make me forget all else in the world except for him, he was succeeding marvelously. Though I did not think that quite what he meant. I took his hand and pressed my lips to his palm. "Thank you."

Happiness sparked briefly in his eyes, followed at once by sorrow, then regret. He pulled his hand away and stepped back, releasing a nearly inaudible sigh. "And now we'd best be about figuring a route to get us safely away from our enemies."

The words the old laird spoke sounded more like a wizard's. It would take magic to do what he suggested—entwining our clans, each dependent upon the other if any were to survive. Then came the vows of betrothal. Katie and I repeated some, her voice the barest whisper in the great hall. Mine was slightly stronger, as I grasped already that I had to be the stronger one of the two of us—for now, anyway. She was to be the seer, I the defender—of Katie, of our people, our very way of life. Even Scotland it seemed. I couldn't imagine what might be coming that could possibly be worse than what we'd just endured with the failed uprising, but Laird Campbell saw something. For a moment, I saw it, too, there in the depths of his steel-grey eyes.

Chapter Seventeen

"I have a route in mind," Collin said. "It will add considerable time to our journey, but we'll be safe, and I think you'll find it a proper introduction to the Highlands." He glanced over and found me adjusting the blanket once more to cover my torn dress. Collin's gaze slid to my shoeless feet. "Some husband I am. Cannot even keep you clothed."

"It isn't your fault I'm parted with my trunk." I pulled the blanket tighter, thankful to have it. "So long as we've Ian's horse, I won't miss not having shoes."

Yesterday's PROMISE

"Hmph." Collin reached into his sporran and took out a handful of oats. "A quick meal before we leave this place?"

"Raw?" I asked, not trying to sound ungrateful, but also not certain how one went about eating uncooked oats.

Collin shook his head. "Not completely. I'll make a cold porridge."

"Yes then, please."

"Wait here." He left me beside Ian's horse and walked toward the moor that had so frightened me. It still did, and I started to call out to him to go another direction in search of water, but only a few paces away Collin knelt and began parting the heather. I watched as he removed a small cup from his pouch and pressed it near to the ground.

He'd found another spring. They seemed to be everywhere here—a good thing. At least we would have enough to drink.

Collin returned with the cup, swirling it around in his hand even as his other dug through his pouch for the lone spoon I knew he kept there. We'd shared it the previous morning and did so again now, Collin making sure I had the first bite once the cold oatmeal had been mixed as well as it could be.

I vow you the first cut of my meat—I'd begun to realize how literally Scots took their promises. What I'd perceived as flowery words were in fact oaths of a practical and even gallant nature.

"Tonight we will have a fire," Collin said, by way of apology, I supposed, for our less-than-palatable lunch.

"And what will we eat?" My shoulder brushed against him as we sat beside one another on the trunk of a fallen tree.

"Not oatmeal." His promise and the sour tone in which it was delivered elicited a laugh.

"I thought Scots never tired of this. Alistair told me himself."

"Alistair's wife is not a good cook," Collin confided. "It is well his tastes are not particular. But I spent too many years at your grandfather's table."

"And will we eat at that same table again?" I asked.

Collin shrugged then looked at me. "I don't know. Will we?"

"I believe we will," I said, for the moment optimistic that we should somehow usurp the castle and be welcomed there. We would need more than confidence to succeed. I needed the gift of my heritage. Alistair had said the sight chose what it wanted to show me, and thus far it had warned me only once of danger. I would have to see more, and soon, for both our safety and strategy.

"You're troubled." Collin held the last bite out to me, but I shook my head, my stomach being full enough, and my mouth unable to gag down any more of the bland paste.

"Not troubled so much as trying to understand why I can see some events of the future but not others. Why didn't I see you coming to England? Why was I not warned of Ian or Malcom last night?"

"I don't know." Collin's brow furrowed, as if he was the one worried now.

Our shoulders brushed again so that even recalling the trauma of the previous night proved no match for my husband's nearness. I felt overwhelmed by it, by having him so close. *Consumed* was perhaps the better word. I imagined a cheery fire blazing within me. This near to Collin I could scarce think of or care about much else, save for him. I felt unburdened, comforted. There was more to it as well, this strangely magnetic pull I felt toward him. I didn't understand these feelings, and in their own way they were frightening. *Best to proceed with caution.*

It seemed he had the same idea, as he rose suddenly. "Best be off." He did not offer a hand to help me rise but instead walked to the brook, where he began to wash out the cup.

I rose and stretched with soreness from both my unexpected swim in the river and my midnight ride. I eyed Ian's horse with resignation. Things were apt to get worse before they got better. How long would it be until I could sink into a hot bath and sleep in a bed again?

Collin returned from the spring, then took my hand to help me mount. I felt better almost instantly. What did a bath, bed, or much of anything else matter, except that he was here? We were together at last.

It was mid-afternoon before we stopped again, having just completed a breathtakingly fast gallop across a field of purple. I laughed as Collin slowed Ian's sweaty stallion. My stomach had tickled during the exhilarating run and now came back to earth, along with the rest of me.

"Oh my." I brought my hand to my head, expecting to discover my hair blown everywhere, but felt only Collin's tightly woven braids, mostly still in place.

"Does your head ache?" Collin asked, concern in his voice.

"Not at all." I felt quite well, considering how long we had ridden. No doubt I'd not feel so fine tomorrow. "I'd forgotten my hair was still plaited. A good thing, or it would be a mess to untangle."

"Glad to know my skills saved you from freezing *and* from tangles." Collin dismounted, then held his hands out to help me do the same.

I leaned over and slid into his arms. He held me an extra few seconds while my legs revolted against standing and I tried to get my footing. Apparently I was a bit sore.

"Your braids did more than that." I placed my hands on Collin's forearms as I looked up at him. "Last night Malcom—" I didn't want to relive those moments. "He tried to grab me by my hair and wasn't able to, and so for a moment, I was free of his grasp. It bought me time—until you arrived."

Collin's lips pressed together in a grim expression.

I let go of his arms and looked down, clasping my hands together. "Your braiding skills did save my life." They had saved more than that. It was perhaps those few seconds gained and the minute that followed when I was out of Malcom's reach that had preserved my virtue.

Collin let out a long breath. He reached a hand out, lifting my chin gently so that I looked at him. "All the same. Let's keep you more than a hair's distance from danger from now on."

"Yes." His simple touch had my heartbeat escalating once more. I tilted my head back, looking up at him, longing—

Yesterday's PROMISE

Collin released me and stepped away. He led Ian's horse to a grassy patch of ground.

I made a pretense of studying our surroundings to hide my hurt and confusion at my husband's abrupt departure and change of mood. He was far more cordial than he'd been the first few days of our marriage, but I sensed he was still holding back. Did he regret confessing his feelings to me? *Something* about us was bothering him. I wished he would tell me what it was.

Instead of asking, I swallowed my hurt and wandered a few steps in each direction. I'd absolutely no idea where we were or even which direction we'd traveled in today, having long since given up trying to make any sense of the route Collin plotted. I trusted that he knew where we were and would get us safely home—if there was to be such a place for us.

If not . . . I found myself strangely content in his presence, concern over all elements of society gone. It was vastly freeing, this not worrying over what anyone else might think of me or being concerned with conventions such as my hair or dress or even the wearing of shoes.

I determined that my mother must have been right when she'd said I secretly longed for adventure. It suited me well.

"We'll camp here tonight," Collin announced when he had secured the horse.

"What may I do to help?" I moved past my moment of disappointment and determined to be of some use to my husband. I didn't know how to hunt or cook. Neither had I any idea of what plants might be edible or which might poison us. I ought to start learning soon, if I intended to survive here.

"Gather wood for a fire," Collin instructed. It appeared he intended to do the same as he began walking, head bent toward the ground as if searching for something.

I retied the blanket about my shoulders and began gathering what I could from the forest floor, be that dried grass, pine needles, or twigs. As I walked I took in the incredible landscape, doing my best to commit this scene to memory. I longed for a paintbrush and would have given much for a canvas just then. Instead I drank in the setting, feasting my eyes on a valley even more beautiful than the one we'd camped in previously.

On three sides a meadow was hemmed in by stands of pine and aspen, the latter just coming into the full green of summer. Their leaves seemed to twinkle in the breeze, and, combined with the heady scent of a pine forest, the effect was intoxicating.

To what I guessed to be the north of the meadow a monolith mountain emerged beyond the sloping hills, jagged peaks disappearing into low-lying clouds. I wondered just how high those peaks went and if anyone ever actually reached their summit. Though the mountain looked formidable, I hoped we might be crossing over at least some point—the views to be had from such heights could only be spectacular.

But it was the meadow itself that held me most entranced. An exquisite carpet of purple, blue, and yellow wildflowers spread from one end to the other, from the forest to the foothills. Their vibrant colors bent with the wind in one continuous ripple that held me spellbound. I wished Timothy was here with me, though no doubt his seven-year-old boyish inquisitiveness would have found the giant boulders at the base of the mountain more fascinating than the flowers.

Mother and Anna would have enjoyed them, though. Nothing Anna might see in Paris could rival this view. And Father? Had he witnessed these wonders, too? Was that part of why he had wished me to return?

Thank you. Whether my gratitude belonged to Father or Grandfather or Collin, I felt it keenly, along with an utter sense of joy that I could not recall having experienced before. A place so astoundingly beautiful could not be entirely bad. No matter what hardships awaited me, I believed I could bear them, if surrounded with such grandeur.

I sensed rather than saw or heard Collin's approach, and the realization that my innate ability seemed to be growing stronger unsettled me a bit.

"What are you looking at?"

"Not looking." I inhaled deeply. "Absorbing."

Collin came to stand beside me, a long, thin branch in his hands. His lips turned down with concern as he studied me.

"Healing," I clarified—or thought I did. His perplexed look grew deeper.

"Last night your Highlands frightened and hurt me. But today—" I couldn't help but smile as my eyes feasted on the colors of the meadow bathed in the glow of the late-afternoon sun. "Today their beauty is restoring."

"They're not just *my* Highlands," Collin reminded me. He took out his knife and began whittling one end of the branch. "You were born here."

"I wish I could remember." *How* I wished.

"Your birth? That could be rather . . . traumatic."

I turned my head in time to see the fleeting smirk on his lips and the sparkle of amusement in his eyes. "Was that a jest I heard—from Collin MacDonald?"

He did not deny it, though his face pinched in a look of extreme discomfort. But I was not about to allow the moment to pass. It was too important.

I dumped the small pile of kindling I'd gathered near his feet, then straightened, hands planted on my hips as I stared up at him. "You *are* possessed of humor," I stated, daring him to deny it, and hoping to glimpse that side of him once more. "It becomes you, you know," I added as an extra enticement.

"All the more reason to keep such frivolous emotion in check," Collin said. "You should not find me becoming or anything else."

"Why ever not?" I demanded. "We are husband and wife. I should hope I find you pleasant. And there is nothing frivolous about happiness, about the ability to experience joy, to smile once in a while." I looked at him pointedly. "Laughter is good for the soul."

"There is precious little to laugh about in this life."

"Then perhaps you are not looking hard enough," I said. "*I* could make you laugh." I had once already. "Together we—"

"You could have been *killed* last night." Collin turned away, scraping wood shavings almost savagely from the end of the stick. "Why are you not angry with me? How can you speak of laughter and—" one hand swept an arc of the field— "and beauty when you are standing here with naught but a torn dress and a borrowed blanket to your name?"

"I have more than that." I strove to bury the stab of dismay I felt about losing my trunk—or, more importantly, the brushes and paints inside. Collin's words had all but confirmed those would not be returned to me.

There are far more important matters. I'd been over this same argument with myself before, on those occasions when my jewelry had been sold, my horse led away, when Anna was bedecked in stunning gowns and I in homespun. All that practice served me well now as I managed to swallow the bitter pill of this latest loss.

"I have this ring on my finger," I said, grateful it hadn't been lost during my swift trip downriver. My fingers closed over the band of silver that meant more to me than any other possession I could recall. "It means a great deal because it means *us*. I don't know exactly what our marriage is to be," I admitted. "I don't know where we are going or what our home will be like. I may be a little hungry just now, and my dress needs mending, but we are surrounded by infinite beauty." I glanced to the meadow as a reminder of the strength I'd derived from it. "I am *alive* because of you. And we have each other." I walked around to stand in front of Collin. "I see plenty of reasons to be grateful—and even happy."

"Would that I could feel the same." His hand with the knife dropped to his side.

"You could," I said. But I was starting to doubt. There was no one around but the two of us, no reason for Collin to pretend indifference to me or our marriage. Yet he seemed determined to remain dour, predisposed to gloom and seriousness. I could think of no excuses for his behavior, especially considering his earlier confessions. Unless they had been untruthful.

"I thought you wanted a friend and confidant?" I made no attempt to hide the hurt in my voice. "Would that not make you happy?"

"It would—it does." He glanced at me briefly. "It's just that I'm sorry, Katie. For your terror of last night. For being upset just now, for bringing you here—for everything."

"I know." I felt the depth of his regret as poignantly as if it had been my own. And with it the depth of his caring. I lifted my chin, then bravely placed my hand over his, taking the initiative to touch him. "I am not sorry that you brought me here. I do not regret our marriage."

"You should," he half growled, and a side of his mouth quirked up. It sent my heart soaring.

"But then I don't suppose I can expect common sense from a lass who's both English and Campbell."

"Perhaps not." Letting my hand slip away, I bent, collecting the shavings he had discarded. "But common sense is often overrated."

"Not here it isn't." He took my arm, pulling me toward him. "It would have saved you from almost being raped and nearly having your throat slit last night. I hope you've sense enough not to go off alone with any man now," Collin said. "Campbell, MacDonald, or otherwise."

"Apparently not." My mouth twisted in a wry grin. "It *is* just the two of us out here, is it not?"

This gave him pause then, "Aye." He thrust the branch to the dirt and threw his head back, sending his gaze heavenward, as if declaring a lost cause. "A worse idea there never was."

"You're to sleep here." Laird Campbell pointed to a spot on the floor directly outside the room I'd seen him carry the lass into just minutes earlier.

"Like a dog," I muttered beneath my breath. The cold, grey stone did not look particularly inviting.

"Like the guardian you are," he corrected. His eyes met mine in the dim torchlight, and understanding passed between us. The lass—Katie—had fallen asleep hours earlier, curled up snugly in her grandfather's lap. I hadn't been afforded the luxury of closing my eyes, though I could scarce recall feeling more exhausted. Or burdened. For reasons I still did not entirely understand, her safety depended upon me. And my life depended upon her safety. And she was in very real danger.

Chapter Eighteen

"If you'll sit here on this rise, I'll always have you in my sight." Collin pointed to a patch of ground that sloped upward, looking over the meadow below.

"And where might you be going?" I much preferred being at his side to merely being in his sight.

"Fishing." Collin held out the branch he'd been whittling, now shaped into a fine spear. "The river's not far, just below—there." He pointed to the eastern edge of the meadow. "I didn't suppose you'd want to camp so close to the water, or go near it at all. You'll be safe here until I get back with our supper."

I was touched that he had considered my feelings, but it was more frightening to think of being separated from him, even for a short time or distance, than it was to be near a river again. "I would like to come. Perhaps you can teach me to catch a fish."

A fleeting smile of pleasant surprise crossed his face. "Maybe. Though if it takes half as long as it did to teach you how to skip stones, we'll starve."

Jesting with me again. I turned away, smiling, and let his teasing go, believing that the less I mentioned it, the more likely his lighter moods were to persist. Collin untied Ian's horse, gathered an armload of the wood we'd gathered, and started off. I followed him eagerly across the meadow, my arms also laden with wood, as Ian's horse trotted along beside.

"I was only five when you taught me to skip stones. Don't you think it possible I'm a faster learner now?"

"I watched you a few days ago at the River Aire," Collin said. "Only a few of your rocks skipped. You still haven't got the hang of it."

"I only *tried* to skip a few," I said, secretly pleased he'd been watching me. "I like seeing ripples."

"Hmph," Collin muttered, obviously unconvinced.

I determined to prove myself. When we reached the river I looked for a suitable stick for my own spear while Collin waded into the shallows, his in hand. The mostly treeless bank was devoid of long branches, and after a few minutes, I gave up searching and sat down to observe Collin instead.

Yesterday's PROMISE

He stood perfectly still, barefoot, legs spread, and breeches rolled up as he held the spear a short distance over the water and leaned forward, his attention focused.

The river was much slower here, forming calm, little pools as it meandered around the large stones which had no doubt tumbled from the mountains above years ago. From my vantage the river appeared shallower and muddier as well. I dared not move closer to look, lest I disturb Collin's concentration. Our evening meal was at stake, and I'd no desire for oatmeal again.

Minutes passed. I wondered at Collin's patience and that his back and neck weren't stiff from holding the same position so long. I thought we might be here until past dark and would indeed be eating oats.

All at once he struck, plunging the spear into the shallow water, then bringing it up a moment later, a good-sized fish writhing on the tip.

I stood and clapped, expressing my delight. "You almost make that look easy." I stepped forward to examine the fish as Collin trudged up on shore.

"Easy, is it?" He sounded insulted as he held his catch away from me. "In that case, this is *my* dinner." He pulled the fish free. "You can try your hand at it now." He thrust the stick at me, and I took it firmly in my hands, trying to show a confidence I did not feel.

With no shoes to remove, I had only my stockings to peel off and my skirt to tie up. This I did, feeling self-conscious about baring my ankles and lower legs. I stepped into the river at the very spot Collin had stood, sinking to my knees as my bare feet squished into the muddy bottom and the cold took my breath away.

"It's freezing!" I jumped up and down, running in place, trying to endure the biting temperature.

"Runoff from the mountain. Of course it's cold." Collin shook his head at me in a manner that indicated he thought I was hopeless. "You've just scared away any fish that were nearby. *Anywhere* nearby."

I followed his gaze down to the murky water, seeing all the sediment my movement had churned up. The cold forgotten, I trudged out of the water, then stomped off down the shoreline, this time looking for a spot more shallow, but not so much so that a fish would never venture there.

When I'd located such a place, I entered the water quietly. I took two silent steps, then stoically clenched my teeth and curled my toes as the chill water swirled about my legs. I was hungry, and this was dinner we were talking about. And my pride. I could endure discomfort for a catch of fresh fish and some respect from my husband.

I leaned forward as I'd seen Collin do, my fist gripping the spear, poised to strike. For several minutes I stared pensively at the river, willing the fish to come. They didn't. Neither did it take long to confirm what I had suspected, that one's back and neck grew stiff maintaining this same position for any length of time. Still, I waited, determined to succeed.

From a short distance away I heard Collin whistling and soon smelled the smoke from a fire. *Good.* I'd need to get warm and dry the bottom of my skirts when I was finished here. I wondered how one went about cooking a fish. Hopefully Collin would be inclined to show me that much at least.

As if he'd read my mind, Collin appeared suddenly at my side.

"Don't move," he said as he dug in his sporran and withdrew a small handful of oats. These he sprinkled across the surface of the water where I stood. Nothing happened at first. Then, from the corner of my eye, I saw not one, but two shadows approaching, swimming back and forth. They entered the pool, mouths up, searching out Collin's offering.

"Now," he whispered.

I struck. The spear plunged just where I thought it should but hit only mud while the fish swam briskly away. My shoulders sagged with disappointment.

Collin chuckled, then came up behind me. He placed his hands on my shoulders and turned me the other direction, then walked us several paces to another, deeper pool. Before tossing his sporran to the shore he removed another pinch of oats.

"Give me your hand," he said.

I held it out, and he dropped the oats into it. He stepped up behind me, his arms circling my waist, his hands resting over mine on the spear. "Sprinkle the oats across the water."

I did as he instructed.

"Now we wait. Follow my lead."

I nodded, hunger, cold, and tiredness replacing my earlier pride. So what if my husband thought me inept at many tasks? It was the truth. I'd never caught a fish or lived outdoors or had any kind of adventure like this before.

I resisted the urge to relax and lean back into him. Already I felt my emotions calming, simply because he was near. Requiring Collin's help wasn't all bad. His breath was warm near my cheek, and having his arms circled around me felt entirely pleasant. If only I would have admitted earlier that I required assistance.

"Here they come," Collin whispered. His hands tightened over mine and then, before the fish had quite reached us, before I thought he ought to, he'd plunged the spear into the river. I felt the difference this time, knew the second we struck. My hands fell away as Collin drew the stick out of the water, an even larger fish than the one he'd first caught flailing on the end of it.

"Success," he pronounced.

"Your success," I corrected, grateful nonetheless that we would have plenty to eat tonight. I turned to face the shore and was surprised when Collin did not step away but kept his arms around me.

"I'm sorry I goaded you on," he said. "That was a mean trick."

I tilted my head back to look up at him and, instead of the triumphant expression I'd expected, found his face flushed with guilt.

"Why was it mean?" I folded my arms across my chest, putting a bit of distance between us and doing my best to conceal my flustered emotions and the exhilarating effects of his nearness.

"It's a difficult thing to spear a fish. When I was learning it probably took me a hundred tries before I finally got it right."

"One *hundred*." I attempted a severe frown. And I'd believed I could accomplish the task in an afternoon. How foolish I must seem to him. "How old were you when you learned this feat?"

"Thirteen—fourteen. It was during the rebellion. We were often without rations and had to fend for ourselves. Da taught me."

"And did a fine job of it." I nodded to the fish on Collin's spear. "I am grateful to you both."

Relief eased the lines of Collin's face. "You're not angry that I—"

"Allowed me to make a fool of myself?" I shook my head. "Not at all." *Not embarrassed. Not shivering with cold and having numb feet for nothing. Not feeling far too attracted to you when you've yet to prove that your feelings—at least in that sense—really are the same.* But it was difficult to feel irritated with Collin, especially when we stood so close. *So close.*

As proof that I wasn't truly upset I leaned forward, intent in my eyes as I focused on his face and then specifically his lips. Collin's look softened further, his eyes darkening and his mouth parting slightly when I tentatively placed my hands on the front of his shirt. Beneath my touch I felt his own heart's staccato beat matching mine, the rapid pitter patters of the desire he aroused within me.

I could kiss him. I wanted to kiss him, or rather wanted him to kiss me, to show he was sorry, to show that he had feelings for me as I couldn't seem to help but have for him. *Is that so impossible?* We had already kissed once, at our wedding, and had both survived. But I knew this time would be different. *So different.* It both thrilled and terrified me.

I wondered briefly what my mother and especially Anna might think were they to see me at this moment, half dressed, standing in the middle of a river, about to kiss a Scottish laird. Our mouths drew closer, Collin's head bent toward mine in anticipation. At the very last second, as if seized by some irrational fear, I pushed him backward instead.

Collin staggered once, then sat down hard in the shallow water. In his effort to catch himself the spear fell from his hand. I caught it before our meal could be lost, then gathered my skirt and ran through the water toward the shore, wanting to be well away before he got up.

I ran all the way to our fire, ignoring the stream of Gaelic filling the air behind me. It was probably best that I didn't understand what he was saying right now. From the corner of my eye, I watched as he approached, water dripping from both his pants and shirt. Collin didn't seem angry exactly, but rather serious and stern as he had on our wedding day, when he'd said I looked just as he expected. Which had been . . .

As a spoiled, naughty child might. What I'd learned of my younger self the past few days was not pleasant, and yet just now had I not acted as the younger Katie would have, spitefully pushing Collin into the water when he had both helped me and apologized for his deceit? I wanted to hang my head in shame but instead forced myself to meet his gaze and apologize.

"I'm sorry. I don't know why I did that. It was unkind of me."

"If was foolish," he said tersely. "What if my sporran and the last of our supplies had become wet? My clothes are soaked, and it's near nightfall. What do you think will happen to you if something happens to me? If I get hurt or become ill?"

"I would deservedly perish." He didn't need to tell me how helpless I'd be out here on my own. With a bravery I did not feel I stepped forward, stopping just in front of him as I had at the river. I reached up, intending to help him take his shirt off, but he pushed my hand away.

"I'll thank you not to touch me."

His words hurt more than any other rebuke might have. Stung, I turned away, fighting tears that were my own fault. "If you'll hand me your shirt I will hold it near the fire to dry."

"I'll see to it myself," Collin said. "With your help I'd likely have *no* shirt come morning."

"I wouldn't do that. I'm sorry I pushed you," I said once more, still perplexed as to why I had. "I only meant to play," I added softly. A poor excuse.

"There is no play here," Collin said tersely. "No frolicking and games as you had in England. In the Highlands there is life and death, and we walk the edge between. We don't need any little thing tipping us to the far side. Can you understand that?"

"Yes." I straightened and held myself rigid, further hurt and now angry that he was treating me like a child. *Don't act like one, then* came the guilty thought. I was no longer five. We no longer had my grandfather's protection. We had only each other and could not afford to be at odds. How I wished I had kissed Collin instead. Dangerous though that might have been, at least it would have united us. Little chance there was for that now.

He tossed his shirt at me as he walked past, and I barely caught it but felt grateful he trusted me with that, at least. I straightened the sleeves and shook the garment out, trying not to take notice of Collin's bare chest as he moved about the fire, adding wood. I'd never seen a man without his shirt on before—not even my father. Mother and a nurse had bathed him during his illness.

Against my will my eyes darted up frequently, admiring the smoothness of Collin's skin and the planes and muscles of his chest. As if he'd sensed me watching him, Collin turned away, his back to me as he knelt on the ground to prepare our meal.

This afforded me a view just as pleasing, and I openly stared, imagining what a portrait I might paint of my husband. I moved nearer to both the fire and Collin, then knelt beside him, his shirt spread across my lap to dry. He turned and found me there, then stood, as if to move farther away.

"Don't. Please—" I reached out to him, then let my hand fall away. "I just want to be near you. You don't have to talk to me or even look at me. I promise to be quiet."

Collin grunted his acceptance of this arrangement and continued preparing our meal while I did my best to dry his shirt, all the while thinking that what I really wished to do was to touch him—to lean my head against his shoulder and wrap my arms around him, to draw the comfort and strength that came so abundantly with his touch.

After several minutes he spoke. "You'll want to move back a ways while I cook the fish."

He didn't have to ask me twice. I stood and moved to the far side of the fire, where I held his shirt by my fingertips, fanning it in the air. It was nearly dry and nearly worn through. Along with my trunk, the clothing he'd worn to our wedding was gone. What would happen when the thin fabric of this shirt tore? As his wife, would I be expected to make another? I'd only ever practiced embroidery—and had little patience with or talent for that—so how was I to properly care for a home and, someday, a family? Being married to a laird in the Highlands, I was quickly discovering, was nothing like being married to a lord in England. I could envision no trips to the dressmakers and at best might hope the castle had a decent cook to prepare our meals.

If we are permitted to stay. I watched Collin laboring over our meal and wondered what I was to do if both clans banished us.

Feeling discouraged with my lack of abilities and particularly my lack of judgment at the river, I sighed out loud.

Collin glanced at me. "What is it? Are you tired of holding my shirt?"

"Not at all," I said, grateful he might be speaking to me again. "I was just thinking of all the things I cannot do and that you did not get a wife who is very useful in the bargain." No doubt Mhairi could mend his shirt and cook a fish for him.

"I did not marry you because you were useful."

"I know." Or hoped I did. Where had the Collin who had spoken so tenderly this morning gone?

"Neither did you marry me for any skill I might possess," Collin said. "I very much doubt this was how you envisioned your wedding trip."

I could tell he meant to make me feel better, but his observation only served to remind me of the settlement I'd believed would be made upon my mother. And of course Collin had known of the dowry provided by my grandfather. We had each done nothing more noble than to attempt to look out for our families. And little good that had done either of us. Mother hadn't received the promised funds, and my dowry would likely fall to Ian who would use it for his own purposes.

Leaving Collin and me without purse or home, and bound to each other in the most unusual of circumstances.

"Are you ready to eat?" Collin held a stick out to me, from which chunks of fish hung lengthwise. During my musings, he had finished cooking our dinner, and now I had only to figure out how to eat it. Without utensils or plates, I would have to improvise. I took the offered stick from Collin.

"Careful. It's hot," he warned.

I held the fish away from me, not particularly enamored of the smell, but hungry enough that I would eat it, regardless.

"We should give thanks." Collin bent his head and offered a simple prayer of gratitude for the blessing of this meal. The sincerity of his words, along with his faith in an unseen God, humbled me.

"Do you really think someone is there and listening?" Across the firelight I searched Collin's eyes, wanting to see the same reassurance I'd heard in his prayer.

"Aye." Collin answered at once. "More than someone, likely. There's God of course. And then those who've gone before who look out for us. My da, your grandfather."

He didn't mention my father, and I knew now was not the time to bring up his possible connection to Collin's past.

"Do you not believe the same?" Collin asked.

"Yes, but believing and knowing seem different. You sound as if you know." I held the fish near my mouth, leaned forward, and nibbled a piece. Flavor burst pleasantly in my mouth, even as the meat seemed to dissolve. "This is good."

Yesterday's PROMISE

"You sound surprised."

"I am. I've never eaten fish caught fresh from a river before. And as you'd no spices or seasonings or a stove on which to cook it . . ."

Collin patted his sporran. "I'd a few things I picked up along the way. Herbs and such."

"Whatever they are, you've done a marvelous job." I took another bite and found it just as good as the first.

"Thank you." Collin didn't exactly smile, but the lines around his eyes crinkled pleasantly, so that I suspected he was pleased with my compliment.

I handed him his now-dry shirt.

He leaned his own stick-fish against a rock and shrugged the shirt over his head. "It's warm."

"But your breeches are not," I said ruefully.

"No," Collin agreed. "I doubt you'd like me to remove them so they can dry."

"You'll have to." I lifted a hand to untie the blanket I'd worn throughout the day, more to keep me modest than warm. It was Collin now who had the greater need for modesty. "You can wear this around your waist."

"I'll be fine," he mumbled through a bite of fish, waving off my concern with his free hand.

"You'll be cold. And if you're cold tonight, I will be, too. This is a purely selfish offer," I insisted, holding the blanket out to him.

"Doubtful." Collin took it from me nonetheless. I stepped back to my side of the fire, where my torn bodice would not be so obvious.

Colder than I wanted to admit without the blanket

around me, I sat on the ground and scooted closer to the flames and continued to nibble my dinner while Collin went off to change. I felt tense and nervous with him out of sight, though he was gone only a minute or two. The river suddenly seemed frighteningly close.

I was glancing uneasily behind me when Collin returned, the blanket tied around his waist.

"Would you prefer to return to the spot I suggested earlier," he asked, as if sensing the direction of my thoughts. Perhaps he, too, had that ability to know my thoughts, as I seemed to with him.

I shook my head. "No. This is good. Being near the water makes sense. I was just—remembering."

"Don't," Collin advised. "Not that, at least. Banish it. There's no sense in being haunted by the past."

"You sound as if you speak from experience."

A minute passed before he acknowledged my unspoken question. "I do. Though I am not sure you wish to hear of it." He retrieved his water pouch from the ground, then came around the fire to hand it to me before taking a drink himself.

The first sip of my wine. "Will you sit by me?" I patted the ground beside me.

Collin crouched down, his legs and the opening of the blanket angled politely away from me. "Ian's horse is acting a bit spooked. Probably nothing, but I'd prefer not to sit in case I need to get up quickly."

After drinking I passed the pouch to Collin, then stared through the dark at the stallion a short distance away. He seemed placid enough to me, munching the grass at his feet. But how many times had I been caught unaware already? What did I know of unseen dangers?

"It's probably wolves. I'll bring him closer to the fire, though that might spook him, too." Collin rose and went to Ian's horse, then moved him nearer to us, but not so close as to have him straining to get away.

When Collin returned I was pleased that he came to my side and sat beside me as if intending to stay a while.

We ate in silence for several minutes while I enjoyed his closeness and pondered which topic—from the ones we'd touched on earlier—I wished to bring up again. When Collin had finished his meal and I was nearly done with mine, I finally decided what I wished to ask him, though I feared the subject might lead to more unpleasantness between us. His father, and specifically his father's death had been on my mind. I needed to know—for better or worse—if *my* father had been involved.

"Collin?" I began tentatively, placing a hand on his arm as he was about to rise. "Will you tell me, if you can, what it was in your past that you've tried to let go of?"

"Telling you might be like bringing it back." He voiced what I had considered already.

"I can see that," I said, choosing my words carefully. "And I don't wish to bring you any harm or sorrow. But if there is something that would be good for me to know, something about you or me or us or our families, I would like to hear it. When you are ready," I answered, realizing that might not be tonight.

"Even if it will be painful for you?" Collin asked.

"Yes. Even then." I withdrew my touch, wishing he would take my hand and hold it close to his heart as he had the previous night.

Collin stared into the fire a while, then rose and went to check on his breeches, spread out on the grass opposite us. "Nearly dry, but not quite. Time enough I suppose."

He sat near me once more, and I was grateful for more than one reason. The night had grown chilly, and I shivered, hugging my arms tight to myself.

"You're cold. You ought to have this." Collin tugged at the blanket covering his legs.

"No!" I flung a hand out to stop him. "You keep it. Please."

He chuckled. "So concerned. And here I thought you might have been—" He stopped abruptly, and I caught the change of tone in his last word. Once more he had slipped casually into pleasantness. Still, it never seemed to last long before the too serious, too solemn Collin returned.

"What had you thought?" I dared ask, hoping whatever it was wouldn't provoke him into one of his dark moods.

"At the river earlier, it almost seemed you intended to kiss me. But I was wrong, obviously, and am currently without breeches to show for my lack of judgment." He tried to make light of it.

"Perhaps you were not wrong." My heartbeat quickened at the confession and even thinking about our close encounter.

"Only perhaps?" Collin asked, turning his head to look at me.

"No," I confessed. "You were right. I did want—to kiss you. I don't know what came over me or why I pushed you instead." I felt thankful for the dark to hide my flaming cheeks.

"It's better that you did not go with your first impulse," Collin said. "Though I appreciate your honesty."

Why was it better? I wished he would be honest with me on that point, particularly if the name Mhairi had something to do with it.

He scooted closer to me. "Come here, Katie." He held his arm up, and I gladly leaned into him, grateful for the warmth and comfort he radiated.

We spoke no more of the almost kiss or his involuntary swim. I sensed he wished it forgotten, as did I. Though I could not forget the feeling of his heart pulsing beneath my hand, or the look in his eyes as his face had descended toward mine. I wasn't the only one who had wished for a kiss in those moments. And was that so wrong? We were husband and wife. Did a married couple not share such intimacies?

If Anna was here, I was certain she would know what was proper and expected between a couple. But I'd not had reason to ask her before she left, and I'd preferred to hear as little on the topic of men and her impending marriage as possible, so I was now left to find my own way in the dark. Literally.

All around us the night had grown black. As dark as the previous night, at the river, with Ian and his knife-wielding henchman. I could no longer see his horse, but heard it nicker occasionally. Collin leaned forward and threw a couple of pieces of wood onto the fire. A wolf howled in the distance, and the stallion snorted and stomped.

"Best to keep the fire going," Collin said. "Just in case. We can sleep beside it."

"Will we have enough wood?" I looked dubiously at the shrinking pile next to Collin's drying breeches.

"To burn low, yes. And that's all we need if the wolves come. Embers could light a pile of grass and small sticks easily and scare them off. I added to it while you were attempting to catch your supper. If the wolves come I'll throw more on the fire, and we'll each light a larger stick as it blazes. It won't last long, but the initial flare up would likely scare them away."

"You've thought of everything," I said, feeling safe and glowing with pride at my husband's survival skills. "Something tells me you don't need a clan or castle. You could survive just fine on your own."

Collin shrugged. "I could. But I had enough of that when I was younger. Sometimes I grow weary with the responsibilities of the clan, but I'd still rather be with them than alone."

"You're not alone anymore," I reminded him.

"It takes some getting used to," he said by way of an answer. I longed for the Collin who had spoken so tenderly last night and this morning, who had talked of friendship between us. But that Collin had been present very little today. I tried to be content that at least we were talking to one another now, a vast improvement over the first few days of our marriage.

"I would like to tell you of my father," Collin said suddenly, leaving me tense and relieved at the same time. This was what I had hoped for, yet also what I dreaded.

"I would like that," I said in an encouraging tone. I snuggled closer, leaning against Collin's side, enjoying the comfort of his arm around me.

"Da raised Ian and me on his own," Collin began. "My mother died birthing us, and though we'd a series of nursemaids and then tutors, it was our father who cared for us much of the time and taught us most everything we needed to know about leading a clan." Collin expounded on what this entailed, from the accounting of coin, to knowing a healthy sheep from an ill one, to being an intent listener, able to hear between the words what a person is really saying.

He told of the trouble he and Ian had caused, among said sheep and various other farm animals, and the switch his father had used to cease those adventures. He spoke of sneaking into places they ought not to and of hearing things they shouldn't have, both amusing and serious. He told a tale of leaving the door open on the granary and the barley crop getting ruined with rain.

"As punishment Ian and I spent the entire next summer, day after day, mashing the malt. I cannot say that I've cared for whisky much since."

"We agree on that," I said, recalling last night's taste that had burned its way down my throat.

When Collin spoke of his education I was surprised at the consideration he'd been given, as the younger twin.

"Your father educated you both equally?" In England to be a younger brother—even minutes younger—was to be a lesser individual and therefore denied equal privileges and opportunities, even from a very young age.

"Taught us both, expected the same of us, gave us the same responsibilities," Collin said. "The only time he treated us differently was at the end. Ian was given over to the Munros a few days before I was taken by the Campbells. He went first, and I believe Da thought Ian was getting the better lot of the two of us. Your grandfather had a terrible reputation, particularly among MacDonalds."

"There's the little matter of our clans hating each other the past century or so."

"There was that," Collin agreed. "And it was no secret that Laird Campbell hosted English soldiers regularly and worked with them in seeking out those who were labeled traitors for siding with bonnie Prince Charles."

"As your father had?" I knew this much already but wanted to hear Collin's side of things.

"Da believed the prince would be the one to finally look out for Scotland and have her interests at heart, particularly the Highlanders and the clans."

"Is that what you and Ian thought as well?" I asked.

"I cannot speak for Ian, but now that time has passed and I have learned both sides of it—I think the prince merely used the Highlanders to accomplish his purposes. He had no real concern for us, but we were easily led to believe he did. Not foolish, exactly, but too trusting. In the end it did not matter if he cared for us or not. We never had the chance to see what he might or might not do on the throne."

I wondered what would have been different had the outcome of the war changed. What would it have meant for England and Scotland? For my father, who'd fought for King George? Would the Campbells have been the hunted outlaws instead of the MacDonalds?

"After Ian was gone, Father and I carried on a few more days. He seemed to have lost his spirit, though. His will to live had gone with Ian, who I believed dead at the time. Only later did I come to realize that Da had purposely given him over to the Munros."

"Giving you both to clans who had sided with the English

was the only way he knew to keep you safe?" The reality of such circumstances set in. I felt ill at the thought of giving Timothy over to an enemy. "What guarantee did your father have that those clans would honor their agreements?"

"None beyond the lairds' word," Collin said. "And as I've told you, Ian did not fare well in his situation. I was fortunate that your grandfather was a man of honor. He kept his promise to my father and went far beyond that, even, raising me almost as if I was one of his own. I had privileges—food, clothing, education, and training—that most clan chiefs reserve for their sons."

"But Grandfather didn't have a son. Only a daughter, and she was dead."

Collin nodded. "But still, doesn't it seem your grandfather's logical choice ought to have been one of his own—a Campbell?"

"Brann?" I guessed. "Was he the one next in line to be laird when my grandfather died?"

"The next male," Collin affirmed. "But he never has been, nor will he ever be a good leader. Like Ian—worse than Ian, in fact—Brann thinks only of himself. Your people have suffered under his governing."

I thought about this a few minutes and of what more I needed to learn of Brann and the Campbells before we arrived. Collin got up and tended the fire. It was dying now, and he raked the coals and embers together toward the center, concentrating their heat to last as long as possible.

Putting aside my immediate concerns about the Campbells, I attempted to return to the topic we'd started with. "We've strayed from talking of your father," I said when

Collin had returned and pulled me close again. It seemed the most natural thing in the world that we would be near to each other like this, and I could only feel grateful for the cool evening and the excuse it gave for us to sit thusly.

"There's not much more to tell. He allowed the Campbells to lead the English to him. In exchange I was to be under your grandfather's care. All happened as each man agreed it would."

"Was your father taken to prison? Or was he—"

"Laird Campbell was merciful," Collin said abruptly. "A firing squad of English soldiers killed him. He didn't have to suffer months of torture and starvation in a prison. Wasn't hanged for his crimes before a crowd of leering English."

A firing squad was showing mercy? I brought a hand to my mouth, holding back the sob I felt in my throat. Tears sprang to my eyes. I didn't need to ask if my father was one of those who had fired his musket at Collin's father. I knew it in my heart already. I knew it and hurt for it, for Collin, for the grievous wrong it seemed.

"Katie?" He leaned away, taking my shoulders and turning me toward him. "What is it?"

"I'm so sorry. No wonder you hate him. You ought to hate me." Tears slipped down my cheeks. I wanted to ask Collin's forgiveness but felt I had no right.

"You're seeing into the past now as well?" Collin pulled me close again, and I buried my face in his side, crying.

"How can you stand to touch me, let alone marry me?" Maybe he couldn't—not really—and that had been the cause for his unhappy temperament.

"You didn't kill him."

"But my father—"

"Was following orders." Collin's chest heaved with a sigh. "I spent a long time hating him and the other men who killed Da. I dreamed of hunting every one of them down. But reliving the past was going to kill *me*. Da died so I could live. I had to stop."

This was what he'd been referring to earlier when he'd told me I needed to forget. "How did you leave it behind?"

"It wasn't easy, and it took time. But there was this little lass. Quite a bossy thing."

"Oh no," I said. "Not her again."

"Yes, her again." Collin gave my shoulder a brief squeeze. "She told me—the very first night I came to live at her home—that even when I am sad or angry, I must still be nice. Then later she told me that I must forget, no matter how hard it was, no matter that I heard the guns firing each night, that I saw Da's crumpled body and ashen face and bloodstained clothes in my dreams. I must work to forget, or to remember only occasionally, when it was important to remember."

"That was not right for her, for me, to tell you such things," I said, once again appalled at my younger self.

"It was very right," Collin said. "She was only four and had been with her mother when she died." He spoke of me as if I wasn't there, as if the child in question was some other girl. But it *was* me, and his words released a floodgate of memories. I gasped as they returned, trumpeting through my mind with a viciousness that struck painfully.

My mother and I together—how beautiful she was, how happy and alive. I was her shadow; we went everywhere together—running through the castle, playing outside, picnicking and chasing butterflies. At night she told me stories. We shared a room. I slept in her bed often, as my father was not there. I didn't mind. We had each other. And Grandfather.

The pleasant memories flew by all too quickly, leaving me with an emptiness and yearning. Then Mother and I were outside again, playing a game with some other children. A hiding game. I was hiding and she was searching. She found—

"Brann!" I sat up suddenly, shaking at the vision hovering in my mind. "Brann killed my mother."

"Are you certain?" Collin grasped my arms, steadying me.

"I saw it. Just now. He came up behind her and strangled her. He used a band of cloth so it wouldn't leave any marks at her throat. I saw him do it. He said I was next. I screamed so loudly that others came, and he couldn't hurt me, too."

"You *are* seeing the past." Collin stood and pulled me with him. "You're certain it's a vision Katie and not—"

"It's not a vision. It's a memory. I *saw* him kill my mother—and I didn't stop him." I clutched my stomach as I turned away. "I was hiding. I was afraid he would hurt me, so I waited to come out, to save her—until it was too late."

I turned to Collin. "That's what I meant when I said you must forget. We had nightmares—both of us—and the only way to be rid of them was to force the memory away."

"You put it from your mind because you were afraid," Collin said.

"I guess—I don't know. But why didn't I stop it or tell someone?"

"Because you were four years old and frightened." Collin gathered me close again, as if that might protect me from the past.

"I remember my mother." My voice broke. "I remember her, Collin." I wept into his chest, uncertain which of my tears were for the happy memories and which were for those best forgotten. I felt so relieved that pieces of my past were returning. I really was a Campbell. I belonged here. But what awaited me? What other memories had I forced into the deep recesses of my mind? If Brann had killed my mother, what was to stop him from doing the same to me?

Collin. The answer had his arms wrapped firmly around me, his head bent near to mine. Grandfather had given him to me—had given us to each other—for comfort and protection. In return, Collin's responsibility for me—the task given him by the laird himself—must have protected him from other clan members who would have done him, an enemy MacDonald, harm.

He claimed I had helped him. But all he had done for the past week was protect and comfort me. It was time I started returning the favor. We had been talking of his father's death, and somehow Collin was still the one comforting me when it should have been the other way around.

I wiped my eyes and leaned away from his embrace. "I'm sorry for falling apart again. It seems all I've done this past week is cry. It is not a regular habit."

"It was when you were a child," he said seriously.

"Oh dear." I sighed again. "From this time forward I shall endeavor to be better than my childhood self." I didn't quite promise that there would never be tears, not trusting my current, fragile state of emotions, to be that stable.

"I don't mind your tears." Collin brushed his fingers

lightly across my cheek. "But I mind that you're hurting. And now I mind that I'm taking you home to a murderer."

"We knew he was that before tonight. Now we've just added my mother to the list of his victims." I drew in a breath and wished the memory away. "Time enough to talk of our plans tomorrow," I said, using a turn of phrase spoken to me more than once over the past days. I felt suddenly tired, drained from the flash flood of recollection.

"Tomorrow," Collin agreed. "Morning, more than night, is a time for clarity." He moved his arm, releasing me completely. "And now I'd best get the rest of my clothes on."

I smiled through the dark. "A good idea," I agreed, though I wouldn't have minded if he'd tried to kiss me goodnight.

"Quit following me around." Katie tossed her long hair over her shoulder as she turned her back on me and broke into a run. She was surprisingly quick for someone so little, but she was no match for my stride.

I caught her by her dress and hauled her back. "I don't like this anymore than you do. Less, in fact." The last few days of traipsing after her—all while receiving looks of disdain from everyone around us—had done little to improve my opinion of the Campbells. That I was mistrusted and hated by everyone but the laird was obvious.

Despite her grandfather's instructions, Katie was fighting our new arrangement vehemently. I'd had very little sleep, given the hardness of the stone and her attempts to sneak past me in the night. If not for the food that was both good and plentiful and helping to restore my strength, I would have made my escape by now, promises to the laird notwithstanding. I would leave soon. Just a day or two more, and I'd be ready.

Chapter Nineteen

"Good morning." Collin glanced at me from his place by the fire.

I thought his lazy smile the perfect way to awaken and returned it with one of my own before a rush of self-consciousness heated my face. We'd spent the night curled up together in the shared blanket. Alone. The two of us. Not even the wolves had ventured close, and Ian's horse hardly counted as a chaperone.

Silly thought. I was married now. The time for chaperones had passed.

"What are you thinking?" Collin dropped oats into his tin cup and began stirring. "You seem upset."

"Oh no," I assured him, sitting up. I pushed the blanket aside before remembering my torn gown. I reached for the corner of the blanket and held it up to me again. "It's somewhat disconcerting to awake like this is all."

"In the middle of the wilderness," Collin said. "Without a bed or even a roof overhead."

"No. It's not that." I twisted the cloth round my fingers. "With a man—with you. I feel as if I'm missing a chaperone— as if I've done something scandalous."

"Ah." Understanding and perhaps a flicker of amusement lightened Collin's eyes.

"Not that it's unpleasant," I hurried to add, not wanting him to feel injured. "I quite like being here—with you. I was warm through the night, and it was nice to . . ." My cheeks had to be positively flaming now.

"Nice to be close," Collin suggested. "To share a bed, as it were."

I nodded, then stood quickly. "Excuse me." I hurried past him, toward the meadow, wondering where I should have a moment of privacy with so few trees about.

Behind me Collin began whistling. "Breakfast is ready when you return. The oats have been cooked this time."

"Thank you," I called and hurried to a spot hidden from

our camp. When finished I came back by way of the river, taking a minute to splash water on my face, pat down my hair, and arrange the dress to cover as much of me as possible.

Collin waited for me near the fire. He held the cup out.

"Thank you." I accepted it, careful to avoid looking at him directly. I wasn't certain what made this morning different from the others we'd spent together. We'd been alone a good part of yesterday as well, and I hadn't felt this awkward.

He'd held my hand. We'd ridden together, he'd stood behind me in the river when we fished. But after spending the entirety of the night curled up beside him, his arms not once moving from their protective embrace, something was definitely different.

I couldn't look at Collin or think of him or talk to him without feeling incredibly aware of our proximity to each other and the distance separating us from the rest of the world. I'd wished for this very thing, and now that I had it, I wasn't certain what to do or how to act.

I took a bite of oatmeal, then held the tin out to Collin. Our fingers brushed as he took it, and even that little touch set my nerves afire. I watched him lift the spoon to his mouth, pressing my own lips together when his closed over our shared utensil.

This time he kept the cup but held the next bite out to me. I opened my mouth and allowed him to feed me and felt it even more intimate than our sharing of the blanket had been.

It's just breakfast, for heaven's sake! What is wrong with me? My knees felt weak, my palms sweaty. I couldn't meet Collin's eye. It was part embarrassment, part feeling like I was about to take flight. Part feeling like I would give anything if he'd just set the cup aside, take my face in his hands, and kiss me instead.

I didn't want oatmeal for breakfast. I wanted him.

I gave a little sigh, accepting that the fluttering in my stomach wasn't about to go away anytime soon but would likely only get worse in his continued presence.

"Are you unwell this morning?" Collin asked when I declined any more of the porridge.

"No." Quite well. Only swoony and infatuated, and feeling guilty about both. It was like I'd snuck into a ball I wasn't supposed to be at and the music was sweeping me away on a cloud of forbidden euphoria. Or I'd stolen the most scrumptious confection imaginable from London's most famous bakery. I held the cake in my hands, already having committed a crime by taking it, yet not having enjoyed that first delicious bite. I anticipated it and basked in the heavenly aroma, almost desperate for the flavor that was to come.

Yet with each of these scenarios, there was wrongdoing. I'd done the forbidden, and there would be a consequence to my actions. That wasn't the case here, was it? I told myself that I'd done nothing wrong by lying in my husband's arms all night. Nor was there anything wrong with wanting him to kiss me.

But last night Collin had almost made it sound as if there was, and that worried and confused me. I might have overcome my embarrassment, but I couldn't overcome the possibility that he might be displeased if he knew my thoughts. Or that somehow they were wrong.

Yesterday's PROMISE

Whether he realized it or not, Collin's intention to tutor me on the history of the Campbells, and particularly on how our passed-down gift of sight affected them, proved the perfect distraction from my morning discomfort. He kept our pace slow and spoke continuously as we rode, going over everything from my genealogy, so far as he knew it, to things the Campbell leaders had foretold and how those had, in turn, impacted their choices.

"You actually believe my grandfather saw the uprising and knew the outcome before it happened?" I asked shortly into Collin's explanation as to why the Campbells had sided with the English during the Jacobite rebellion of '45. Being aware of danger to oneself was one thing; predicting the outcome of a war seemed another entirely.

"You don't?" Collin asked. "Even after what happened to you yesterday?"

"That was different. I saw two groups of people—Brann and his followers, and those at our camp with the MacDonalds and Campbells." That had been more than enough to crowd my mind with dialogues to keep straight, facial expressions to judge, locations to remember. It had been like being in two places at once, with multiple conversations going on around me, each filled with details I'd been expected to recall. "I can't imagine how one could see more than that—the battles, the commanders and men on both sides . . . to know the dates and locations."

"Yet he did," Collin said patiently. "I admit to being skeptical at first as well. But many a night I sat with your grandfather while he told me every detail of the uprising from its earliest inception to the final outcome. I wasn't truly convinced until the night he sat down with me and recalled a meeting my father had led. It was like being with him again, as Liam Campbell literally said, word for word, what my father had that night. After that, I could not doubt that your grandfather spoke the truth and his gift was real."

"What a terrible burden for him." I couldn't imagine the pain that must have accompanied those visions or the weight my grandfather had to have felt, knowing what was in store for Scotland. "If he knew so much, why didn't he do more to stop the uprising? Or why didn't he fight for Scotland instead of fighting against many of the other clans?"

"Good questions, and some I asked him myself," Collin said. "Think on it a minute. If you knew that, no matter what you did, Scotland was to lose the war, what would you have done?"

"Gone somewhere else to live." I suggested the first thing that came to mind.

"Perhaps, if you had only yourself to think of, that would have been a viable solution." Collin said. "But what if you loved your country fiercely? Even more than that, what if you loved your people, and you had a great many depending upon you for their well-being and survival? Would you choose to send men, your own kin, to their deaths for a hopeless cause? Or would you do everything you could to keep them and your entire clan safe? Would you side with those you knew would win and do what you must to preserve your land and livestock and crops beyond the years of the rebellion?"

I didn't answer, and Collin didn't seem to expect me to. The truth of his words settled over me, this heritage I hadn't known of and still didn't necessarily want to claim, mine whether I wished it or not. My grandfather had done the best he could in the dangerous times he'd lived in. *I must do the same.*

"We aren't at war now and, God willing, won't be again," I said. "So I don't understand what good my gift—limited as it seems to be—will do anyone, other than perhaps the two of us, in keeping us clear of Brann and Ian."

"It will show us what must be done with your clan. It will show us not only how to avoid Brann, but how to be rid of him as well." Collin's faith in me was unnerving.

"And you're wrong," he continued. "We are at war. Only this time, the war isn't between England and Scotland or even between clans. It's between Brann and those like him, and the rest of your kin and other Highlanders whose families have lived on this land for centuries. The fight is very real—families fighting for their homes, the ability to provide for themselves, their very lives."

My head was starting to hurt again, though I wasn't having any visions at the moment. Dread and worry over what was to come, what it seemed Collin and others expected me to accomplish, sent tension through every part of my body.

"What if my visions aren't so precise as Grandfather's? What if I miss something?" I'd missed several things already.

"Liam's visions weren't always detailed," Collin said. "In some instances he knew everything; in others, only vague outlines. For example, he knew Ian MacDonald's son was to come live with him. But he didn't know which of us would be given into his care."

"You mean I could have been stuck with Ian?" I shuddered.

Behind me Collin shrugged. "He might have been a different man if he had spent the years with your grandfather that I did. And I might have been as he is now, had I been abused."

I leaned back into Collin and felt his hand tighten around my waist. "I don't believe you could ever be as he is. You were inherently good before coming to my grandfather. His guidance perhaps improved upon that, but you were already well on your way to becoming the man you are."

"Sure about that, are you?" There was teasing in Collin's voice.

"Oh yes," I declared. "I remember everything of our time together now."

"Really? You remember that I made you muck out a horse's stall every day for a month straight, all for the promise of one ride, if the animal became mine?"

"An entire month for one ride?" I exclaimed. "That hardly seems fair."

"Of course it wasn't," Collin said. "But you'd been behaving poorly again, a right little tart, and I wanted to show your grandfather that you weren't completely hopeless. More than that, I wanted to show you who was in charge—and it wasn't you any longer." Collin pinched my side, and I jumped and swatted his hand away.

"Hmph," I said, sounding particularly Scottish. "It seems like it should have been my horse instead, as I was the one doing all of the work."

"It was to have been yours." Collin's voice fell serious

again. "It was what your grandfather intended for your sixth birthday, providing your behavior improved. But I couldn't tell you that and spoil the surprise, so I convinced you it was to be mine, and you would only get to ride if you worked for it."

"What about you? You weren't to have your own horse as well?" This couldn't have sat well with a fifteen-year-old boy. Why should some snippet of a girl have such a privilege and he not the same?

But Collin was shaking his head. "I wasn't promised one of the spring foals. Your grandfather hadn't planned to trust me with a horse so soon, not when I'd planned to steal one and make my escape shortly after I arrived—a plan you foiled, I might add." He spoke lightly of the event, though I could only imagine it must have been anything but.

"A little over a year had passed since I'd been there, and though we had each made great progress in our relationship, I still had fourteen years as a MacDonald weighing against just one with the Campbells."

"And this didn't make you angry—or jealous?" He *was* a good man. Much better than me.

"It probably would have," Collin admitted. "But I never had the chance to find out. You were taken by your father before your birthday."

Taken. I hadn't gone willingly?

"Your grandfather felt bad for me, I think," Collin said. "I'd been injured . . . Collin's voice trailed off, and I recognized the distant look in his eyes once more, as he revisited the past.

"Anyway," he continued after a moment, "Liam decided

to trust me. I never betrayed that trust. Never left Campbell land until your grandfather sent me away."

I needed to learn about those years, too, but my mind was already full of the morning's revelations. I needed time to think. And I just wanted to be held. Feeling bold, I reached for Collin's hand that I'd swatted away earlier and pulled it around me again. Collin leaned forward, his face close to mine.

"We were each gone, and now we're both coming back—together. We're going home, Katie, and we're going to help your people, and mine, too. It's all right to doubt right now, but know this. Your grandfather saw *us*. He saw our day, too."

I took the evening meal at the far end of the main table, with the lass, who alternated between making faces at me and signaling to her grandfather, trying to gain his attention.

"What is it, Katie?" he said at last, when she'd taken to standing on her seat and waving her plaid about like a banner. Thankfully, I was responsible for her safety and not her behavior.

"Collin is thinking to escape this night," she announced loudly.

Conversation in the hall ceased as the laird and the other Campbells turned sharp eyes on me. Beneath the table my hands clenched into fists. Meddlesome little brat. Not even my thoughts were my own anymore. I was going to kill her.

"He's figured out how to get past the guards, and he knows which horse he plans to take," Katie said.

Hers would be a slow, painful death. If mine wasn't first.

"Thievery, too, in the bargain?" Laird Campbell frowned at me.

Katie gasped. "Now he's wishing he could put his hands around my neck and strangle me." She jumped from her chair, even as her hands went protectively to her throat.

To my astonishment Laird Campbell threw his head back and laughed. "I don't imagine it's the last time Collin will think such a thing about you."

Chapter Twenty

The next days passed in a haze of happiness—at our budding relationship—and worry over the problems awaiting us. By the fourth day of our travel alone I came to realize that Collin was not only prolonging our journey, but showing me some of his favorite places in the Highlands and leading me toward one of mine, though I had only ever seen it in my painting. This morning we meandered through the Forest of Atholl.

"You'll find the best and worst of the Highlands all right here," Collin explained. He held my hand as we picked our way over boulders and between stately trees. Ian's horse trotted along obediently, grateful, I supposed, for relief from riders. I, too, was relieved to walk, especially now that Collin had used the last of his coin to purchase shoes for me during a brief stop at Blair Castle the previous evening. I'd spent a nervous hour alone in hiding while Collin had gone on his errand, believing it safest for me if the Murrays didn't realize there was a Campbell among them. Apparently there was some truth to the concern Alistair had voiced days earlier.

When Collin had returned he'd apologized that he'd been unable to obtain a gown for me as well. The shoes were enough, though, allowing for this detour.

"Much of the Highlands is moorland, pretty in its own way. But you cannot deny there is something about a forest." Collin smiled with delight. "Were I to have my choice, I should like to build a home surrounded by trees such as this, Scotch pine with its fresh scent, silver birch, and larch."

"There are no forests on MacDonald land?" I lifted my skirt and stepped over a fallen tree trunk.

"There is very little of anything on MacDonald land anymore," Collin said. "I fear that soon we will have nothing."

I tugged on his hand and stopped so that he was forced to do the same. "Should we not be getting home, then?

Should we not go straight to the MacDonalds, or to the Campbells at least and begin to work out what must be done?" I didn't like the idea any more than I had a few days ago, but the possibility that Collin's family might be suffering while I was enjoying a pleasant tour of the Highlands did not sit well with me either.

"We'll be there soon enough," Collin said. "These hours and days of travel my mind has not been idle. I've been thinking on a solution to the troubles of our clans—both of them."

"And have you come up with anything?" I tilted my face toward his, eager to hear what he might have thought of, what solution there might be to his continuing as laird of the MacDonalds while being married to me and keeping Brann from doing more harm.

"If it comes to it . . . there is something that may work, something your grandfather said in passing long ago." Collin made as if to walk again, but I refused to move.

"Will you share it with me?" I asked hopefully. He had spoken of wanting someone to confide in.

Collin stood unmoving for several seconds, as if considering my request. When he spoke it was with words carefully measured. "Someday I will, Katie. But not now. It is for your own good, as well as mine and our people. I need you to trust that I will act as I see best for all, but most especially for you."

I swallowed the hurt his words caused. I did trust Collin, but could he not say the same of me? Was my gift of sight no use to him after all? Thus far it had been the only thing I had to offer for our assistance, and it pained me to think he did not even need that. *Or me.* With effort I nodded my agreement to his request, and we continued on our way.

We were in a deep glen now, the solemn pines more sparse here, but the plentiful stone making me once again thankful to be wearing shoes. Ahead I could hear the rushing of water growing closer.

A roe deer darted across our path quite suddenly, spooking both Ian's horse and me. Collin seemed unfazed by its appearance and merely remarked that venison would have been a nice change from fish.

The river was roaring now, and a few minutes more brought us in view of a lovely waterfall cascading over stone like that on which we stood. The gorge below the falls was quite narrow, giving the impression that it was the water itself that had cut the rock away and formed its path over the centuries.

"I present to you The Falls of Bruar." Collin bowed gallantly in front of me, as if presenting me at court.

"Beautiful." I clapped with sincere delight.

"Only the best for my lady fair."

I was not at all certain I was looking so fair, after days in the sun without any sort of hat, and with only fingers to comb out my hair. But I had washed it, and my dress, the previous day, when I'd taken my own, involuntary swim while making yet another attempt to catch our supper. The accident had turned out to be a happy one, as I'd discovered—once my garments were dried and I had put them on again—that wearing my shift backward took care of the most pressing of my modesty problems. Collin had further solved them by carefully cutting holes on either side of the front of my torn dress, then using my old corset laces, previously tied in my braids, to lace the front of my gown together. I was not likely to start any new fashion, but at least I had been able to shed the blanket during the warmer daylight hours.

"Is something wrong?" Collin's lips pressed together with concern. "Do you not like the falls?"

"I love them." To prove my point I sat on the ground right where I was. "I think we should take our luncheon in this very spot." I was not particularly hungry, for either oats or fish, yet I would eat both to appease Collin's worry. He had enough troubles without thinking his wife ungrateful or unhappy. Especially when I was neither.

He settled beside me and opened his sporran.

Oats then. He'd replenished his supply when purchasing my shoes. But instead of our usual fare Collin withdrew a tied cloth, inside which were a few slices of cheese and the end piece of a loaf of bread. A veritable feast.

"Where did you get those?" I did not attempt to hide either my smile or eagerness.

"They came with the shoes." He wouldn't quite meet my eye as he said this, alerting me to his falsehood.

"Is that so?"

"Aye," he insisted, handing me two slices of cheese. "Slipped right away from the table and into the shoes did they."

"*In* the shoes?" The cheese suddenly did not taste quite as good.

Collin laughed. "Not to worry. They were in the cloth the whole time. And it wasn't really stealing. They charged too much for the shoes, anyway."

It was my turn to laugh. "I must say that I feel a bit like Maid Marian, traipsing about Sherwood Forest and married to the outlaw Robin Hood."

"Be sure not to write that to your sister." Collin broke the bread in two pieces and handed the larger one to me.

"When and how am I to write her at all?" I asked, surprised that he had mentioned Anna or even remembered I had a sister.

"When we've reached the Campbells' of course," Collin said. "They've the post there, though it'll take some weeks, if not a month or more, for a letter to reach London."

"I hadn't thought on that." My life in England seemed so far away now. "I must write Timothy first. He is the one I miss the most. I shall tell him of your outlawish behavior. He will find it quite thrilling." I smiled encouragingly at Collin. "I suppose I should write to Anna and Mother as well."

"You can tell your sister of the falls." Collin looked past me to the rushing water. "And the moorlands and lochs. After today you can tell her that you have been to the place in your painting. That you have stood atop Bealach Druim Uachdair and seen the grass of the sloping hills bending in the wind, that you've tasted the rivers running on either side. You've climbed the path as near to the heavens as one can get here, and you've felt the power of them in the grand stones planted in the earth."

"You are more poetic than Finlay." Collin's words seemed as beautiful as the land itself and expressed the depth of his feelings for the Highlands. I found myself longing to share that with him. I had enjoyed what I'd seen, been moved by the wonders and creations surrounding us, but Scotland had not yet penetrated my soul as it had Collin's. That he had tried, these past few days, to share that with me touched me deeply.

"I wanted you to have something to tell your sister." Collin looked away as if embarrassed. "I know she has been visiting the continent with her husband and this cannot compare, but I wanted you to have something of a wedding trip as well."

"Oh, Collin." I leaned forward and threw my arms about him, hugging him fiercely as my feelings—those that *had* penetrated my soul—overflowed. "That is the kindest thing. You are too good to me." Here I thought he had been avoiding going home, and instead he had been doing this for me. *A wedding trip. As if we are a real married couple.* Perhaps we were, or would come to that stage eventually.

I drew back a little and looked into his eyes. "This has been the best week of my life."

His brows lifted, and half of his lip rose in a doubtful smirk. "I thought you said your father was good to you."

"He was," I insisted. "Very good. I had a most pleasant upbringing. But it wasn't here. I wasn't with *you.*" I slid one hand from his shoulder and patted his chest, so that my fingers were just above his heart. Right where they had been the last time we almost kissed.

We were even closer now, with me on his lap, our faces just a breath away from one another.

I looked into his eyes. *Please, Collin.* There was no river to push him in this time. I would not run away. I was brave enough now. I thought he was, too. My eyes fluttered closed in invitation.

"Katie, I—"

I dared to look at him and read the desire burning in his eyes. My heart soared. *He does care for me.*

"Collin," I whispered. Would he make me beg? I didn't care if he did. His nearness didn't seem enough anymore. It was his affection I craved, in word and deed.

"Katie, I—I'm glad you're here. That you've come home." He leaned forward, pressing a quick kiss to my forehead. "But you're sitting on the only bread I've had to eat in five days."

"Oh." I jumped up, fighting a surge of disappointment and feeling guilty as I saw the smashed piece and scattered crumbs on his leg. "Here. Have mine." I retrieved it from the ground where it had fallen when I'd made the sudden leap to his lap. "I've only taken a bite. It isn't very good, actually. Crumbly and dry."

"It's not fish or oatmeal," Collin said lightheartedly, accepting my offering. I saw through his attempt to ease the tension between us.

Once again I did not understand his reluctance to be close to me, to behave as a husband and wife ought. For the more I thought about it, the more certain I felt it must be all right for a married couple to kiss one another. I believed my father and step mother had—in those earlier, happier years. I knew Collin felt the same hunger as I. And he continued to prove he cared for me. Yet he would not trust me with his secret. Or with his heart, it seemed. I thought back to my sketchbook and how I had vowed to make him smile.

Perhaps I ought to have made a different goal. It was much more than a smile that he needed. I glanced at Collin as I stood and shook the crumbs from my skirt. *I promise to teach you of love.*

Yesterday's PROMISE

We lingered too long—entirely my fault—on Bealach Druim Uachdair. It was everything I had imagined when I had painted it. One really could see forever, and Collin took his time pointing out things on both sides of the pass to me. On our way up he told me about the Battle of Killiecrankie, the sight of the first Jacobite rebellion in 1689.

"Over seventy years now this has been going on." I shook my head, utterly displeased to learn this and worried that it wasn't truly over yet.

"Scotland's never had a peaceful past," Collin said. "It isn't in our nature."

"Or it has to do with our neighbors—to the south," I suggested.

"At times, yes," Collin said. "But at others we have no one but ourselves to blame. We are our own worst enemies."

I thought on this as Ian's stallion steadily picked his way up the moor. Did Collin speak of the conflict between the clans? Or was there something more, something even worse, happening here? Were men like Brann and Ian at the root of it?

"The English have done a few good turns for us," Collin said, giving credit to General Wade for the military road we traveled. "Even if he did build it to stop the Jacobites."

"Is that one of the reasons the English won? Because of these roads?"

"No." Collin was swift to answer. "They won because the

Highlanders were divided. A divided people can never win." We'd reached the final peak, and Collin stopped the horse. He dismounted, then held his hands out to me. I slid easily into his embrace and felt pleased when he kept my hand in his and walked us a distance from the road where we could truly look out over what seemed the edge of the world.

"It's beautiful," I said, wishing for a word that would do the landscape before me justice. "Someday I wish to sit up here and paint it."

"It couldn't look any better than the painting you did already," Collin said. "You've a real talent, Katie."

"Thank you." My heart warmed with his compliment. "It, and the other painting I'd brought, were my favorites. I often imagined this was a real place. It was where I would escape to in my thoughts whenever I was troubled. I never imagined that I was painting my future." I realized my abilities with charcoal and brush would help us little in our new life and land. My art did not seem a reliable or timely way to predict any dangers we might be facing.

"Such a magical place needs a people who care for it," I said. "Are the Highlanders that people? Are we any better than we were at the end of the war? Will the wounds ever heal and the clans band together?"

"Is Ian's hair the shade of Alistair's?" Collin gave a grim bark of laughter. "Nothing much has changed in that regard. MacDonalds and Campbells are still enemies."

"Except us. We aren't." I squeezed his hand, loving that he was both a MacDonald and mine.

"It was what your grandfather hoped." Collin's gaze grew tender. "Those many years ago when he joined our hands and made us speak solemn vows to one another."

Yesterday's PROMISE

"What did we promise?" I asked, unable to remember much of that night.

"That we would care for one another and always put the other first, and that we would care for our people and do what we must to unite them and see that they continued on for generations to come."

"Rather a lot to ask of a fourteen-year-old and a four-year-old, don't you think?"

"Aye, but we're not fourteen and four any longer. We've already done one hard thing. We can do another."

"And what was that?" I couldn't see that we'd accomplished much toward our goal yet, other than to successfully avoid both of our families the past several days.

"We married each other without bloodshed—almost," Collin added.

I supposed he spoke of Malcom. "Marrying you was not difficult—not as I'd expected it might be." I thought back to the day of our wedding and the moment I had first laid eyes on Collin. My heart had known him at once, even if my mind did not then remember him.

"It wasn't," Collin agreed. "But quite a feat nonetheless when, for many years, I wondered if I would ever see you again." He turned my hand over and traced the thin scar running across my palm.

"Do you know how I got that?" I asked, realizing he might know the answer to one of the mysteries of my life. "I asked Father a few times, but he never would tell me, so I supposed it must have happened when I was very young."

"You were five. He is the one who gave you that scar. Mine as well." Collin turned his own hand over, matching ours together so that the line on his continued where mine left off.

I stared at them together and saw them no longer white and thin but blood red, deep, and painful.

"I thought you lost your hand because of me. Because I wouldn't let go." Collin folded my fingers over the scar and raised my hand to his lips, holding it there. "Your father and a small group of English soldiers had been chasing us, tracking us for three nights. I'd done everything I knew of to keep you hidden and safe. I'd circled back around toward the Campbell keep, hoping that if I could get you inside the walls of the church I could plead sanctuary and your grandfather could do something to prevent them from taking you. We didn't make it that far. Your father found us hiding in the graveyard." Collin's eyes met mine, pleading for forgiveness and understanding he didn't need to ask for.

"It wasn't your—"

"I refused to let you go," he continued. "Even when one of the redcoats held a gun to my head. Even when your father grabbed you and was pulling you away. You were begging him to stop, begging me not to let go of you, and so I didn't. Until your father threatened to cut off your hand. He said I could keep that and he would take the rest of you. I had no choice but to let you go then. I couldn't let him cut off your hand, Katie."

"He didn't. It's all right, Collin." I placed that hand on his cheek, wanting to comfort, to erase the painful memory from his mind.

"I let go of you, but you still held on. He struck our joined hands then carried you away screaming and bleeding."

Yesterday's PROMISE

"I remember." I sucked in a breath and closed my eyes, seeing my five-year-old self pressing a bloody hand to a carriage window, trying to get out.

"I ran after you. I ran and ran," Collin said. "But I was no match for a carriage, and the soldiers started shooting at me, and soon you were gone. I didn't know if I would ever see you again."

Thunder echoed in the sky above, and we both looked up to see grey clouds hovering. A storm had moved in, stealing what hours of daylight we'd left.

Wordlessly Collin grabbed my hand, and we both ran to Ian's horse. The trip down the north side of the mountain was no less treacherous, and we were not yet halfway down when fat drops began falling from the sky. Collin steered us off the road onto a side path, then directly across the moor to an outcropping of rock. He led us to an overhang not deep enough to qualify as a cave, but substantial enough to shelter us from most of the rain.

The steady drops turned to a downpour as Collin unfolded our shared blanket and wrapped it around us. We sat on the ground, huddled together for warmth as streams of water began cascading over the rock on either side and in front of us. Two waterfalls in one day.

"Is this still the best week of your life?" Collin asked above the sounds of the storm.

"Yes," I insisted, though my mood was melancholy. I had unraveled the mystery of why Collin hated my father. It had nothing to do with Collin's own loss and everything to do with me.

Fourteen years I had been gone. Years in which Collin

did not know if he would ever see me again. Years which had seen my grandfather's death and ought to have released Collin from any promise he had made. Years when he might have chosen another as his bride. But he had not. Against logic and odds, he had hoped and waited and chosen me.

I twisted the wedding band around my finger. "How long did it take you to make this?" I held my hand up, admiring the ring.

"Your grandfather gave me a bit of silver about a month after you'd gone. He said I could spend it, or he suggested it might make a nice wedding band for you someday. I was grieving badly—I cannot explain it, you being such a little scrap of a thing and ornery and annoying much of the time." Collin nudged my shoulder playfully. "But somehow you'd become my family, my purpose after losing first my home and clan, then Ian and Da. I'd been charged with your safekeeping and felt I had failed, and it nearly crushed me."

"You didn't fail." I rested my head against his shoulder. "I'm here, am I not? Safe all these years, probably because I was with my father instead of here. Besides, that was a terrible lot of responsibility for my grandfather to put on a boy. What was he thinking?"

"It wasn't just him," Collin said. "I came to understand that the night he betrothed us. There was a higher power at work among us, One who intended us to unite for his purposes."

I sat up and turned to him. "Are you speaking of God? Do you really believe that?"

"I know it, Katie." Collin was as serious as I'd ever seen

him. "You would, too, if you'd been a little older or could remember that night."

"Why us?" I asked. The way he spoke made us sound like we were akin to Joan of Arc or King Arthur.

He shrugged. "That I don't know. But you've been given a gift. And I've been given you, so we'd best figure out how to fulfill our parts of the bargain."

I liked the way he said I'd been given to him. As if he treasured me as one would a gift. I twisted the ring on my finger, once more admiring the delicate carving.

"I was grieving, and making you a ring was something I could do," Collin continued. "A little thing, to be sure, but it brought solace, because I thought if I made it, then someday you must wear it, and then I should be with you again." Collin brushed his fingers over the silver band and smiled sadly, as if remembering. "It took months, every evening by the fire. I worked at it off and on over the years, putting it away when I returned to the MacDonalds. When your father's letter arrived, I took the ring out once more and polished it."

"You are an artist, too. A craftsman."

"If only I could conjure a house right now." The sheeting rain had encroached on our shelter, the rock wet right up to the tight circle we sat in.

"That wouldn't be any good," I said. "No trees around, and you want to live in a forest."

Collin grinned. "Anywhere you are will do fine."

Anywhere you are. Anywhere. His words were freeing somehow, suggesting that if all did not go well with the Campbells or MacDonalds we might go elsewhere. We were not tied to any spot of land or people. Only to each other, though I could see that Collin felt a responsibility far beyond that. I'd felt it, too, since learning that Brann was the one who had taken my grandfather's place.

But for now, for these few minutes alone, with the water falling all around us, sealing us away from the rest of the world, we were safe and content with each other, and the future could wait.

Liam Campbell's laughter ceased abruptly. He stood and began removing his belt. My eyes tracked his movements and knew what was coming. The urge to flee or fight nearly overpowered me, but some deep-rooted sense of self-preservation held me in place. I was surrounded by the enemy. But I would only be beaten. Unless I resisted. Then I'd be shot instead.

Chapter Twenty-one

With utmost care I lifted Collin's arm from its usual position, draped across my middle, assumed these many nights we had shared a blanket together with only the grass below as our bed and the stars overhead for a canopy. We had done nothing more than sleep on the handful of nights we'd shared alone, and while I appreciated Collin's patience with me—with us as husband and wife—I was beginning to wonder if he ever would expect more. Or even wish for it.

On our wedding night he had made it clear that nothing more was required to make our union legal. After Collin's explanations regarding his aloof behavior those first few days, I wasn't entirely certain whether his wedding-night statement stood or not. I wasn't sure I wanted it to. Sleeping beside Collin, with his arm wrapped protectively around me, the steady assurance of his heartbeat as my lullaby, had proved both comforting and exhilarating—instead of awkward and discomfiting.

But there had been times the past couple of nights when, instead of his mumbled, 'Goodnight, Katie,' I wished desperately that he would kiss me instead. But he had not even attempted such or brought up the subject since the night I'd lost my nerve and shoved him in the river. *Oh, that I had that moment back.*

Perhaps Collin's reluctance was my penance for the deed. But how long was I to be punished? And what was wrong with me that I saw his considerate behavior as *punishment?* I categorized it with my apparent need for adventure, one I'd been largely enjoying the past few days—with one exception. We were very near to facing danger head on, and I had no notion of how we were to protect ourselves. Or, more precisely, I'd had no additional visions and had little confidence in my ability to predict anything of the future and thus help us navigate the dangers safely.

By nightfall we would be on Campbell land. Tomorrow I would have to face Brann and who knew how many hostile others. Not only that, I would have to do something about them as well.

Having extricated myself from beneath Collin's arm, I eased out from beneath the blanket. If I intended to claim my right to my grandfather's castle and oust its current occupant, it seemed the least I ought to be able to do was to begin such endeavors by catching my own breakfast, and Collin's, too.

I crawled away into the grey predawn light—one of the best times to catch a fish, Collin had explained on the numerous mornings he'd risen before me and had breakfast waiting by the time I awoke. Today it was my turn.

Not bothering with my shoes, I crept down to the loch. I tied my dress up, braced myself for the cold, and stepped into the freezing water, pressing my lips together to contain any number of epithets I might have expressed about the shocking temperature.

One hundred tries. Collin believed that was how long it had taken him to acquire the skill of spearing a fish. With grim determination I stared down at the still water pooling at my feet, wondering how close I'd come to that number already over the past week. Surely catching a fish here would be easier than catching one in a river, no matter how gentle the current. I didn't have the luxury of weeks to learn—how to fish or anything else.

I sprinkled a tiny ration of oats across the top of the water, then readied the spear. *Here, little fishies.* Long minutes passed, but I held my pose, ignoring the ache in my back. Only my eyes moved, darting back and forth until at last they caught sight of a shadow in the water, a shape moving toward me slowly. Ever so slowly.

Patience. Closer now. Here. Here . . . now! I struck and felt the difference at once, as the spear pierced the fish instead of the bottom of the lake.

"Collin! I did it. I caught one. Look!" With loud, splashing steps I slogged up to the shore, heedless of the fact that I'd intended to let him sleep while I caught and prepared our breakfast—all before dawn.

He sat up quickly. Too quickly—he'd been feigning sleep this entire time. I was too excited over my catch to mind.

"Let's see," he said with an eager smile.

I held the spear tip with the dead fish near his face. "I think it's big enough to feed both of us. Maybe I'll go catch another one anyway. It wasn't that hard after all. It's just knowing the right time and angle at which to strike." I couldn't remember ever feeling so pleased with myself.

Collin's mouth turned down as he examined the fish. After a few seconds he looked up at me. "It's dead, Katie."

"I know. I killed it." Who would have believed, a few weeks ago, how thrilled I'd be with such an accomplishment? *Anna would be positively horrified.* The thought provided a sort of gleeful satisfaction.

"Actually . . ." Collin rubbed the back of his neck. "I don't think it was alive when you speared it. This fish looks like it's been dead for some time."

"What do you mean?" It looked just like all the others he'd caught, didn't it?

"Rainbow trout have color," Collin said. "This one looks like a ghost. It's rotting already."

"Maybe it's a different species."

"One that doesn't bend?" Collin poked at the stiff, unmoving fish. "This one's been dead at least a day, Katie."

I *hadn't* done anything worthwhile. I couldn't even catch a stupid fish. We were doomed. With a grunt of frustration I turned from him and threw the entire thing—fish and spear—back into the loch. "Fine. We'll have oats for breakfast. Again. I'm tired of fish anyway."

Collin came up beside me and put his hand on my shoulder. I shrugged it off. "Don't touch me. None of your mind-soothing tricks. I'm angry and I've every right to be."

"Who are you angry at?" Collin asked. "The fish?"

Yesterday's PROMISE

"Yes. For dying before I could kill it." I rolled my eyes. "I'm upset with myself. If I can't accomplish something simple like catching our breakfast, how I am supposed to deal with Brann?"

"Ah—" Instead of leaving me alone as I'd requested, Collin turned me to him.

I crossed my arms in front and stared at the ground, refusing to give in to his offer of comfort, though I wanted to. "I can't run to you every time I need something or there's some kind of trouble. I'm not five anymore."

"I've noticed." Collin's voice held a hint of amusement.

"Have you?" It seemed doubtful, the way he spoke to me sometimes and how he avoided any intimacy between us. I raised my head to glare at him and saw that he was fighting back laughter.

"Go ahead." I raised my hands, giving him permission to enjoy a good laugh at my expense. "There certainly won't be anything amusing about tomorrow, when we arrive on Campbell land with absolutely no idea what to do next."

"You're right. That won't be amusing." Instead of sobering him, this only seemed to add to his mirth. Collin spluttered a time or two, noises escaping out the sides of his mouth. He brought a hand up, coughing into it.

"Maybe you did kill that fish. Maybe the sight of your spear frightened it death." Full-blown laughter erupted then, great choking gasps of amusement.

I watched, nonplussed that the dead fish incident, of all things, had wrought such a change in my husband. *It's been building for years*, I reasoned, thinking of how very little cause Collin had had for any sort of happiness in his past. Maybe this is what happened to a person who'd been only serious his entire life.

"At least I'm good at making you smile and laugh. I suppose that's something."

"It's more than something." He pulled me close in a hug. "I much prefer it over you bringing me a fish in the morning—even if it had been fresh caught."

"That's good," I mumbled into his chest. "If our survival were up to me, we'd starve."

"No worries over that. Fetch your spear, and we'll catch something together. I'll be back in a minute." Collin released me and turned toward the surrounding forest, whistling as he went. A minute later he'd disappeared into the trees, leaving me alone with my thoughts and the speared, rotting fish still floating on the surface not far from shore.

I looked at the water with disdain, my earlier enthusiasm gone and with it my willingness to submit my feet and legs to the cold—even for a minute or two. But Collin had asked it of me, so I would. *For him.* I was coming to feel that I would do a lot for him, anything perhaps. There was something about Collin, about us. Together. Even the short distance separating us at the moment created a void. I felt a pull toward him, an inexplicable and constant yearning to be with my husband of two weeks. *How did I survive all these years without him?* He was my first thought in the morning and my last at night. I wanted nothing so much as to be at his side always.

Had Collin felt that way, too, all these years of our separation? Did Anna feel the same about her husband? Recalling all the fuss about her trousseau and decorating her fiancé's town home, and planning her wedding and wedding trip in the weeks before she married, I somehow doubted that her feelings ran as deeply as mine. For the first time I felt sorry for her.

Collin and I had only each other. Nearly everything else had been stripped away, leaving only our relationship—each other to rely upon and navigate toward. There was something raw and beautiful in that.

Two steps toward the loch the hairs on the back of my neck and arms stood up. Fear sped along my spine, sending tingles of warning to every nerve ending. I felt the same as I had that evening at the river and whirled around, half expecting to see Ian or Brann. Instead I saw only our meager camp—the lone blanket, my discarded shoes, Collin's sporran, knife, and pistol.

Where moments before there had been the sound of birdsong and Collin whistling, there was now only silence. Whatever or whoever it was that was coming was nearby, but not yet close enough for me to hear.

Collin. He was out there in the trees, between me and the unseen danger. It was right there, at the edge of my vision, but I hadn't the skills or time to reel the image in closer where I might see more clearly.

Don't you dare faint. I fought the pounding in my head as I grabbed my shoes. I had the sudden thought that Collin's pistol and knife should not be left out in the open, so I snatched those up, too, then stole toward the loch, uncertain in my movements while equally certain that some unseen force guided me.

Get in the water. Alistair's somewhat lengthy and tiresome explanation of how he tracked people and had been able to find Malcom and me came to mind.

Water would hide my scent. The dogs wouldn't be able to find me. *Dogs?* In my mind I saw two brutish animals, racing ahead of three men on horseback. *Three!* My heart sank. What was I doing leaving Collin alone, unarmed to face three men?

I can do more good this way. I prayed whatever intuition was guiding me was right. Holding both the weapons and shoes overhead I sloshed into the waist-high water. I trudged along, parallel to the shore, searching for a place where I might cross. But nowhere seemed shallow enough, and my swimming skills were poor. Being this far out was risk enough.

With continual glances over my shoulder, I hurried forward, fearful that Collin would return to encounter those men, worried that he had already met with trouble.

The loch widened considerably up ahead. My chance to cross had passed. The best I could hope for was to hide somewhere on shore. I pushed on, seeing the men in my mind drawing closer to our camp. A boulder field loomed ahead, more stones fallen from a nearby mountain, some of which had landed in the loch itself. The largest ones were near the shore. I strained to reach them when sounds from the forest reached my ears. *Too late.* I dove behind the closest boulder, crouching low in the freezing water.

Clutching the gun, knife and shoes to my chest, I waited and listened to the distant sounds of men arguing. Keeping my head low, I angled my body so I could hear and partially see. The dogs ran around camp in apparent agitation, and the three men on horseback clustered together as if in consultation with one another.

Yesterday's PROMISE

A minute or two later Collin strode into camp, nodded to the men, then dumped a handful of something on the blanket. "Hamish, Rab, Gordon, good to see you again. Care to join me for breakfast?" He spoke loudly. *For my benefit?*

"It's your Campbell bride we've come for. Where is she?" The man dismounted and walked toward Collin.

"Gone," Collin said.

"Ian said she was traveling this way with you," one of the men still on horseback accused.

"I'm surprised at you, Hamish." Collin shook his head. "Since when did you start believing anything my brother says? Did it never occur to you that Ian might be up to something else, and sending you after me was a convenient way to be rid of you?"

Hamish cast an uneasy glance toward the others.

"Though as it happens, she was traveling with me," Collin said.

What? What was he doing? It seemed they might have believed him. But now . . .

"I still wouldn't trust Ian," Collin added. He picked something up from the blanket, popped it in his mouth, and began chewing. "Blaeberries. A bit early for the first of July. Still, these aren't too bad. Help yourself, Rab." Collin gestured to the pile on the blanket.

"Your wife, Collin." Rab withdrew his dirk. "We've come to take her off your hands."

Images of Ian and Malcom flashed in my mind. Bile rose in my throat. My breath came in short, panicked spurts. I forced the memories back. *Never again.* To that end, Collin had been teaching me to defend myself. But how was I to defend him?

"She's here all right. And we've an old score to settle with the Campbells." The other man slid from his horse. He knelt before the whining dogs and held a wad of fabric to their noses. "Find her, boys." He tossed the fabric—what appeared to be a dress—to Collin. "You can bury your Campbell wife in this after we've killed her."

I shrank farther down in the water.

Collin tossed the dress back to the man. "If that's your plan you'd best get going to Fort William. That's where the English patrol we met yesterday was headed."

The barking dogs didn't allow me to hear any more. From my hiding place I glimpsed them occasionally as they ran around the camp, then ended up at the water's edge each time.

"Where is she?" Rab took a menacing step toward Collin.

"I couldn't say," Collin said. "Neither was there much I could do when the English took her last night. There were a half dozen of them and only one of me. They didn't believe for a minute that an Englishwoman was my wife—and she did precious little to persuade them—so they took her."

"A patrol on Murray land?" Hamish looked around as if expecting to see them appear while the man called Gordon beckoned the dogs back.

"The English go where they like, take what they like. You ken that as well as I." Collin knelt and began scooping berries into his sporran.

"What else have you got in there?" Rab demanded. "Let me see it."

Yesterday's PROMISE

Collin handed the pouch to Rab without argument.

Rab dug through it quickly. "Not even a dirk to your name? No wonder you're eating berries." He and the others laughed.

"English took that, too," Collin muttered as Rab returned the satchel. "It was only my wife's last minute pleading that allowed me to go on my way unhindered, without being taken in for possessing a weapon." He picked up our shared blanket and began folding it.

"Sounds like she was eager to be parted from you," Hamish noted.

"Aye," Collin said. "We were not well suited. Didn't expect that we would be, but I had planned to collect the purse that was her dowry. Now I've to go home with nothing to show for my efforts." He shook his head, and I imagined the dour expression upon his face. "Two weeks wasted. Never met a woman who traveled slower or who was more exasperating to travel with."

"It's been a poor lot of luck for the MacDonalds," Rab agreed. "Cannot say I feel sorry for you exactly, taking up with Campbells as you did all those years."

"I'd no choice in the matter," Collin said. "Nor did I this time, needing that money as we do. I'm not sure what we'll do without it now. The land's been so poor for planting, and I've not enough men to work it." He placed the blanket on Ian's horse and mounted.

"You're headed home then?" Rab asked, sounding skeptical.

"Aye." Collin reined Ian's horse in the opposite direction from me. "Many days I'd be more than happy to turn the whole clan over to Ian, but my conscience will not let me do that. He's liable to do something foolish, as you well know." He let the suggestion hang in the air a moment. "Good day to you, gentlemen." With a nod Collin started off, leaving the others to linger at our camp.

Numb with shock and cold, and uncertain whether or not his charade had worked, I watched as Collin rode away, disappearing into the forest, leaving me truly alone.

"Grandfather?" Katie's hands dropped from her neck to hang limply at her side as she watched his progress down the length of the table toward us. Her eyes, even larger than usual, stared up at him, a flicker of worry within.

He wasn't looking at her, nor did he even acknowledge her presence. His attention was all for me—on me. I forced myself to finish chewing the bit of bread in my mouth, then lifted my cup and swallowed the last of my water. It did little to soothe my throat swollen with fear.

A few paces from me Laird Campbell stopped. His stance was summons enough, and I pushed back my chair and stood, then turned to face him.

He snapped the belt loudly, silencing any last whispers in the hall. "A promise given is a promise to be kept."

It sounded like something Father would have said. It was what he would have expected of me—even though it was to the enemy that I'd pledged my troth.

Chapter Twenty-two

Long minutes passed while I stayed crouched behind the boulders in the loch, shivering with cold, my heart and mind frozen with fear. My fingers clenched around the gun and the knife handle. I strained to listen, hearing snatches of conversation among the men. It seemed they believed Collin's story but were in no hurry to leave.

What would happen if they stayed all day and into the night? I'd freeze if I remained in the water much longer. Yet I dared not move.

After a while there was no more conversation, but I heard the dogs still; then I realized they were getting closer. *They're searching for me.* I pressed my elbows in tight and tried to shrink even more. *They'll find me.* Walking along the shore, it wouldn't take them long at all to spot my hiding place. Panic kept me bound. I couldn't move. My choices were to be seen or to go deeper into the water. *Drown or be shot—or worse.* The memory of Malcom and the cave made my decision. I would rather drown.

Pressing my lips together, I slid my feet along the floor of the loch, edging around the stone that hid me. Only two steps, and the bottom fell away. I hadn't a free hand to grasp at the rock and only just managed to keep Collin's gun above the surface. Water lapped below my chin. I ducked lower, worried my light hair might be visible from shore. My jaw clenched to keep my teeth from chattering.

"The MacDonald's not turning back," one of the Murrays called. "Followed him as far as the cut off, and he's headed home."

"Maybe he was telling the truth," another who sounded very close said. "Dogs can't find her."

"What if he was telling the truth about his brother? Ian could be at the keep, and we're not there to stop him taking what he wants."

A bark sounded just in front of me. I jumped, banging the pistol against the rock.

"What was that?" one of the Murrays asked.

I held my breath. Water rippled around me, disturbed from my sudden movement.

The bark came again, followed by splashing then the sounds of a tongue greedily lapping.

From the corner of my eye I spotted one of the dogs, little more than an arm's distance away, standing in the loch, drinking water. *If he looks up.* I sank into the water, leaving only my hand with the gun hovering on the surface.

"It's just the dogs," one of the men yelled. "Come on. Let's go. Ian MacDonald is of more concern than a Campbell wench."

Their grumbled conversation continued on, growing more distant.

I raised up out of the water allowing my forehead to rest against the rock while I took in great breaths of air. I scooted around the rock, cold, but alive, and I could touch the bottom here. I would wait, all day if necessary, to come out of hiding.

Minutes passed. Hoofbeats sounded. *They're leaving.* Tears of relief streamed from my eyes. Still, I stayed put, waiting until I could stand the cold no longer or until I felt some reassurance that it was safe to reveal myself.

What if they came back? What if Collin *never* did? My thoughts tormented me. No longer did I wish for home. I merely wanted Collin to return.

I'd proven numerous times already that I was incapable of taking care of myself. How was I to eat? To protect myself? To ever get out of this forsaken forest? *What would Collin do?*

It was the thought of him and the danger *he* might find

himself in, weaponless as he was, that finally prodded me from the water. Still clutching his gun and my precious shoes I slogged to shore, what was left of my grey dress trailing behind, weighing me down. Once on shore I hid behind the larger boulders, crouched and shivering, then waited probably another hour in case the men returned. It wasn't until a twittering hawfinch alerted me that the danger had passed that I allowed myself to set the pistol and knife aside and remove my wet dress.

If the birds deemed it safe to resume their song, then it was likely no one else was near. I wrung my grey gown out as thoroughly as I could and spread it across a boulder to dry. At least I could keep from catching my death of cold. *Today.*

Tonight would be another matter. *Collin will return by then,* I told myself resolutely. If not, it was unlikely I would be able to start a fire. I had his knife, but the flint was in his sporran.

I slipped on my wet shoes and, wearing only those and my damp shift, returned the way I'd come, Collin's pistol in my hand as I kept to the shore. My spear with the dead fish had floated to within easy reach, and I retrieved it now, grimacing as I peeled the stiff fish away. How had I not noticed before how poorly it looked?

With the spear in one hand and the pistol in my other, I continued to our camp. Nothing remained except a handful of berries scattered on the ground and the dress the Murrays had tossed at Collin. I knelt and picked it up, not surprised to discover it was one of my own faded, too short frocks. No doubt Ian had given it to the Murrays when encouraging them to hunt me down.

Yesterday's PROMISE

I wasted no time putting the dress on and felt immediately better—warmer and safer, now that I was properly covered again. How considerate of Ian to provide the Murrays with a dress for me, and how kind of them to have left it behind. I almost smiled.

Be grateful in all the little things. One of my old pastor's sermons came to mind. I doubted that being grateful for an old dress, a sharp stick, and a few berries were what he'd been referring to. Still, I found myself near to tears for the blessing of a dress that wasn't soaked and the promise of something to eat.

I gathered the few berries in my hand, then returned to my hiding place among the rocks. I traded the spear for Collin's knife and went in search of the berries Collin had found. Surely the handfuls he'd returned with hadn't been all that there were. With a clear example of what I was looking for squished in my palm, I felt confident I could find something that wasn't going to poison me.

It did not take long to locate the berry bushes. I alternately ate and stored the fruit, dropping every other berry I picked into a corner of my tied-up skirt. I wished I had Collin's sporran with me, then instantly regretted the thought. That I'd left him defenseless was bad enough. I reasoned that the Murrays would have taken at least his pistol from him anyway, and perhaps they would not have believed his story as well, had Collin been discovered in better circumstances. But I'd done him wrong—not only in taking his weapons and abandoning him, but in my early morning grumpiness.

Silently I berated myself as I recalled with angst my

frustration with Collin's laughter just hours before. What was the last thing I'd said to him? Had it been kind or hurtful? Had I still been upset?

He'd left me behind because it was the only way to protect me. I believed that with all my heart. But it didn't ease my fear or make my situation any less dire. *Please come back to me. I'm sorry.*

I felt lonely and scared, too—more so when the sun reached its zenith, then started its trek west. *Please don't let me be alone tonight.*

With all the berries I could carry, and with the hawfinches still chirping their assurance that all was well in this part of the wood, I began to make my way back toward the beach. Maybe I could try to catch another fish. Perhaps I should gather wood for a fire—that I'd not be able to light. Definitely I should find a better place to hide and one in which I might stay warm and dry if the clouds threatening from the north turned to rain.

Just before I left the forest, the chittering of the birds became increasingly loud. I looked to my left and saw the reason why—a nest lay in a clump of wild bushes. It rested nearly on its side, at an odd angle, giving the impression that it had fallen from the tree above. I was close enough to touch the nest, and the mama bird was not pleased.

Eggs. I hesitated and met her eyes, pleading with me to leave her family alone, untouched. But those eggs might be the difference between me starving or not, and the nest would make a fine kindling. I hesitated, some deep-rooted survival instincts having taken hold in me the past hours. This felt like a gift from God. Yet I did not want to take it. Killing a fish was one thing. Taking a mother's eggs and home was another.

Yesterday's PROMISE

With a sigh that was part relief, part an admission of failure, I continued on, leaving the nest behind. It might be that I had to come back for it. But for now, berries would suffice for the one meal of my day.

The nest gave me an idea that I spent the remainder of the day focused on. I would build a nest for myself, using the pine needles and last season's leaves that were plentiful on the forest floor. I gathered pile after pile and hauled them to a crevice between the rock—the spot I'd deemed close enough to our previous camp that I could see if Collin returned. It was also near to the water—important, as I had no pouch to hold water, and it was a place to stay hidden and also sheltered from the wind. If the rain came, I would be wet, but there was nothing to be done for that. I'd solved two of three problems and told myself it was the best I could do.

Night came, and my head pounded, not from any impending danger or warning, but from true hunger. I'd not been particularly full on our journey, but neither had I felt the gnawing ache or nausea I experienced now. I thought of the MacDonalds, of women like me, and especially of little children. Collin had said they were starving. I had not understood—perhaps I still didn't. But I felt a kinship with them now and a concern for their plight. I *wanted* Collin to have my grandfather's money to help them.

I curled up between the rocks and raked the leaves and needles over my feet and legs. It wasn't comfortable, but it did bring a little warmth. My grey dress had long since dried. I wrapped it around my shoulders, though it was a poor substitute for Collin, a fire, and our shared blanket.

Where are you? Are you all right? Tears fell, and yearning overtook me. If ever I saw my husband again, if Collin returned to me safely, I *would* kiss him. I would tell him how I felt. I would allow myself to love him freely and trust that we could conquer whatever obstacles lay in our path to happiness, be they Campbells, MacDonalds, Murrays or anyone else. I'd told Collin he didn't have to walk alone anymore, but I hadn't truly shown that with my actions yet.

Please give me the chance to, I prayed throughout the long, cold night.

With the knowledge that I was in the wrong, that somehow—since the turn of events binding me with his granddaughter—my life was no longer my first priority, I turned away from the laird and bent over my chair.

His first strike felt like fire. I clenched my teeth and stared straight ahead, past the leering face of a lad about my age who stood at the far wall.

In planning to leave this place, I had ignored what was now the single truth guiding my actions: Katie's life came first.

The second strike came, harder than the first. Then another and another, each swift and strong. My fingers curled around the back of the chair, and I tasted blood on my lip as I bit down to keep from crying out. He intended to beat the promise into me, to make certain I never forgot again.

Chapter Twenty-three

It wasn't birdsong, but a horse's nickering that woke me in the morning. The sun was barely up, and someone—or more than one someone possibly—was nearby. Pine needles poked through my already torn stockings, prickling my skin, some drawing blood. Silently I plucked a few away, realizing too late the noise they would make when I moved.

I'd slept with Collin's pistol in hand and kept it there

now while my other grabbed clumps of the needles and pushed them aside. I would have to move to see who or what was nearby.

My hope that it was Collin was quickly fading, as he hadn't called out to me. I maneuvered slowly in the small space until I could look through a crack in the side. Ian's horse was the first thing that came into view, and tears of relief sprang to my eyes.

Where is Collin?

I spied him a second later, moving laboriously along the shore, then back to the wood, then to shore again. He was tracking me, looking for clues—clues I had not been as careful to cover as I should have. Were the dogs to return, my scent would have been everywhere and eventually led them to this very spot. In my consuming desire to spend a warm night, I had neglected other, equally important survival skills.

"Col—" The joyous cry died in my throat. An all-too-familiar warning crept along my spine.

He glanced my direction, and my heart thudded painfully. I had to be wrong. No one else was around. Why had I sensed danger? *Why is Collin not calling out for me?* The feeling persisted, spiking between my eyes in a painful burst.

Perhaps deciding he hadn't heard anything after all, Collin continued his methodical search while behind him—

I bit back a scream as I scrambled to my knees and took aim at one of the men from the previous day, knife in his hand as he shadowed Collin's movements.

My hands shook. I wedged the pistol in the crevice of rock to steady it. *One chance.* My finger wrapped around the trigger in an eerie replay of that night in the carriage.

Yesterday's PROMISE

Collin was perhaps twenty paces away now. His face appeared haggard, eyes ringed with dark circles as he focused on his search. His hands hung at his side, clenching and unclenching.

This way. Come this way, I willed silently when his tracking led him to the right. *No room for error.* I dared not lower the gun. Collin paused, spied something on the ground, squatted. I pulled the trigger.

The shot echoed. I flew back, landing on the bed of pine needles. I grabbed the knife and jumped up to meet Collin's astonished face as he leapt over the rock toward me.

"Katie!"

I reached for him. He tumbled into my hiding place on top of me.

I clutched his shoulders. "There was a man behind you."

Collin wrenched the pistol from the crevice where it had stuck and took the knife from me. "Stay here." He was gone as quickly as he'd come. I feared for him, for us both. Where were the other two Murrays he'd encountered yesterday?

Keeping low, Collin dodged between the boulders, then scurried behind the tree line. I glimpsed him as he ran in the direction I'd fired.

Please let him be all right. I prayed for both Collin and the man I'd shot. I'd felt so relieved when Malcom died, but I didn't feel that now. I didn't want to have killed someone. I only wanted to keep him from harming Collin.

Minutes passed. I felt like a coward waiting when Collin might need me. When I hadn't listened to him, I'd endangered both of us. But sitting here doing nothing felt wrong, too. At last Collin reappeared, walking briskly toward me. I stood up and ran to meet him. My expression must have asked what I could not voice, for he shook his head.

"Your aim has improved," he said solemnly. "Rab will have a devil of a time riding with that shoulder. But he'll live. I've patched him up enough that he'll be all right until he gets help."

I let out a breath of relief. "Does he know who shot him?"

"He does now," Collin said, his expression grim. "All the more reason for us to leave Murray land as quickly as possible."

"Where are his brothers?" I asked uneasily. We were still outnumbered, and now they had even more reason to hate me.

"Headed to find Ian, if I'm correct. In any case, they're not here. They split up yesterday afternoon." Collin reached behind me to grab the grey dress that had fallen from my shoulders when I ran to him. He helped me onto Ian's horse, put the dress across my lap, and climbed up behind me.

"We've got to ride hard," he said. "They argued last night whether or not to return to our camp. Rab drew the short straw and had to go back. But when he doesn't return they'll come looking for him."

My stomach churned in spite of its emptiness. Collin reached around me and took the reins, heading us in the opposite direction he had gone yesterday.

"Won't this way take us deeper into Murray land?" I recalled the crude clan map he'd drawn for me in the dirt a few days past.

"It will, but the other direction leads us straight to

Hamish and Gordon. We'll cut over at some point. Though we'll not be to your home today as I'd promised."

Another delay before we confronted Brann. I ought to have felt relieved. Instead the reality that I'd just earned us another, very real enemy settled inside of me like a stone in the bottom of a river.

In all our days of travel we'd never ridden so hard. Several times Collin had to coax Ian's horse along.

"I do not like to abuse the animal," Collin said the one time he allowed us to rest and Ian's horse to stop and take water. "I rode him like a madman yesterday—far enough out that the Murrays could follow my trail and be convinced I'd truly gone on my way. Then I drove the poor creature through the night over the worst possible terrain so I could end at the loch again by morning."

Collin's night had been worse than mine. He had to be as exhausted as the horse.

Instead of complaining, he stroked the animal. "Apples, carrots, and oats for you my friend, when we've completed our journey."

When would that be? I could no longer fathom how far we'd traveled. I trusted that Collin knew how to get us home—wherever that might be—and despite our dire circumstances took a moment to appreciate his knowledge of the land, the clans, and our country.

"You must be starved. When did you last eat?" Collin had

dug through his sporran and produced a handful of oats, likely our last.

"Give them to him." I nodded toward the stallion. "He has more need than I."

Collin hesitated only a second, then held his hand out to the horse. "A paltry offering, I know, boy." When his palm was empty he stroked the animal again.

Belatedly I remembered my own paltry offering, forgotten in the haste of the morning's flight. I bent down and untied the corner of my dress. "Berries," I offered, pressing the fabric back as I held it up. Only days ago I would have been appalled at such immodesty, but now the thought that Collin might see my ankles was of little consequence.

"You found them, I see." Collin stuck a finger in and came up with some of the well-mashed concoction. "Too bad we don't have a crust for a pie."

"Don't speak of pies." I held an arm across my empty stomach. "Did you drop a few of the berries on purpose for me to find?"

"Aye. It was the only thing I could think to do for you. That and leave the dress behind and hope the Murrays did as well. When the dogs lost your scent at the loch, I figured you were hidden somewhere wet."

"Did you see where I'd gone?" I asked.

Collin shook his head. "At first I didn't know what had become of you. My heart near stopped when I came out of the wood and saw only Murrays. I've never been so relieved in all my life as when Rab asked where you were. I knew then that you must be all right. You had a bit of warning, aye?"

"Yes. A very last-minute warning." My stomach clenched

at the reminder, lessening my appetite for smashed berries or anything else. I tied up the corner of my dress again.

"I am sorry I had to leave you and sorry you had to use the pistol today," Collin said. "I knew Rab was following me and was hoping to reach you before he did. I'm not sure what I would have done if you'd used that shot already."

"I didn't dare. I didn't attempt a fire either. Not that I'd have been able to get one started," I added.

A corner of Collin's mouth lifted. "In that tinder pile you were sitting on, and with a few strikes of my knife against a rock, it's very likely you could have started one. But I'm glad you didn't. Murrays are cunning devils. I knew when they let me go so easily they were up to no good."

"They stayed another hour at least and came very close to finding me." I hugged my arms to myself, remembering the dog so close I might have reached out to touch him. Yet again, somehow Collin and I had both survived. I also remembered the promises I'd made to myself were we to be reunited.

I hesitated another second, then stepped forward. As I had after our fishing lesson, I placed my hands on his shirt front and looked up at him, hoping the intent was clear in my eyes. Raising up on my toes, I shyly pressed my lips to his, lingering perhaps a second or two longer than was proper. Then I wrapped my arms around his waist and held tight. His arms came around me, crushing me to him.

"Katie." My whispered name sounded like an endearment as he bent his head close to mine.

"I love you, Collin MacDonald. Don't ever leave me again."

"I won't. I was so frightened I'd lost y—" He stepped back

suddenly, holding me away from him as he looked into my eyes. "What did you say?"

"I—love you." My eyes filled with tears. So much for promising not to cry all the time. "I don't know what will happen to us—if the Murrays will find us first or Ian, or if Brann is lying in wait somewhere. I don't want to wait anymore to tell you what I feel. I want you to know, now and always, no matter how long that is. I'll take whatever time we have together." I wiped my cheeks with the back of my hand. "A few weeks ago I didn't even remember who Collin MacDonald was. But now I do, and being together is so much more, much *better*, than anything I ever imagined." The words tumbling from me didn't sound right. They weren't enough. I felt helpless to adequately explain and worried I had ruined the kiss by following it with such an awkward, impassioned speech.

Collin took my face in his hands. "It nearly killed me to leave you yesterday. It was as if a part of me was ripped out and left behind, too. I knew I couldn't survive it this time. I've loved you so long, Katie. I've waited so long for the *privilege* of loving you." He lowered his lips to mine, returning my shy effort with one that spoke of years of pent-up yearning. His lips were soft and slow, exploring every surface. They lingered and caressed, fulfilling the promise only hinted at on our wedding day.

I sighed with contentment, causing Collin to pause, lean back, and study my face.

"It *is* all right for a woman to kiss her husband, isn't it?" If he told me otherwise I wasn't certain I would care.

Collin's eyes darkened briefly, the ever-present

seriousness attempting to surface. I grasped his shirt front and pulled him close to me again. I couldn't lose him to that darkness. Not now.

"*Today* it is all right for you to kiss me." His look remained dark, but it was passion I saw simmering there now. "And for me to kiss you." He did so again, his mouth more insistent this time. My hands slid up to his shoulders, then around the back of his neck, holding tight when he lifted me from the ground.

I was out of breath but didn't care. Collin's lips parted suddenly, inviting. I gasped. With a shaky laugh he released me to kiss the bridge of my nose and my forehead.

"I'm not entirely certain that type of kiss is proper." I stared at the front of his shirt instead of his face.

Collin lifted one of my tousled curls. "And does that concern you over much?"

"No." I didn't need to consider. He kissed me a third time, long and slow and luxuriously until I thought I would melt in his arms. "Collin," I breathed. "I love—kissing."

He laughed, then gathered me close, resting his chin on top of my head.

"For years I heard nothing of you or your whereabouts, but I pictured you a grown-up young lady, dancing at balls on the arm of some well-bred, English nobleman. Countless nights I tortured myself with such images. Others I spent dreaming of this very moment."

"The time for dreaming is over." Euphoria wrapped me in the snug cocoon of his arms. I never wanted to leave this spot or his embrace. But at last Collin stepped away, holding me at arms' length.

"We should continue on. It isn't safe here."

"I'm not certain anywhere with you will ever be safe again." I smiled as I brought a hand to my forehead, damp with perspiration.

"True." A corner of his mouth lifted. "You are a danger I shall be constantly wary of."

"*Me?*" I looked up at him through my lashes, as Anna had once taught me about flirting.

"Aye, lass. You started it." Collin swept me in his arms and pretended to toss me towards the horse. I reached up and hoisted myself the rest of the way.

"Remember that," I said pertly as I settled my weary legs for another long ride. "Next time it is your turn to begin the kissing." I looked away, blushing at my boldness, before I could gauge Collin's reaction to my invitation. I'd laid my heart and soul bare, utterly exposed for him to do as he wished.

How long, I wondered restlessly, would I have to wait.

"Grandfather, no!"

I sensed a different kind of movement behind me and whirled to see the lass standing between me and the belt. I grabbed her arm and pulled her out of the way a second before the leather slapped smartly across the front of my thigh.

"Stay back," I ordered, even as she flung herself at her grandfather, arms wrapped around his legs.

He pried her fingers away and held her sternly from him. "And now yours. For flaunting a gift meant to be used with wisdom. He shoved her toward me. "Hold her."

"No." I pulled Katie behind me, the sound of her weeping filling the silence of the hall. "You charged me with protecting her, and so I will."

"I'll do no lasting harm," the laird promised.

I shook my head. "She's but a child, and the wrong here is not hers. Let her be."

Chapter Twenty-four

"There." Collin stood behind me on a bluff, a thick forest of trees at our back, protecting us from being visible to anyone below. He pointed to a distant castle and outlying crofts, both sparsely spread and with less farmland between than I had imagined.

"We've been on Campbell land for some time now," Collin continued. "But this is the best vantage point of your home."

"*Our* home," I corrected, wrapping my arms tight around my middle. I didn't want to go there alone, or at all really. *Brann is there now.* As were others who would do us harm. It would be up to me to be aware of their movements if we were to stay safe. But save for the brief, almost too late warning at the loch, I had sensed or seen nothing since the vision at the moor.

"I turned and buried my face in Collin's chest. "Must we go?"

He held me close and stroked the back of my head as I imagined he might have when I was a child. "No one is here to force us."

"But—" I'd heard the lilt in his voice and knew he wished to say more.

"Your grandfather expected we would." Collin held me away from him and looked directly at me. "He counted on us, and there are many others there looking for you to return as well."

I groaned. "Let us hope they are not terribly disappointed."

"I haven't been, so why should they be? You're going to help them, Katie. Why—" A mischievous smile lit Collin's face. "You may even be able to feed them, with your recently acquired skill, locating already dead fish."

"Unjust," I cried, punching him lightly, feeling immensely grateful that the solemn Collin was slowly being replaced by this man who could smile and tease and even laugh. I prayed he might stay like this, once we were no longer by ourselves.

"You're not going there alone. We are in this together," Collin reminded me. He'd turned me away from him once more, and his hands rested on my shoulders as they had that night at the inn. As I had then, I felt a calm and confidence flow from him into me.

"How do you *do* that?" I asked, as I had previously, still waiting for a satisfactory explanation.

"It is my gift, so you may use yours. You must be calm to see what is coming. I help your mind and heart to be still."

"But *how* do you do it?" I persisted.

"It's very simple. Something your grandfather taught me."

"Is it a secret? Am I not to know?"

"You can now." Collin leaned close, brushing my hair aside to whisper in my ear. "I love you. That is the secret. I gather my feelings for you, concentrate them into my touch, and the love you feel from me provides the peace you need."

More tears. *Oh dear.* His simple, beautiful explanation buoyed me above our worries. I reached up, placing one of my hands over Collin's. "Thank you." It seemed I would be forever in his debt. I wished there was something I could give in return. He had my love, but I wasn't certain he felt it, as I felt his.

"Never doubt my devotion to you, Katie. No matter what may come."

"I won't." I dashed a hand over my cheeks, hoping he hadn't seen my tears. "Now then," I acquiesced, "I shall do my best to see what Brann is up to." Concentrating my mind on him seemed the best chance I had to see anything. He'd been the first person in my vision at the moor. I closed my eyes, reaching out to the land spread below us, expecting I would have the bird's-eye view of my previous sight, where it felt as if I had hovered above the land and people and was privy to their actions and conversation. But this time it was different.

In my mind I found a path and followed it, not to the castle, but to a cottage where I saw not Brann, but a woman.

Uncertain if this was my imagination or actually seeing something, I allowed myself to daydream that the cottage was ours. Maybe we should live happily there instead. The idea of having our own little home was suddenly very appealing. A castle would house many people, whereas a cottage might just be for the two of us.

Was the little house in my mind real? Did it already exist, either here or on MacDonald land? There was only one way to find out.

"Will you find me some sticks, please?" I opened my eyes and walked to a spot of ground mostly devoid of grass. I knelt and began using my hand to smooth the dirt.

Collin brought me a sharp rock and two sticks, one thicker than the other.

"Thank you." I dragged the rock through the dirt, marking off a square in which to work. Then I picked the thinner of the two sticks and began scratching it across the ground, making lines that in turn showed the small home I'd seen, simply built. Humble. I wouldn't care what it looked like if it was ours. "Hmm. This roof must leak. Look how poorly it's patched." I dug deeper, using the darker earth beneath to shade the thatching in places.

Collin said nothing but sat nearby and watched as I drew the main cottage and then the smaller outbuildings. I thought about adding a chicken or two next to the coop in the yard, but the sticks didn't allow me to provide that much detail. There was a woman there that I felt I had to draw. I began sketching her, my heart falling with each stroke. This wasn't to be our cottage. It belonged to someone else. The name that had haunted me for days came to mind again. I stopped midway through crafting her skirt and turned to Collin.

"Who is Mhairi?" If I was soon to meet her, now was the time to ask about everything that had been troubling me. "Ian made it sound as if the two of you were—"

"Friends," Collin said. "Mhairi's father was killed at Culloden. Her family is one I've tried to help, like many in our clan. There has never been more to it than that."

I imagined Collin repairing a roof or bringing meat to the family and being asked to stay for dinner. Of course Mhairi would see him as her own, personal hero. I knew the feeling well. Perhaps Collin hadn't thought there was more to their friendship, but it seemed likely Mhairi had felt there was.

Ian had believed so, anyway.

"Is this her house?" I leaned away from my drawing so Collin could see all of it.

He shook his head and pretended a frown. "Your sight isn't working all that well if you think the woman standing there is Mhairi. I said her *father* died at Culloden, not her grandson." He leaned back on his elbows, as if expecting to be here awhile. "Not to mention that Mhairi is on MacDonald land, and the croft you've drawn is down there—if it's the place I'm thinking of." He pointed to the valley below. "What else can you see?"

Not Mhairi, or her house. Good. I couldn't seem to help the flare up of jealousy but now happily pushed it aside as I turned back to my drawing. The woman I'd sketched showed no indication of age. Her face was little more than an oval, given the crude implements with which I had to work. Discarding the stick, I drew my knees up to my chest, closed my eyes, and searched again.

Collin joined me, scooting close to sit behind me and kneading the tension from my shoulders. "You can do this," he encouraged quietly. "I know you can."

I wanted to. For him. For my grandfather. For the people down there I hadn't even met.

As before the cottage appeared in my mind, the edges fuzzy at first. As they grew clearer the door of the house came into sharp focus. A woman stood before it, her face lifted as if searching for someone. *For us?* Hands wrinkled with age gripped her apron while her mouth moved wordlessly. White hair topped her head. Her eyes stared at everything—and nothing.

"She's—blind." I opened my own eyes and scrambled to my feet. Collin followed, holding out a hand to steady me.

"The cottage *is* down there," I said, excitedly. "Not too far from Grandfather's castle. The woman's name is Liusaidh, and she is looking for us. Waiting. Expecting us. But she cannot see . . . as we can."

Collin's lips parted, and his grip at my elbow tightened.

He breathed in deeply before saying anything. "Liusaidh is real, and she is blind." He smiled, but it was filled with sadness.

I thought I understood why. "We really are going there, aren't we? This—us helping our people as my grandfather saw it—is actually going to happen." Even with the dangers we'd faced and all that Collin had told me the past week, it still hadn't seemed real—until now.

"Aye, Katie. It is going to happen. Just as your grandfather saw it." Collin took my hands in his, gently rubbing his thumbs across the tops. "I thought it might take you a little more time . . . But that was foolish of me. Selfish. I've got to get your dowry to Ian before he brings MacDonalds raiding at our door. And we've got to prevent Brann from harming any more of your people." Collin drew in another deep breath. "Together we will face whatever problems await." His mouth lifted in a fleeting smile. "I feel much better with your gift and knowledge on our side."

"Me, too." My smile lingered longer than his. "I wish I could describe to you how it feels." I gestured to the picture in the dirt. "I *saw* all of that. I saw Liusaidh—someone I don't even know." My new ability felt amazing, exciting.

"I'm grateful for your confidence," he said. "But remember, this is not a game. We are like Daniel walking into the lion's den. I believe we have the Lord's favor, but only the most careful actions will stay the beasts."

"I understand." I squeezed Collin's hands. "I wish I still had my paints and brushes," I said, for the first time voicing my regret at losing the contents of my trunk. "It feels like I've just passed a preliminary test. I want to try again, to see if there is more of importance I can summon and draw or paint."

"One thing at a time," Collin said. "First, I think we each need some new clothes."

"And something to eat that isn't fish or oatmeal." I tugged at his hands. "And a real bath! Come on. Let's go."

"In a minute." Collin pulled me back toward him. "And we can't just walk down the path. We've got to stay hidden, remember."

"Of course." I felt foolish. I hadn't seen Brann, but that didn't mean that he, or someone else who would do us harm, wasn't nearby. "Why do you suppose I saw Liusaidh? She is waiting for us, but might it be a trap?"

Collin shook his head. "Liusaidh is an old friend and loyal to your grandfather. You probably saw her because that is where we are to go first. She will be able to appraise us of the state of things."

"Oh, good." I smiled my relief at not having to wait longer. My reluctance had fled. Only a short while earlier I hadn't wanted to go down there at all. Now I felt impatient to meet this Liusaidh, to see my grandfather's castle—my childhood home—to learn more of my past.

It seemed Collin did not share my enthusiasm. His eyes betrayed a deep sorrow.

"What is it? What's wrong?" I placed a hand on his cheek.

He covered my hand with his, then brought it to his mouth, kissing the back of my knuckles lightly. "It will not be just the two of us after this. Our wedding trip is over."

"Oh." I'd forgotten that he viewed our days together as such. While the last two had been fraught with danger, those before he had planned thoughtfully for my pleasure. "They were the best days of my life," I reaffirmed. "But I expect that some in the future will surpass them. We will be together, and someday the difficulties we face will be resolved."

"You're right, of course." He didn't sound convinced.

For a second I worried that he knew something of the future as well, something troubling. But no, that was my burden. Not Collin's. *I* was his and wanted very much not to add to his troubles but to take them from him, to be the friend who kept him from being lonely.

"I should think a celebration is in order," I suggested, thinking of something that might pull him from his melancholy. "You've brought me safely all the way from England—no small feat, given the opposition we've faced. And I've just found our lodging for tonight. Surely that ought to be worth something."

"What did you have in mind?" Collin asked, his gaze straying to my mouth. "Perhaps you could show me."

"Oh no." I shook my head. "It's your turn to start. I kissed you first yesterday."

"So you did." He pressed his lips to my fingers once more, then turned my hand over and lowered his mouth to my wrist.

I closed my eyes, sliding easily into bliss. "What is it about your lips? Is there another secret to them that my grandfather taught you?"

Collin laughed. "Same one. My kisses are given with love. Makes them better than any you might have had before."

My eyes flew open. "I *never* kissed anyone before you."

"Never? At a ball, or while strolling about a garden on some not-so-proper gentleman's arm?"

"Of course not." I pulled my hand away. "It was Anna who had suitors and a season. Not I."

"What do you mean?" Collin frowned. "There's no need to pretend with me. Your father was well connected. I know what your life was like. Yesterday when you declared that you loved kissing, I assumed—"

"Father saw to it that I never had any suitors. I thought it was only because we couldn't afford it—though Anna *was* granted a season. Now I realize it had to do with more than money, and I can only be thankful. As you should be. Father prevented me from meeting any eligible men, let alone kissing one. And I am certain his actions were because of you."

Collin didn't speak for a moment then cleared his throat. "I may have to reconsider my opinion of your father."

"I am glad to hear it. As I am glad to know I'm not the only one who feels jealous." I felt so again suddenly, wondering whether or not I had been Collin's first kiss. "Did *you* ever kiss anyone before me?"

His shifting eyes told me the answer before his reluctant "Aye."

"Who?" *Please don't let it be—*

"Mhairi," he admitted. "Just once. It was wrong of me. A mistake. Considering that I was already betrothed . . ."

All of the insecurity and hurt of the previous days rebounded inside of me. I tried to turn away, but Collin wouldn't allow it.

"Katie, I'm sorry. I was telling the truth when I said Mhairi and I are just friends. I'm human and was lonely, and I never loved her like I love you."

"You loved her, too?" My voice escalated along with my efforts to break free of his grasp.

"No! You misunderstand. Please, Katie. Listen to me."

I stopped moving and stared at his chest.

"It was about a year ago—a good six months before your father's letter arrived. Laird Campbell had died. I hadn't seen you or heard any word from you in over thirteen years. I had only my faith to go on that we would be together again. And one day that faltered. Just for a minute. I felt remorse at once and told Mhairi it must never happen again."

No doubt Mhairi had felt differently.

"Forgive me? Please?" Collin tipped my chin up, so that I met his gaze.

"I'm not angry." *Not exactly, anyhow.* "Just—hurt." And oh, so jealous. How many years had Mhairi had with Collin, while I had been away?

"I think it would be best if we were to each thoroughly convince the other that there is no cause for such emotion, that our commitment to one another is complete." Collin caught me around the waist and pulled me close.

"An excellent idea," I agreed, though my heart wasn't in it, as it had been a moment ago. Now I was the gloomy one.

"It has always been you, Katie. Only you. From the very first moment we met, when you scolded me, it was as if *I* could see the future, the woman you would become and the love we would have. I've never loved any other."

At Collin's tender admission, tears burst to the surface. I clung to him and allowed him to kiss me. It didn't take long before I was convinced of all that he'd said.

When we finally broke apart he moved back, an almost pained look upon his face, his breathing heavy. "We shouldn't—we can't—" He threw his hands up in surrender, then stepped forward again.

I wasn't certain who kissed the other first this time. I reached for him as he came to me, then once again we were swept away in consuming passion that left no room for anything but each other in the world. My castle, a hot bath, real food . . . it could all wait. Forever, if necessary. So long as I had Collin. So long as we had each other.

When our kiss ended, he did not release me but held me tightly to him. I lay my head against his chest, over his heart, comforted once more by its steadiness. Every beat seemed to echo his declaration. *I love you.*

And though this did not begin to solve all of our problems, it provided our strength. My home was where Collin was. And for now, it was enough.

A collective gasp reverberated throughout the hall. Laird Campbell and I faced off, his expression a peculiar mixture of fury and relief.

"Very well," he said quietly after several tense seconds had passed. "If you don't wish Katie to be punished, you may take her thrashing for her."

"Please, Grandfather, no!" She ran out from behind me, but I snatched her gown and hauled her back.

"I'm sorry," she wailed. "I won't boast of what I see again. I won't."

"I believe you, lass." He snapped the belt once more. "But to make certain you understand, this has to be done. There are consequences..."

I saw in the stoic resignation of Katie's face that she was prepared to accept her punishment. I couldn't allow it, couldn't imagine anything worse than seeing her hurt. Wincing, I crouched down, grasped her slight shoulders and turned her toward me.

"You must permit me to do this. After all, you saved me a beating the first day I was here. I've been in your debt since. And nothing is worse for a man than owing a favor to a lass."

"But you're not a man." Katie's lip trembled, and a tear slid down her cheek.

"I disagree," Laird Campbell said quietly. "Tonight, Collin has proven himself worthy of that title."

It felt almost as if the compliment had come from my father. I thought of him as the next lashes fell. His approval made them easier to bear, as did the sight of the child on her knees before me, crying as if her heart would break.

MICHELE PAIGE HOLMES

My backside stung, but my soul felt more peace than it had in the nights since the old laird and his priest had betrothed the lass to me. My father had sent me to this place, but it was she who would keep me here. Aligning my will to that purpose, to the higher power Who orchestrated it all, was my only hope, and hers as well.

DON'T MISS THE SEQUEL TO

Yesterday's Promise:

A Hearthfire Historical Romance

A Promise for Tomorrow,

Book 2

MICHELE PAIGE HOLMES

A final note,

Thank you for reading *Yesterday's Promise*.

I continue to appreciate those who take the time to read my stories and those who post reviews as well. You make it possible for me to continue doing what I love.

If you would like more information about my other books and future releases, please visit michelepaigeholmes.com. You can also follow me on Twitter at @MichelePHolmes.

Happy reading!

Michele

About Michele Paige Holmes

MICHELE PAIGE HOLMES spent her childhood and youth in Arizona and northern California, often curled up with a good book instead of out enjoying the sunshine. She graduated from Brigham Young University with a degree in elementary education and found it an excellent major with which to indulge her love of children's literature.

Her first novel, *Counting Stars*, won the 2007 Whitney Award for Best Romance. Its companion novel, a romantic suspense titled *All the Stars in Heaven*, was a Whitney Award finalist, as was her first historical romance, *Captive Heart*. *My Lucky Stars* completed the Stars series.

In 2014 Michele launched the Hearthfire Historical Romance line, with the debut title, *Saving Grace*. *Loving Helen* is the companion novel, with a third, *Marrying Christopher*, followed by the companion novella *Twelve Days in December*.

When not reading or writing romance, Michele is busy with her full-time job as a wife and mother. She and her husband live in Utah with their five high-maintenance children, and a Shitzu that resembles a teddy bear, in a house with a wonderful view of the mountains.

You can find Michele on the web: MichelePaigeHolmes.com

Facebook: Michele Holmes

Twitter: @MichelePHolmes

www.ingramcontent.com/pod-product-compliance
Lightning Source LLC
LaVergne TN
LVHW021232080526
838199LV00088B/4314